Nic Tatano

I've always been a writer of some sort, having spent my career working as a reporter, anchor or producer in television news. Fiction is a lot more fun, since you don't have to deal with those pesky things known as facts.

I spent fifteen years as a television news reporter and anchor. My work has taken me from the floors of the Democratic and Republican National Conventions to Ground Zero in New York to Jay Leno's backyard. My stories have been seen on NBC, ABC and CNN. I still work as a freelance network field producer for FOX, NBC, CBS and ABC.

I grew up in the New York City metropolitan area and now live on the Gulf Coast where I will never shovel snow again. I'm happily married to a math teacher and we share our wonderful home with our tortoiseshell tabby cat, Gypsy.

You can follow me on Twitter @NicTatano.

PRAISE FOR NIC TATANO'S DEBUT WING GIRL

The Love Triangle

NIC TATANO

A division of HarperCollins*Publishers*
www.harpercollins.co.uk

Harper*Impulse* an imprint of
HarperCollins*Publishers*
1 London Bridge Street
London SE1 9GF

www.harpercollins.co.uk

A Paperback Original 2016

First published in Great Britain in ebook format by Harper*Impulse* 2016

Copyright © Nic Tatano 2016

Nic Tatano asserts the moral right to
be identified as the author of this work

A catalogue record for this book
is available from the British Library

ISBN: 9780008173654

Set in Minion by Palimpsest Book Production Limited, Falkirk, Stirlingshire

Printed and bound in Great Britain

MIX
Paper from
responsible sources

FSC
www.fsc.org
FSC™ C007454

FSC™ is a non-profit international organisation established to promote
the responsible management of the world's forests. Products carrying the
FSC label are independently certified to assure consumers that they come
from forests that are managed to meet the social, economic and
ecological needs of present and future generations,
and other controlled sources.

Find out more about HarperCollins and the environment at
www.harpercollins.co.uk/green

For Myra, always my shining light...

CHAPTER ONE

"Let me get this straight. Your *family values* candidate, the United States Congressman, who is the paragon of conservatism, gets caught by his wife having an affair with a hooker, who used to be a man in a previous life. But wait, there's more! Said Congressman was bent over the hooker's knee being spanked with a riding crop, while he's wearing a pink tu-tu, and you want to know how we can *spin this*?" Lexi Harlow shoved her shoulder-length red tangles behind her ears as she stared at the speakerphone.

"Lexi, you're in charge of our public relations. I thought you might have a suggestion to make this situation disappear."

She rubbed her temples as she glanced at the one-word front page headline of *The New York Post*, which featured a cartoon of the Congressman and read *Giddyup*. It told her that her biggest client was history and serious money problems were on the way. "You wanna make this disappear? Try looking in the Yellow Pages under *magicians*."

"Be serious, Lexi. I'm the New York state party chairman and we need to make this go away."

"Go away? Todd, that barn door has sailed. The Congressman is a national joke. *No one* can make this go away. He's toast. And please don't use the typical politician excuse and call it an error in judgment and have his wife sing the stand-by-your-man tune."

"How about something saying we're being a more inclusive party?"

She rolled her emerald green eyes. "Sure, we'll call it the

1

rainbow coalition for prostitutes. Look, Todd, I like you and have enjoyed working with you. But trust me, this one is un-fixable. Every other PR person in town will tell you the same thing. The guy is radioactive." She looked up and saw her assistant standing in the doorway. "And I gotta go. My advice to you is to have the man resign and get him off the front page and the late night talk shows before it does more damage to the party and the future candidates you will *hopefully* send me next year."

She heard the man sigh. "Lexi, I'm sorry this happened. I know you just started your agency and how much work you put into the campaign. And your work was terrific."

"Thanks, I appreciate that."

"If it weren't so close to election day, I'd get you another account, but everything is set. But I promise I'll have something for you next year."

"Thank you."

"Well, if you do think of anything, give me a call."

"Sure. Hang in there, Todd. Bye." She hit the button on her speakerphone, shook her head, leaned back in her chair and stretched out her five-foot-five frame as she turned to her assistant. "What?"

"And good morning to you too." Chandler, her tall, British, slender thirty-year-old assistant moved into her office, took a seat opposite her desk and studied her face with his pale blue eyes as he swept his mop of sandy hair out of his face. "From your current expression along with the front page of *The Post* I would surmise there was a significant amount of ammonia covering the rolled bits of grain in your morning meal."

"Chandler, I know you're smarter than me and like showing it off, but next time just say *you look like someone pissed in your corn flakes.*"

He shrugged and offered a slight smile. "This from the woman who just said *that barn door has sailed.*"

"Fine, point taken. But, my dear assistant, as you no doubt

2

have *surmised*, we lost our biggest client when the Congressman decided to play *Fifty Shades of Politics*. I was up all night knowing we were in trouble. Which is why I look like I just had a colonoscopy with an umbrella."

Chandler slowly nodded. "There was nothing you could do. The Congressman was a bad, bad boy."

"Yeah, but usually you get spanked *after* you're bad. Anyway, the big problem we need to immediately address is how to replace a client who made up more than seventy percent of our income."

He gave her a soulful look. "Lexi, we're in this for the long haul. My salary increase can wait, if that will help. Or you can hold back a couple of paychecks."

"That's a wonderful gesture, Chandler, but don't be ridiculous. We'll find some new clients. And you're more than my assistant. You've become like an extra brother."

"But if—"

She put up her hand. "End of discussion. We'll make do. I'll eat mac and cheese for a month to keep this place afloat. I've worked too hard to get this business started and I'm not going to let a kinky client sink it." A drop of water pinged into the steel bucket in the corner. She looked up at the stained ceiling. "Considering the leaks in this dump, that remark might turn out to be literal. Dammit, if the Congressman had won we would have gotten the bonus and we could have moved to a decent office. Hopefully one where we can't hear the people upstairs through the air vent."

"So what's the game plan?"

"Find some new clients. Plural. I've just discovered what happens when you put all your eggs in one basket. You would think a woman who just turned thirty would have learned that already."

He nodded. "I agree. Multiple small and medium-sized clients would be best. Perhaps you'll find a few at that conference this afternoon. You're quite adept at face-to-face interaction."

She stood up. "Maybe so. But right now I need to think. So I'm going to shoot some hoops."

"We just lost our biggest client and you're going to play basketball?"

"Everything becomes perfectly clear to me when I'm doing something mindless. Besides, I need to blow off some steam. I don't need to approach potential clients or give a talk to a few hundred people when I'm this pissed off. And right now my Irish temper is at DEFCON 1."

***

Kyle Caruso, known by Kasey to close friends thanks to his initials, laced up his sneakers as he sat on the bench next to his buddies. The weekly basketball game did wonders for his stress levels, especially since the thirty-year-old sports agent refused to deal with clients behaving badly. Million dollar contracts and immaturity did not mix well. The gym was pretty deserted at this time of the morning, the only sounds coming from a woman bouncing a basketball at the other end of the court. He watched her for a moment as he wrapped a headband around his thick black hair, olive green eyes wide as he noted she was nailing every shot with nothing but net. His best friend Jim Baldwin grabbed the seat next to him. "Hey, Jimbo, ready to go?"

"Kasey, we got a problem. Jackson is stuck in court all day. So we only got nine players. We're one short."

"Well, shit. Anyone else wandering around the gym?"

He shook his head. "Already checked." Jim cocked his head at the woman playing at the other end. "How about that redhead. Looks like she's got a killer jump shot."

Kyle furrowed his brow as he looked at her. "She's only a little thing. Might get hurt."

"You know, at five-seven and one-fifty you're not exactly LeBron James and we let you play."

"Very funny."

"Well, it's either ask her to join us or one of us sits out. And you know damn well no one wants to sit out."

"Fine, let's see if she'll play."

The two men got up and headed toward the slender woman, who was totally focused on the basket. Kyle couldn't help but note she was beyond cute, despite being soaked with sweat, flaming red hair gathered up behind her head, matching headband and a ton of freckles, while her movements were incredibly fluid. "Excuse me…"

She took a shot, made it and turned to face them.

Damn, what spectacular eyes… they look like the Caribbean.

"Yeah?"

Jim took the lead. "We're short one guy for a game. Wanna join us?"

She mopped her brow. "If you're short one *guy*, why you asking me?"

"Cause you look like you've got game," said Jim.

She scrunched up her face a bit as she tapped her chin with one finger. "Let me guess. There aren't any other men in the gym, right?"

Kyle rolled his eyes and put up his hands in surrender. "Hey, forget it. Sorry we bothered you—"

"No, please forgive the attitude. It's already been a rough day. Sure, I'll play." She moved closer and looked up at him. "But only if this one thinks he can guard me."

Jim started to laugh. "Ooooh, she's thrown down the gauntlet. I want Little Red on my team."

She locked eyes with Kyle for a moment and smiled. "Okay then. Let's rock."

Jim stuck out his hand to shake. "He's Kasey. I'm Jimbo."

She shook Jim's hand, then did the same to Kyle. "Nice to meet you guys."

"And you are?" asked Kyle.

"Didn't you hear your friend? Just call me Little Red."

***

The redhead moved toward Kyle as the game started, at one point dribbling between her legs and behind her back, like one of the Harlem Globetrotters, while totally focused on him. He couldn't help but be impressed as he moved forward to guard her. Her eyes looked at him for a moment, then darted around the court as it was obvious she was going to pass the ball. She raised her hand slightly and he knew she was about to pass to his right. He reached for the ball and found nothing but air as she dribbled behind her back in the other direction and left him in the dust, then pulled up and sank a long three-pointer as his feet got tangled up. He hit the floor and one of his sneakers came off.

Everyone laughed as her teammates moved forward and gave her a high five.

Jim offered a hand to help Kyle off the floor as he put his sneaker back on. "Damn, Little Red faked you out of your shoes."

Kyle glared at Jim as he took his friend's hand and stood up, finding the redhead looking at him while she had the ball pressed between her forearm and her side. She didn't say anything to rub it in, didn't smile. Just looked at him.

"What?"

She shrugged. "Your ball." She tossed it to him.

Then gave him a wink.

Okay, the gloves are coming off.

Kyle took the ball out of bounds, then started dribbling up the court. She moved forward to guard him, her arms wide. He stopped and held the ball up over his head, where she couldn't get it since he guessed she was a couple inches shorter. He turned away for a moment to look for an open teammate—

And she jumped, slapped it out of his hands, headed in the other direction and sank an easy layup shot.

Everyone laughed again.

Jim slapped Kyle on the back. "Never thought I'd see the day when you got your ass kicked by a hundred pound woman."

***

Kyle sat on the bench after the game, totally exhausted with his head against the cool concrete wall, dripping sweat and out of breath. The redhead had totally wiped the floor with him. He looked over as everyone gathered up their gym bags and headed for the showers. The woman was smiling and laughing as she shook hands with the guys, then headed in his direction.

She stopped right in front of him. "You need some oxygen? Paramedic? CPR?"

"Funny."

She stuck out her hand. "Hey, I'm kidding. Good game."

"Yeah, right. Maybe for you."

"I said *good game*. You're supposed to shake the hand of your opponent after we're done. Unless you're some sort of sore loser."

"No. You played great and I admit you kicked my ass." He shook her hand as he studied her face. "You play in college or something?"

"Nope."

"High school?"

"Uh-uh. Just the court in the old neighborhood. And I've got four brothers well over six feet tall. So I had to learn to shoot three-pointers and control the ball or I was toast."

"Well, you're a hell of a player."

"Thank you."

"You come here often?" he asked.

"That the best line you can come up with? We're not in a bar."

"I didn't mean it that way—"

"Again, I'm kidding! I like to shoot to blow off steam and, like I said, the day got off to a really bad start. Anyway, this was fun. Hadn't played an actual game in a while. Thanks for inviting me." She waved at him. "Well, see ya—"

She started to walk away. "Hey. I didn't get your name."

She turned and smiled. "Sure you did. Little Red." She winked and headed for the women's locker room.

Jim came over and patted him on the back as they both watched her walk away. "Girl sure had your number today."

"Yeah. Wish I had hers."

***

Lexi looked out at the crowd of about two hundred in the large hotel meeting room and grabbed the sides of the podium. "Okay, that's my take on spin doctoring, and we've got a few minutes left, so I'll be happy to take questions."

A woman in the front row raised her hand. "You didn't mention that you handle the PR for Congressman Bensen. How are you going to deal—"

"*Handled*, past tense. As of this morning, he is no longer my client. There are simply some situations that are not spinnable, if that's even a word, and this was one of them. I officially cut ties with his campaign this morning. While political accounts can be very lucrative, being associated with a situation like that isn't worth the money or the trouble. And it wouldn't do much for my reputation. While all of us in public relations occasionally have to deal with people and companies we don't particularly like, there are some lines I personally can't cross. Meanwhile, if there's a politician in the audience who does not own an outfit from the Joffrey Ballet and doesn't have anyone going to the whip at the top of the stretch, I'll be happy to talk to you."

The crowd laughed as she pointed to a woman in the back with her hand raised. "Yes…"

"Suppose this was your garden variety cheating politician, without the tu-tu and riding crop and all the ridicule that came with that. How would you have handled it?"

"Same outcome. I would have quit. But told his wife to clean him out on the way. Honestly, I have no tolerance for infidelity, personally or professionally. I may be old-fashioned in that respect, but that's a deal-breaker for me. So there's no such thing as a garden-variety extra-marital affair. If you're breaking a sacred vow, which I consider marriage to be, it doesn't matter if you wanna play prima ballerina or pretend you're running in the Kentucky Derby while you're cheating. I realize there have been plenty of politicians who have resurrected their careers after being caught, but I'm not interested in that kind of client. I have to look myself in the mirror at the end of the day. One more question." She pointed to a very young man in the middle of the auditorium. "Yes."

"Ms. Harlow, I'm about to graduate with a degree in public relations and I'd like to learn from a real-life spin girl. Can I come work for you?"

The crowd laughed as she smiled. "Now how did you know I needed a nickname? But sadly, young man, I do not have any openings as I run a two-person agency. But that's the kind of spunk you need to survive in this business. Be bold and believe in yourself. That's half the battle. And, remember, it is never the wrong time to do the right thing."

***

Lexi bounded up the stairs to her apartment carrying a grocery bag of goodies. Knocking off work early after a sleepless night and a tough Friday and cooking dinner for her boyfriend would take her mind off the money situation. She'd gotten a great reception

9

at the conference, handed out a ton of business cards and met some possible future clients. Things would get better for her agency.

And people had started calling her Spin Girl. The name had stuck. Hopefully it would get around and help to single her out from her competition.

But right now she desperately needed a hug from Dave. And probably a lot more from the hunky actor on the hot new sitcom who turned her on like no man ever had and was the best-looking guy she'd ever dated. Their two-year relationship was a bright spot in her life, as he had been her oasis when things were going rough for her professionally. Tonight was the night she would ask him to move in with her. Hell, because he had roommates and she lived by herself, he spent most nights at her apartment anyway and had a key to the place. She had two hours to get dinner and herself ready.

She heard voices as she put the key in the door. "Dammit, I left the TV on again." She opened it and what she saw made her jaw drop along with the groceries.

The television set was off.

The voices were coming from behind the bedroom door. And there was no TV in that room.

Her pulse spiked as she quickly moved to the bedroom, opened the door and found the source of the noise.

Dave, naked, his amazing physique bathed in candlelight. Wrists tied to the bedposts with neckties that she'd given him as gifts.

With a top-heavy blonde she recognized as his co-star strad-dling him.

Lexi put her hands on her hips as her emotions exploded. "You sonofabitch!"

Dave's eyes went wide. "Oh, shit! Babe, I can explain. We're rehearsing a scene—"

"Oh, give me a friggin' break!"

The blonde quickly pulled the sheets around her as Dave

managed to get one arm free and tried to reach over the edge of the bed for his pants.

Lexi was quicker and snatched them off the floor. "Oh, you need these?" She held the slacks in front of him.

"Lexi, please. This means nothing—"

"It means a helluva lot to me. It means you can't be trusted." She pointed at the door as her blood reached the boiling point. "Get! Out!"

"Lexi, calm down—"

"Out!"

"Fine, just give me my pants." He turned to the blonde. "Untie my other wrist."

Lexi kept her eyes locked on him as she reached behind her and opened the window that led to the fire escape. She held his linen slacks over the burning candle and they went up like a torch. She tossed them out on the fire escape, where they quickly became a ball of flame.

"Dammit, Lexi, there was five hundred bucks in the pocket!"

"Hey, you're on a hit TV show. Call it *money to burn*, asshole. Besides, she only looks like a twenty-dollar whore, so go hit an ATM if you need to pay her." She saw the blonde start to creep around the bed for her own clothes, but Lexi grabbed them as well and tossed them out the window into the fire. "Wow, silk goes up even faster! Who knew? Now both of you get the hell out of my apartment!"

The blonde slipped on a bra and panties. "In our underwear?"

Lexi whipped out her cell phone and placed a call. "Yeah, sorry, I don't own anything from the fall Extreme Silicone collection." The call connected. "Hey, Frankie, grab your camera and get outside our building right now. Catch a rising sitcom star in his tighty whiteys. And his bimbo co-star spilling out of a bra."

Dave's eyes went wide. "Who the hell did you call?"

"Paparazzo who lives downstairs. I owed him a favor. Now get out before I set *you* on fire!"

CHAPTER TWO

Kyle Caruso knew what was coming when he opened the door to his office on Monday morning.

One of his new clients had gotten in trouble late Saturday night and needed damage control, quick.

His executive assistant, who also happened to be his older sister, Donna, looked up as he entered the office. "Busy already?" he asked.

"Fuhgeddaboudit," she said, in her familiar thick New York accent. She handed him a fistful of pink message slips. "Phone's been ringin' off the hook. I've been tryin' to keep the media at bay."

"Yeah, I figured as much. Never expected him to do something so stupid. He seemed like a straight arrow."

The petite curvy brunette took his arms. "Well, you need to take care of the situation before you get on that plane. The media aint goin' away on this."

"Yeah, you're right."

"Look, Kyle, with you on the road so much looking for new clients, I think it's time we got some public relations help, and I think I found the right person. Did you listen to the podcast I gave you from the PR conference I went to on Friday?"

He nodded. "Yeah. Interesting stuff."

"I particularly liked that woman who dumped the Congressman as a client. The one they were calling Spin Girl after her talk. Sounds like she's got some high standards. Just what we need."

"You're right. She was impressive."

"Of course I'm right. I'm your older, wiser sister and I know how to look out for my little brother. That's why I grabbed her business card." Donna handed it to him. "Why don't you give her a call? Maybe she's free today and can help you out."

***

Lexi entered her office, head held high despite the events of the weekend. While walking in on her boyfriend was emotionally crushing, her revenge chromosome was a dominant one, and she took pleasure in the aftermath thanks to her neighbor the paparazzo, who had taken some terrific photos which ended up splashed across a major newspaper. Chandler looked up and studied her face as he stood up to greet her holding a handful of pink message slips. "Lexi, are you okay?"

She nodded and smiled. "Yeah, I'm good."

"I surmised that after catching your significant other *in flagrante delicto* with a woman whose hourglass figure has a good deal of sand in the top that your mood might be a somewhat dour one."

"In other words, you thought I'd be pissed off after catching the sonofabitch nailing a woman who defies the laws of gravity as they apply to halter tops."

"Basically."

"Hey, better I know now that I can't trust someone than after I go down the aisle with him. And I got even."

"He got what he deserved. I knew he was wrong for you."

"You've said that so many times."

"Perhaps someday in the future you might start listening to me." He folded his arms. "Alexandra Rebecca Harlow, you're too trusting with men. You have to be careful. You're too much of an open book with men you just meet. You have to play your cards closer to the vest."

13

"Yeah, I know. And stop doing the full name thing with me. You're not my dad."

"And you knew Dave had a reputation as a player—"

"Okay! I get it! I'll have the CIA vet the next guy who asks me out and send me a dossier."

"I'm just looking out for your future endeavors in the romance department."

"Fine, Chandler, enough about my love life, or lack thereof right now. What's with all the messages this early in the day?"

"Your talk at the conference seems to be paying dividends. We've already had a few calls from prospective new clients." He handed her the message slips as the phone rang.

Chandler answered the call as she headed for her office while looking at the messages. One decent-sized corporation, a couple of small businesses and a politician she knew to be a decent human being mounting a campaign for next year. She was about to reach for the phone to return the calls when Chandler stuck his head in the door. "Yes, Chandler?"

"Interesting prospect on the line. Sports agent for Noah Washington, the young man from the New York Jets who found himself in a difficult situation Saturday night."

"Yeah, I read the paper. Sports agent, huh?"

"They usually have deep pockets. At least the players do. Anyway, a gentleman named Kyle Caruso is on the phone and needs immediate help. And he sounds like he needs it yesterday."

"Great, thanks." She grabbed a pen to take notes as she answered the call. "Hi, Mister Caruso, this is Lexi Harlow. What can I do for you?"

"Thanks for taking my call, Lexi. And please call me Kyle. I realize I'm not a client but I heard the podcast of your talk Friday and really liked what I heard. My executive assistant was there and she liked your talk as well. Anyway, I thought you might be the right person to help me with Noah Washington of the Jets. Are you familiar with the situation?"

14

"Yeah, I'm a big sports fan and I saw that in the paper. Yet another member of the Jets in the news for the wrong reason. It's not like he got behind the wheel drunk, but that nightclub incident is still not good for his reputation. Especially since he'd never been in trouble before."

"Anyway, Noah's really a good kid but a bit immature. This often happens to rookies when they suddenly become rich and get an entourage. And while what he did qualifies as stupid, he's remorseful and wants to make things right. I thought you might have some ideas on how we can make that happen. I realize you don't know me or my client and this is ridiculously short notice but I need someone to be the point person on this today since I'm about to get on a plane. We need to spin this one quick."

"Can I meet with him right away?"

"Sure. I already told him to expect your call."

"How did you know I'd take you as a client?"

"I didn't but I figured you had some free time without the Congressman on your dance card."

She couldn't help but laugh. "You're right about that."

"Actually, the fact that you cut ties with him immediately speaks volumes about you."

"Thank you. I can't deal with sleazy clients."

"We're on the same page on that." She went over her rates and he quickly agreed to pay what she requested. They exchanged cell numbers and other pertinent information. "Lexi, can't tell you how much I appreciate this, especially on such short notice. Hope to meet you sometime when I'm back in town."

"You too. Thanks, Kyle." The call ended and she threw up her hands. "Yes!"

Chandler poked his head in the door. "I assume that was good news?"

"Yep, we can pay the rent for another month."

***

Several hours later Kyle's phone buzzed with a text as he started to unpack in the California hotel room.

News conference. Two-minute warning. Fox Sports One.
-Lexi

He turned on the hotel room television and tuned to the sports channel. An anchor was doing a voiceover as half of the screen showed an empty podium while the other side was filled with the video of his client's arrest. The image of the rookie being led away in handcuffs while screaming at police had gone viral and made Kyle cringe. The bottom of the screen read *Noah Washington to address media regarding arrest.*

He continued unpacking, keeping one eye on the TV. He saw his client head for the podium, sat on the edge of the bed and turned up the sound.

The anchor stopped talking as New York Jets rookie Noah Washington adjusted the microphone up a bit. "Good afternoon, and thank you all for coming. As everyone knows by now, I was at a club late Saturday night when a brawl broke out involving my best friend. I was not involved in the fight. After the police arrived, I attempted to protect my friend by trying to keep the police from getting to him, and in doing so I pushed an officer, who fell to the ground. I was arrested for assault and obstruction of a police investigation. When I saw the video of the arrest I was embarrassed that I acted with such a lack of maturity. This is not how my parents raised me, as I was taught to respect authority. And while I did not mean for the officer to fall or to hurt him, what I did was wrong and there was no excuse for my behavior."

Kyle's eyes went wide. "No excuses. I like that. Off to a good start."

The football player continued. "First, I apologize to the officer involved and the New York City police department. These men and women risk their lives every day to keep us safe, and I didn't show them the proper respect. For that, I am sorry. And while I can chalk this up to youthful indiscretion or having a few drinks too many, I will not. I am done with clubbing, drinking, and being out after midnight. That said, actions have consequences and I must face those I have brought on myself. First, I am going to save the court some trouble by pleading guilty to both charges. While my court date is not for two months, I am going to do two things that will hopefully show my remorse and prove to our fans and the people of New York that I have learned my lesson. First, I will donate my next game check to the policemen's benevolent association. But I don't want you to think I'm just another rich athlete who can write a check to make problems go away. So I am volunteering to do one hundred hours of community service by working on my off days on the NYPD project that's currently underway building a house for officers who have fallen on hard times. I hope that in some small way this will serve as an acceptable apology and please know I will do my best to be a model citizen going forward. You will never see my name on the police blotter again. Finally, should my head coach decide to suspend or fine me, I would ask the players' union to not challenge this as I will accept whatever punishment he thinks appropriate."

The player moved toward an officer and shook his hand while handing him a check, then went back to the podium to take questions.

Kyle's jaw hung open. "Sonofabitch. That was incredible." He watched the rest of the news conference as his client politely took every single question, never dodging the issue.

***

Lexi smiled as she read the text.

Terrific job, thank you! Will call this evening.
-Kyle Caruso

She looked up as the football player, conservatively dressed in a gray three-piece suit, calmly took question after question from the media, whose hostility had been drained with the announcement of his self-imposed sentence. Whatever blood had been in the water had been washed out to sea by the man's contrition. Number eighty-eight was now a human being who was sorry for his behavior. Very sorry.

She felt a hand lightly touch her forearm. "Excuse me, is this your handiwork?"

Lexi turned and found herself staring into the chest of a very tall man. She looked up and immediately recognized him as the veteran quarterback of the Jets, Jake Frost. "I'm his public relations person, if that's what you're asking."

"Well, then, thank you for diffusing the situation and turning it into a positive." He stuck out his hand. "Jake Frost."

"Yeah, I know."

"And you are?"

"Lexi Harlow."

"How long have you been working with my teammate?"

"About four hours. I got hired this morning by his agent."

"Wow. Well, this is a stroke of genius. The poor kid was getting beat to hell on talk radio all weekend and this morning. I know this will turn things around."

"So what are you doing here?"

"Team captain. And I've been trying to mentor the kid. Though obviously I didn't do a very good job. Maybe you need to travel with the team."

"You said it yourself, he's a kid. You couldn't watch him twenty-four seven."

"Well, this will make him grow up fast. So, did the agent have you set this up or did you come up with this strategy all by yourself?"

"My idea."

"I'm impressed. Especially with the *actions have consequences* thing. The rest of the world needs to learn that, especially parents. Hell, the rest of the NFL needs to learn it."

"Sounds like we're on the same page." She glanced back at the news conference and saw that the questions had finally stopped. "Well, looks like we're done here. Nice meeting you."

She started to walk away, but he put his hand lightly on her shoulder. "Listen, I wouldn't mind getting to know the woman who seems to think like I do. May I have your phone number?"

"You need a PR person?"

"No, I need a dinner date." He flashed a crooked smile, which made him look like a shy high school boy.

She backed up a step, surprised at his answer. She stared into the deep-set gray eyes of this Greek god and saw a look that was sincere. Though she knew the reputation of athletes, something told her this one might be okay. She couldn't remember reading anything about the guy breaking the law. Besides, she'd barbecued all of her boyfriend's clothes and was now a free agent. She smiled at him, reached into her purse, pulled out a business card but didn't give it to him, holding it near her face. "I don't usually give my number to perfect strangers."

He shrugged. "I never said I was perfect. I have an awful lot of flaws. I mean, besides throwing interceptions from time to time. Off the field I'm a total disaster. I really need a woman to fix me."

She couldn't help but laugh. His answer lowered her inhibitions and she handed him the card. "Every woman's dream, to mold a man into perfection. But if you're a typical bed-hopping athlete you should know that this weekend I torched the clothes of the boyfriend who cheated on me, so you either treat me right or wear a flame-retardant suit."

His eyes widened. "That was you? The thing with the sitcom guy on the front page of *The Post*?"

She put one finger to her lips. "Shhhh. Not common knowledge, but I confess to being the arsonist."

"I'll consider myself warned." He put the card in his pocket. "And I *will* call you. I guess there will be a penalty if I don't."

She moved closer and craned her neck as she locked eyes with him. "You'd better believe it, Mister."

***

Lexi poured herself a glass of wine, stretched out on the couch and put her feet up, then turned on Fox Sports One. She wanted to see a replay of the news conference. Talk radio had done a complete about-face, the callers all impressed that her new client had taken responsibility for his actions and was doing something tangible to apologize. Even a few cops called in to compliment the young man. The local news showed Nate Washington in jeans and a tee-shirt working on the construction of a house alongside a bunch of police officers.

Her strategy had worked perfectly.

And a pro quarterback, possibly the most eligible bachelor in New York and one who was (hard to believe) even better-looking than Dave, had asked for her phone number. Whether he would actually call was beside the point. It felt good to have a man like that interested in her. Greek gods didn't grow on trees.

Three days ago her world had gone ablaze, literally and figuratively.

Now, in what seemed like an instant, things had turned around. Though possibly getting into bed with a professional athlete, literally and figuratively, was something that demanded she tread with caution. For now, though, the rose-colored glasses provided by possibly the most gorgeous man she'd ever met remained in place.

She took a sip of the cold red wine and settled in to watch the replay when her cell rang. She didn't recognize the number and hit the pause button on the TV. "Hello, this is Lexi."

"Hi, Lexi, it's Kyle Caruso. Am I catching you at a bad time?"

"No, not at all. Just watching TV. Your trip go okay?"

"Too early to tell. I'm at San Diego State, hoping to sign their star running back. But right now it takes a back seat to all the goodwill you got for my client today, and that all reflects really well on me as his agent. I can't thank you enough and tell you how impressed I am with your strategy, especially on such short notice."

"Thank you, I'm glad you're pleased. Noah was a pleasure to work with."

"I told you, he's a good kid. But you made him look like a saint."

"That's why they call me Spin Girl. I can usually spin most situations. Though not cheating politicians."

He laughed a bit. "Yeah, I can't imagine anyone could fix that. Anyway, did the Jets treat you okay setting things up? I gave them a heads-up that you were working with me."

"They were very nice, thank you for calling ahead. The head coach was happy we were being so pro-active and taking control of the situation. So was the quarterback."

"Oh, I didn't see Frost at the news conference."

"He was there, but off camera. He said he'd been mentoring Noah and was glad to see him take responsibility for what he'd done. Seemed like a good guy."

"Man, I'd love to have him as a client. Talk about deep pockets. By the way, are you a fan?"

"Of who, the Jets?"

"Yeah."

"Nope, lifelong Giants fan. Got season tickets. But I like to see the Jets do well. A subway Super Bowl would be seriously cool, even though it wouldn't be in New York."

"Season tickets, huh? So what's your take on the team? The Giants, I mean."

She relaxed a bit, the business part of the conversation apparently over. Her new client was happy, and obviously liked to talk. She gave him her opinion on the Giants, then the conversation segued to football announcers, TV shows, movies, politics, why she got into PR, how he became an agent. The conversation was easy and flowed, like she was talking to an old friend. She picked up her iPad and did a search of his name, hoping to find a photo to see the face behind the voice.

The search turned up nothing but a plain business website with pictures of his clients. No photos of him.

Her phone beeped. "Hang on a minute, Kyle."

"Sure."

She looked at her phone expecting to see an incoming call, but instead found a low battery warning. "Hey, my cell is about to die. Guess we've been talking awhile." She looked at the clock and her eyes widened. "Like, an hour and a half. You give good phone."

He laughed. "Never heard that one before. I enjoyed talking to you too. Anyway, I'm sure I'll have more work for you in the future if you're up for more stuff with athletes."

"Thanks, I appreciate that. Would love to sit down with you in person."

"It will probably be awhile. I travel a lot this time of year and only manage to get home a day at a time. I'm back Friday night and out first thing Sunday morning. But we'll get together eventually."

"Look forward to it." The phone beeped twice, telling her it was about to die. "Okay, my cell is about to flatline, so, bye."

"Thanks again, Lexi."

The phone went dead.

She got up, put her phone back on the charger and headed for the kitchen to get some celebratory Häagen Dazs rum raisin with the obligatory extra splash of rum. She couldn't help but smile. Her agency was off life support for the moment, a Greek god wanted to take her to dinner (well, maybe) and she'd made a new friend out of a client.

All was right in the universe.

At least for now.

CHAPTER THREE

Though still bleary-eyed Saturday morning after taking the Friday red-eye from California, Kyle needed to shake off his jet lag at the gym. Shooting hoops for an hour or so and an afternoon nap would hopefully regulate his body clock before his next trip. He stopped at the desk to check out a basketball and heard the rhythmic thump from the court. "Is there actually a game going on at this hour?"

The shaggy clerk, who looked to be about eighteen, shook his head. "Just a young woman, but that's it. You can each have a half court. I'll be right back with a ball."

A young woman?

He walked across the hall, looked through the plexiglass down at the court and saw the little redhead hitting shot after shot.

I'm gonna get my ass kicked again. Then again, maybe this time I can get her number...

He moved back to the desk as the clerk handed him a basketball. He wrote his name on the sign-out sheet, then looked at the clerk as he cocked his head at the court. "By the way, you know her name?"

"Sir, I can't give out that information."

"Sure, I understand."

"But she's very nice."

He took a quick look at the sloppy signature above his. It looked like *Alexandra* followed by a scribble. He headed down the stairs to the basketball court and found her sitting on the bench, dripping with sweat, sipping a bottle of water. She looked up and smiled. "Well, look who's here. Back for a re-match?"

He pretended to study her face for a moment. "I'm sorry, I don't believe we've met."

She laughed. "Very funny. It's Kasey, right?"

"Yeah. And I still don't know your name." He noticed a light jacket with monogrammed initials draped over her gym bag and pointed at it. "Ah, but it begins with A."

She nodded. "Very perceptive, Columbo. You've narrowed it down."

"Wait, don't tell me… Amy?"

"Nope."

"Agatha?"

She furrowed her brow and pointed to her face. "Do I look eighty years old to you?"

"Sorry. Actually about fifty-five years younger."

"Hang on, let me do the math… eighty minus fifty-five… zero minus five, borrow the one… why thank you, kind sir."

"You're welcome. But back to your name… you look like you'd have something really classy."

She pointed at her face. "This sweaty mug looks classy to you?"

"Women don't sweat, they glow."

"Yeah, and I'm glowin' like Secretariat."

"Anyway, back to your name… Alexandra?"

Her eyes widened. "Damn, you're good."

"Really, that's it?"

She nodded. "Yep. Mom wanted a boy and was going to name him Alex, so Alexandra was the next best thing."

"So, do friends call you Alex? I hope not because I think Alexandra suits you better."

"Nope." She grabbed a towel and wiped her face. "You can totally call me Alexandra if you like."

"I like."

25

"Well, I'm about done here, but if you're up for a little one-on-one, I'm game."

"Why, you need to start your weekend beating the hell out of a guy?"

"Thought you might be one of those alpha males who hates losing to a woman and needs to get even."

"Nah, I'm one of those renaissance men who treats women as equals. Though in your case I will admit you're better than me at one thing."

"Just one?"

"So far that's the only thing we have to go on. I'm willing to bet I'm better at something than you are."

She sat up straight. "What? Shooting pool? Poker? Let's rock."

"Planning a date."

"Excuse me?"

"I'm an expert at planning fantastic dates."

"So, you're saying you're a great date?"

"You might not fall in love with me, but women are always entertained when I take them out. I'm a Jedi date master. I'm sure you couldn't possibly beat me planning the ultimate fun date."

She backed up a bit. "You asking me out?"

He shrugged. "Depends."

"Depends? On what?"

"If you think you're better than me at planning a date."

"So what exactly are you proposing?"

"Two dates. We each plan one. Then decide which was the most enjoyable."

"I must admit, I have not run into this clever tactic before. You're taking advantage of my competitive nature as a backdoor method of asking me out. Surely you realize that I realize what you're doing."

"Of course. But the beauty of this is that if you decline I can simply assume you're worried about losing the bet, rather than not being interested in me. And my fragile male ego wouldn't be bruised, since, as you know, men can be devastated for weeks when turned down for a date. But you strike me as a woman who can't turn down a challenge."

She locked eyes with him for a moment with those fantastic eyes, sending a shiver through his body. "Okay. But I wanna see how creative you are, so let's make this interesting. Hundred-dollar limit on the dates. And that includes a nice dinner."

"A hundred bucks? We're in New York City. If we do anything besides dinner we'll be eating at a hot dog cart."

"Then we'll find out who's more creative." She stuck out her hand. "You agree to the terms?"

He shook. "It's a bet. Oh, what does the winner get?"

"If I win, you buy me another dinner with no expense limit at the restaurant of my choice."

"And if I win?"

She shot him a wicked grin and batted her eyes. "You would have already won by having the pleasure of my company for two evenings."

"Something tells me that will be enough. You're not a very good gambler since I win either way."

"Aw, you're such a sweetie. So, when does this happen?"

"I'm out of town all week, but free next Saturday night. After that I'll be gone for two more weeks."

"Okay. Next Saturday."

"Ladies first?"

"Hell no. I wanna see what I've gotta beat. And it will give me two weeks to plan."

"Fine. I'll pick you up at six, so I'll need your number and address."

She wagged a finger at him. "Not yet, Mister. Meet me outside the gym and you will be dressed nice, not in the Occupy Wall Street collection. If you're one minute late, I'm gone."

"You want me to pick you up in front of this place?"

"Yeah. Girl's gotta be careful these days, you know?"

"Sure, I understand. You don't really know me. Okay, so if either of us has to cancel for any reason, leave a note at the front desk."

"Okay, see you in a week." She got up and grabbed her bag. "Well, I'm outta here. By the way, remember that I have four very large brothers. Treat me badly and one of them will break you in half."

He stood up. "You're a spunky little thing, you know that?"

"Part of my charm, as you will soon discover. And watch who you're calling little, you're not much taller than me." She moved closer and looked up at him, then got up on her tiptoes so she actually looked down at him. "And I've got lots of four-inch heels."

He didn't back up. "Hey, I said I treat women as equals. Bring it."

***

The dropping temperatures of October had chilled Lexi's apartment, but she had a fire going, and Dave's remaining belongings had made wonderful kindling. For the first time in two years she was spending Saturday night alone, but without regret. It was time to regroup and consider the interesting possibilities that had presented themselves in the past week.

New York's most eligible bachelor had asked for her phone number. Sure, he hadn't called yet, and probably wouldn't, but it had still lifted her spirits at a time she needed a boost.

Her agency was off life support thanks to a new client from out of the blue. And one with whom she seemed to have a connection on the phone that went beyond a business relationship. Since they hadn't met and she couldn't even find a photo, the physical attraction part was still a mystery.

What the hell, a guy who gave good phone was always nice to have.

She settled in to binge-watch Netflix with a bottle of chilled wine, turned on the TV—

And the phone rang.

She looked at her cell, which read *private number* then furrowed her brow as she answered the call. "Hello, this is Lexi—"

"Hi, Lexi, Jake Frost. Hope I'm not calling you at a bad time."

"No, not at all."

Curious. Guy calling me at seven on a Saturday night. Did his date cancel and is he expecting me to drop what I'm doing to go out with him? I knew athletes were arrogant, but seriously?

"Great. Well, I told you I'd call and I'd like to get together—"

"I'm staying in tonight, Jake."

He chuckled a bit. "No, not tonight. I've got a game tomorrow at one and during the season I don't go out on weekends. Getting good rest is important and I have a feeling I wouldn't get much with you around."

Half compliment, half come-on? "And… why would you say that?"

"Cause you strike me as someone I'd stay up talking with till one in the morning."

"Oh. I was wondering where you were going with that."

"Sorry, guess it came out wrong. Like I said, I'm pretty much a mess off the field."

"I'll let it slide, but try and watch the double entendres in the future."

"Yes, ma'am."

"And please don't call me ma'am, I'm not that old!"

"Sorry. Force of habit, since I'm from Texas. We try to be polite to our women folk."

"I see. So, what did you have in mind?"

"Well, Monday after a game I pretty much resemble an extra from *The Walking Dead* and since we're playing the Patriots tomorrow I know I'm gonna get hammered. But I'm usually okay on a Tuesday. I realize that's not a traditional date night, but it's the best I can do this time of year. So, I'd love to have dinner with you Tuesday night, if you're interested and didn't have any other plans."

"Sure, Tuesday sounds good. Where do you want to meet?"

"Uh, I was gonna pick you up."

"Jake, don't take this the wrong way, but these days I'm being extra careful about giving out my address after my most recent experience with a boyfriend."

"Oh, right. The guy with hot pants. Sure, Lexi, I understand. Then how about you meet me at Reston's on fifty-fourth, say around seven?"

"Sure. Hey, I'll need your number just in case something comes up."

"Oh, so you can have *my* number but I can't have *your* address?"

"Them's the rules if you want a date with Spin Girl."

"That's what they call you?"

"Damage control is my game, Spin Girl is my name."

"Cute. Anyway, I will abide by your rules. I can already tell you're gonna be a handful."

"I am a redhead, Jake. We're all a handful."

He laughed, gave her his phone number and ended the call. She leaned back and sipped wine, wondering if getting involved with a pro athlete was a smart thing to do, but feeling damned attractive knowing that this one was interested in her.

Then she grabbed her tablet and did a search on Jake Frost, finding hundreds of images.

Many of the pro quarterback with a supermodel on his arm.

***

Lexi took a deep breath as she reached for the brass handle of the upscale restaurant door. It was her first date with someone different in two years, and she knew the dangers of starting a possible new relationship on the rebound. But the ego factor of dinner with someone like Jake Frost had the rose-colored glasses firmly in place, despite continued warnings from her trusty assistant.

She entered the dimly lit restaurant at exactly seven o'clock, looking around the lobby and not seeing anyone but the host in a tuxedo at an oak podium. The middle-aged gentleman looked up at her and smiled. "Good evening, Miss. Do you have a reservation?"

"I'm supposedly meeting someone, but I'll need a table for one and a big bottle of wine if I get stood up."

He studied her face. "Ah, yes, you're obviously Mister Frost's dining companion."

"How did you know?"

"He told me to keep an eye out for an attractive flame-haired woman with an attitude to match."

She couldn't help but laugh. "Yeah, that's pretty much spot on. Is he here?"

"Yes, he enters through the back door to avoid the paparazzi. We have a nice secluded table for you. Right this way."

She followed the host through a maze of tables, already filled as the scent of seared beef and the sounds from a piano filled the air. Lexi had only read about this place, with its thousand-dollar dinners and well-heeled clientele, mostly old guys with young trophy wives. As she looked at the patrons her best emerald green dress suddenly felt like something from a close-out store. Luckily no one paid attention to her. The host led her around a corner, where she found Jake Frost in a gray three-piece suit seated at a table. He smiled and stood up, then pulled out her chair. "Right on time."

"In my business you have to be."

The host gave a slight nod. "Enjoy your evening."

"Thanks, Frederick," said Jake, as he sat opposite her. "You look great, Lexi."

31

"Thank you, but I think I'm a little underdressed for this place."

"Don't be ridiculous, you'd look fabulous in a burlap sack."

"Okay, Mister, you can dial down the compliments. A little, anyway." He smiled at her, his dazzling look sending an electric charge through her body. "So, you won Sunday."

"Yeah, had a good game. Didn't get beat up too bad. You have a good week?"

"Yes, things went well." She turned her attention to the leather-bound menu with a gold tassel running down the middle. She opened it and read the list of elaborate entrees, none of which had prices next to them. "Uh-oh."

"What?"

"No prices on the menu. I always worry about ordering a hamburger and getting a bill for fifty bucks."

"Well, they don't serve burgers here. But I know what you mean. My family didn't have much growing up and I guess that stays with you forever. It took me a while to stop clipping coupons."

"You clipped coupons?"

"My rookie year. My financial advisor finally told me to loosen up a bit."

"I've noted you give a lot of it away."

"Ah, you've vetted me."

"Girl's gotta know who's taking her out. But yes, I checked you out and was very impressed at your considerable amount of charitable donations."

"Lexi, I couldn't possibly spend all the money I've made in a dozen lifetimes. May as well do something good with it."

"Very noble."

"And at this point I have no one to leave it to."

"I see."

"So obviously since you're here, I survived your investigation." She scrunched up her face a bit and looked at the ceiling.

"Well, there was one thing in your dossier that raised a red flag just a bit off the ground."

His eyes filled with worry. "Red flag? I've never been in trouble—"

"Your seeming affinity for tall, slinky blonde supermodels who appear in swimsuit issues wearing very little."

He blushed a bit. "Those, uh, were youthful indiscretions. Fame and fortune do strange things to guys and when women like that throw themselves at you – well, you can imagine."

"So you no longer think with the wrong head."

He shook his head and smiled. "You're not exactly shy about expressing yourself, are you?"

"As you said, I'm a handful. Anyway, this bikini babe thing is in the past, huh?"

"Well, if your investigation turned up dates along with those photos, you would have noted all those so-called relationships were nearly ten years ago. I've grown up and my tastes have changed."

"Ah, I see. Changed to what?"

"Right now I seem to be into smartass redheads with a brain. But they're so damn hard to find."

***

Two and a half hours later they emerged through the back door into the chilly night.

The waiting limo was surrounded with photographers and autograph-seekers.

"Aw, hell," said Jake.

"I thought no one knew you were here since you came in the back door."

"Damn Twitter. There's a hashtag called *where is Jake Frost* and when I get spotted, a flash mob shows up." He put his arm around her shoulders and ushered her toward the waiting car.

The flashes from the cameras blinded her and she felt herself being pushed into the limo. Jake slid in beside her as the chauffeur closed the door. Her vision cleared and she looked through the windows as the vehicle pulled away. "Damn, you go through that every day?"

"Yeah. Pretty hard to hide when you're six-five and play for a New York football team. Some days I wish I'd get traded to a place like Kansas City."

"I'm sure you don't."

"Of course not. But I'm always reminded of the old saying about fame. People dream of being famous and then when it happens they go through life with sunglasses on."

"I wouldn't know, but it sounds about right."

"That's one reason I like to vacation out of the country, where no one watches American football and I can be anonymous."

She looked out the window. "So where are we going?"

"Up to you. But I need to be asleep by midnight."

"What, is it a school night?"

"No, we're in the middle of the season and athletes need proper rest. Besides, we have team meetings and workouts tomorrow at ten."

"Right, forgot about that. So what did you have in mind?"

"We can ride around the city, go to a club, go to my place and talk, or I can take you home."

"Well, I get the idea that after the scene we just left you're not wild about going to a club, but then again, neither am I. I think I've outgrown that stuff. And though I have enjoyed our evening so far I'm still not ready to tell you where I live. Hope you're not offended by that."

"Not at all. I meant I could have the driver take you home after he drops me off. Wouldn't want you to feel uncomfortable."

She reached over and patted his hand. "I don't feel uncomfortable at all. I guess we could go to your place for a while and talk. If that's actually what you have in mind. Talking."

"Regardless of what I might have in mind, you've been in control of things the entire night, wouldn't you agree?"

She laughed a bit. "Yeah, I guess so." She leaned forward toward the driver. "Home, James."

"Yours or his?" asked the driver.

"His, first. But mine later."

"My pleasure, Miss."

***

Lexi's eyes bugged out as the elevator opened into a spectacular penthouse. She stepped out onto the polished white marble floor and took in the amazing panoramic view of Manhattan through floor-to-ceiling windows. "Whoa."

"Welcome to my humble abode."

"Let me guess… you're house-sitting for Donald Trump?"

He laughed. "Nope, it's mine. Make yourself comfortable. Would you like a glass of champagne?"

"Bring it on." *Even though champagne makes me let my guard down and I've already had two glasses at the restaurant.*

"Meet you in the living room."

She stepped down into the sunken living room, amazed at the decor. It sure didn't look like any bachelor apartment she'd ever seen, as he obviously had a decorator and a maid. She grabbed a seat on one end of the white-leather sectional couch, took off her heels, curled her legs under her and put a pillow on her lap. Jake returned carrying two glasses of champagne, handed one to her, studied her for a moment, then took a seat at the opposite end of the couch. She furrowed her brow.

"What are you doing way over there? Am I supposed to yell, or call you on the phone?"

"I thought you'd be more comfortable if I sat here."

"Why would you think that?"

"My sister is a body language expert. Woman with a pillow in her lap means *look but don't touch*. At least that's what she told me."

"So, your sister taught you how to read women?"

"Of course not. Your logic is in a foreign language."

"Very funny. As for said pillow in lap, I was just getting comfortable."

"Well, I thought in light of the fact that you didn't give me your address, I didn't want to scare you away."

"Men don't scare me, Jake. I can take care of myself. And if I didn't want to be here, I would have gone home." She patted the seat next to her. "C'mon, I won't bite."

He smiled, got up and sat next to her, then clinked her glass. "To new relationships."

"We're off to a good start."

"Good to know."

She looked around the room. "So I was expecting something that looked like a sports bar. Where are all the trophies, awards, autographed jerseys?"

Jake shrugged. "I was never much for that stuff. They're really just things. Memories are more important. Every award I've gotten I've auctioned off for charity. The total raised is up to six hundred thousand now."

"Damn, your stock just went up."

"Hey, if an inanimate object can help someone in need, why not? And it's not like I need anything. Other than a woman to fix me."

***

About two hours later his grandfather clock chime signaled it was the witching hour. Jake turned and looked at the clock. "Damn, it's twelve already?"

"And we haven't even gotten to a discussion about favorite TV shows."

"Well, I hate to kick you out but—"

"I know, you need your beauty sleep during the season. Not a problem." She put her champagne glass on the glass coffee table, put her heels back on and stood up. The room began to spin a bit. "Whoa."

He stood up and took her arm. "You okay?"

"Between the drinks at dinner and three glasses of champagne here I've got a nice buzz going."

"Well, thankfully you have two options to get home. I can send you in the limo, which means my driver will know your address, or I can give you the cab fare."

She studied his face. "I think you've proven yourself trustworthy enough to know where I live. Besides, that limo beats the hell out of a cab."

"Very true."

"By the way, you didn't have to order one on my account."

"Oh, it's part of my contract. It also insures I'll never be behind the wheel after having a drink, and I do like a drink or two. Sometimes three."

"Smart man."

"By the way, before I was hounded by the paparazzi I would always walk a girl to the door, but you're already going to be on *Page Six* tomorrow."

"Seriously?"

"Yep. I spotted the photographer from *The Post*. Caption will probably read *Jake Frost at upscale restaurant with unidentified stunning redhead*."

She tried to hold back a smile but couldn't. "Stop it, I'm not stunning. Especially considering your previous dinner companions were in the Victoria's Secret TV fashion show and on the covers of swimsuit issues."

"You're not going to let that go, are you?"

"Nope. Need something to hold over your head. And not the one you used to think with."

"Very funny." He walked her to the elevator, put his hands on her shoulders and turned her so she was facing him. "Lexi, I really enjoyed tonight."

"Me too."

"I'm not sure I've ever been out on a date and just talked to a woman for five hours."

"So when you were out with a garden-variety supermodel you talked for two minutes and then—"

"Sorry, that didn't come out right. Just another example of me being a total mess off the field. I meant I really enjoyed talking with a woman as smart and funny as you."

"Ah, so you're only interested in my mind."

"Oh, I'm definitely interested in the rest of you too, but your mind is certainly intriguing. So, can I see you again?"

She tapped her chin with one finger and looked to the side. "Hmmm… I think you've behaved well enough to merit a second date."

"Have I behaved well enough to merit a goodnight kiss?"

She moved closer to him. Lexi craned her neck to look up at the man who towered over her. "Sure, if you've got a stepladder handy."

"When you're six-five, you don't need one. But I can fix the problem." He reached down, placed his hands on her sides and effortlessly lifted her up so that she was at eye level with him. She took his head in her hands and gave him a soft kiss. Their lips parted and she locked eyes with him, getting a look that went right into her soul. The kiss from an incredibly attractive man, along with too much champagne and a subconscious desire to get even with Dave, all dropped her inhibitions down to near zero. She slid her arms around his neck and their lips met again as she instinctively wrapped her legs around his waist. His hands slid under her hips, supporting her as she kissed him with a hunger she'd never known with anyone else.

Ten minutes later she stopped, rested her head on his shoulder as she ran her hands across his back, savoring the feel of the massive, rock-hard muscles under his shirt. "Damn."

"Yeah. So much for the *look but don't touch* body language."

I was referring to the fact that your muscles have muscles, but whatever. She leaned back and smiled at him. "I told you I was just getting comfortable."

"You comfortable now?"

"Very. But you need your sleep and I've gotta work tomorrow too."

"And if you stay here any longer I'm not going to get any sleep at all." She tried not to blush but her freckles caught fire. He set her back down and pressed the button on the elevator. "Next Tuesday, then?"

"To be continued." The elevator door opened and she backed into it, not breaking eye contact.

And as soon as the door closed, she knew she'd gone too far.

CHAPTER FOUR

"Well, if it isn't the unidentified stunning redhead."

Lexi studied Chandler's face. "What the hell are you talking about?"

He handed her the day's edition of the *New York Post*, open to the gossip section known as *Page Six*. Her eyes went wide as she saw the photo of herself with Jake Frost getting into the limo. "Holy shit!" Then a smile slowly grew. "Hmmm… they actually called me stunning."

"My sentiments exactly."

"The *holy shit* part or the fact that you're surprised they called me stunning?"

"I'm not at all surprised at your description in the publication, as you have, since the day I met you, consistently underestimated your appeal to those of the male persuasion. As for the expletive involving excrement, since when are you being escorted about town by a professional athlete? Were you unable to log on to Ashley Madison's website?"

"Oh, stop it. I don't need to visit an affair website. I met him at the Jets' news conference the other day. He asked me out and seemed like a good guy." She pulled off her sunglasses. "Damn, it's bright in here."

Chandler moved closer to get a good look at her bloodshot eyes. "Ah, revenge of the grape."

"Don't remind me. But *do* remind me not to drink champagne on a weeknight when I have to go to work the next day. I feel like someone's hitting a Chinese gong in my head. I think I'll just work on those press releases all day."

"Perhaps not. Mister Caruso called again with yet another emergency request for your help with one of his clients."

"When did he call?"

"Five minutes ago." He handed her a message slip.

"Okay, let me see what he needs. This could be a very lucrative client. And he seems like a really good guy."

"You met him?"

"No, we talked on the phone forever the other night. Really had a connection."

"Speaking of connections, what's the story with the aforementioned professional athlete?"

"Yeah, we had a connection as well, but I'm regretting it this morning."

"Since you're wearing a different outfit than yesterday, I assumed you were not doing the proverbial walk of shame."

"Hey, what kind of a girl do you think I am? No, I meant that since I'm on the rebound I should be taking things slow and they got a bit out of hand last night. But not *that* far out of hand. Champagne on a first date is a bad idea for me. Anyway, let me get back to Kyle and see what he's got for me."

"Meanwhile, I'll work up a dossier on the weekend gladiator."

"He's a football player, not a guy fighting lions in the Coliseum."

"Similar occupation, different era. Regardless, I wish you to know who you might be getting into bed with. Literally and/or figuratively."

"You don't have to do that—"

"I should have done it with your last paramour."

"Point taken, Chandler. Knock yourself out. Dig up as much dirt as you can find. Hopefully you won't discover anything, but better safe than sorry."

She headed into her office, pulled her cell from her purse and dialed Kyle's number. He picked up on the first ring. "Lexi, thanks for calling back so quick."

"Not a problem, Kyle, what do you need?"

"One more athlete who needs an attitude adjustment. But at least this one's not in trouble with the police." Lexi took notes as he went over the situation. "Anyway, as usual I'm stuck out of town and was hoping you could knock some sense into the kid."

"Sure, happy to do it."

"Great. He can be at my office later this morning if your schedule permits you to meet him there. Oh, and I've told my executive assistant, Donna, to cut you a check for last week and today."

"Kyle, you're my kind of client."

"Hey, you dropped what you were doing for me at the last minute, so the least I can do is pay you quick."

"Thanks, I appreciate it. So give me the address for your office." Her eyes went wide as he told her. "Are you kidding me?"

"Why would I kid about my address?"

"You're not gonna believe this, but we're in the same building!"

"Are you kidding me?"

"That's my line. Anyway, you're one floor up from me."

"Damn, small world. We both share office space in the same dump."

"No argument here," she said with a sigh.

"The rent's cheap and since I just went out on my own, I have to keep expenses down," he explained.

"Same story here, so I know where you're coming from."

"Well, I guess I won't have to reimburse you for a cab fare."

She laughed. "Yeah. Anyway, I'll wander upstairs in a couple of hours and make your problem go away."

"Thanks, Lexi, I cannot thank you enough. One of these days I'll do it in person."

Lexi took the stairs, since Kyle's office was only one flight up. Besides, the elevator in the old building was always an adventure, and the standing joke was that if the hamster fell off the treadmill that powered the ancient thing you'd get stuck.

She found the door marked "Caruso Agency", which turned out to be right over her own office. She entered the office and found a sharp-looking thirty-something brunette manning the reception desk. The woman looked up and smiled as she stood up and extended her hand. "I'll bet you're Lexi. I'm Donna, Kyle's executive assistant."

Lexi shook her hand. "So nice to meet you, Donna." Though she hadn't met Kyle, he certainly had good taste in assistants. The woman was petite, maybe five-two, with huge brown eyes, high cheekbones and long, wavy mahogany hair down to the middle of her back. Very exotic. Very Italian. "So, where's the guy I'm here to fix?"

"Every woman's dream, huh? And you get paid to do it. Right this way." Donna led her into a small meeting room occupied by a large blonde man, who was busy staring at his cell phone. "This is Franklin Jessup. Franklin, this is Lexi Harlow, the woman Kyle sent over for you."

The guy looked up from his phone and stood up, towering over both women, and built like a Coke machine. "Nice to meet you."

Lexi looked up at the hulk. "You might not think so when we're done."

"Can I get you anything to drink?" asked Donna.

Lexi sat at the small round table. "Big glass of water, thanks." She gestured to the chair opposite her. "Have a seat, Franklin. So, you're in trouble for your tweets and Facebook posts."

The guy exhaled as he sat down with a hangdog look. "Yeah. I've been getting into arguments with fans and I guess some

43

people took my last tweet the wrong way and got offended. I was just joking around. Coach fined me and then called Mister Caruso. Mister Caruso told me I should do exactly what you tell me to do."

"Why don't you just stay off the Internet?"

He shrugged. "I dunno. I guess I'm addicted, like most young people. Fans start saying hurtful things about me and I have to fight back."

"Actually, you don't. Do you go into the stands and fight the fans when they boo you on the field?"

"Of course not."

"Then you shouldn't do it online. It's nothing more than digital road rage, like flipping the bird at someone from your car." Donna returned and slid the glass of water next to Lexi, then leaned against the wall to listen. "Are all your accounts logged in with apps?" She pointed at his phone.

"Yeah. Twitter, Facebook, Instagram and Snapchat."

Lexi reached across the table and grabbed the phone. "Franklin, you need a cleanse to fix your problem."

"What, like drinking juice all day?"

"Nope. Social media cleanse." She tapped his phone a few times. "Okay, that takes care of Twitter."

"What do you mean?"

"I just deleted your account."

His eyes went wide. "Why would you do that? I had thousands of followers!"

"So you won't get in any more trouble. By the way, you've got seventy thousand *real* followers in the stadium stands and millions more on TV every Sunday." She tapped the phone a little more. "Okay, *hasta la vista* Facebook."

"No!"

A few more taps. "And it's *sayonara* to Instagram. Say bye-bye to Snapchat."

The player bit his lower lip as Lexi continued to tap on his phone. Then she turned it over, opened it, and pulled out the SIM card. "What are you doing now?"

"First, you owe me fifty bucks."

"For what?"

She reached in her purse and pulled out a simple flip phone. "Your new phone." She opened the back and slid the SIM card inside, then closed it and slid it over to Franklin.

He opened it and shook his head. "No way. This is one of those phones for old people with the big numbers. All it does is make calls."

"No shit, Sherlock." She took his smartphone, held it over the glass of water and dropped it in.

"What the hell did you do that for?"

"So you can't get in trouble. You wanna talk to someone, or someone wants to talk to you, you now have this wonderful thing called a telephone call. No more social media, no more texting. You are cleansed and off the grid. And therefore... wait for it..."

"I can't get in trouble."

"Very good. So what's more important, Franklin... your cell phone and playing on the Internet or your career and keeping your coach and fans happy?"

He slowly nodded. "My career."

"Good."

"You do realize I could simply go out and buy another phone."

"You do realize that if you do I'll kick your ass."

He was speechless.

"Now get your butt back to practice and knock the hell out of the Falcons this weekend."

Franklin got up and shook her hand. "Thank you, Miss Harlow."

"You can thank me by staying off the Internet and out of trouble." He nodded and left the office.

Donna patted Lexi on the back, then sat down next to her.

"Oh my God, the look on his face when you dropped his phone in the water! You, young lady, are worth your weight in gold."

"Thank you. Just a matter of tough love."

"Well, it worked. Hey, you wanna go to lunch?"

***

Lexi hadn't realized how much she needed simple girl talk. Chandler was an okay sounding board, but too much like her dad and very protective of her when it came to matters of the heart. And most of her friends were male. But she immediately sensed a kindred spirit in Donna, who seemed to be as spunky and snarky as she was.

Donna picked at her grilled-chicken salad. "So, I don't see a ring on your finger. What's the story here?"

"Just got out of a two-year relationship."

"Ah, rebound city. So, taking time off from the dating pool?"

"Ya know, when I was younger I might have, but I've decided to simply bury the past right away and play the field for a while. Dating one guy didn't work out… I mean, I put all my eggs in one basket and ended up with an omelet on my face."

"Interesting visual. So, you already back on the horse? Or still looking at the racing form?"

"Got a couple of new guys on my dance card who I just met. But I simply need to have a bit of fun without anything serious."

"I hear ya. Think you might have room for a third on that dance card? You're perfect for my brother."

Her face tightened a bit. "No offense, but I'm not big on fix-ups, Donna."

"Well, I'm obviously biased, but he's a catch and I think you two would be a great match. He loves spunky girls and he's got this thing for redheads. Oh my gawd, he would luv ya. He's around your age, just turned thirty. Cute as hell. Got that boy- next-door thing going. And a real sweetheart. He's my younger brother but

46

he's very protective of me as if he was the older one. We're really close."

"That's nice. So why hasn't this great catch been caught yet?"

"Well, he's never had any problems getting dates because he's so much fun, but when it comes to getting serious... I dunno, I don't think girls see him as what they envisioned in a husband."

"Why, what's wrong with him?"

"Nothing. But he's got several factors working against him. He's, well... he's a little guy. I don't mean as short as me, but he's only five-seven and slender. Not the traditional big macho guy many women want. He also doesn't have a lot of money. He just opened his new business a year ago and finances are tight. In fact, the only way he could go out on his own was by ditching his apartment and moving in with me. So I'm searching for a girl who can look past a short guy with no money who lives with his sister and realizes good things come in small packages."

"I don't have any problem dating short guys. In fact, one of the guys I'm seeing this weekend isn't much taller than me."

"See, I knew you were open-minded. Anyway, if those two guys on that dance card of yours don't work out, let me know. Seriously, you're perfect for him."

"So how did you feel about him moving in with you?"

"It was my idea. He needed the twenty-five hundred he was blowing on an apartment each month to rent an office, and I had a house all to myself. Pretty much thanks to him."

"Not sure I follow."

Donna grabbed her drink and leaned back. "Well, I got married when I was twenty-two to a handsome rich guy and it wasn't working out. I caught him cheating and the sonofabitch hits me like it's my fault. So I left the house and went over to my brother's apartment. When he saw the black eye he was livid, went to my house and kicked the living crap out of my ex-husband, who was twice his size. My brother had been bullied a lot in school so he got a black belt in karate. Anyway, a few weeks later we show up with our lawyers for the first divorce meeting, my brother cracks his knuckles, shoots my ex the death stare and he immediately caves. Gives me the house and most of the cash. So I owe my little brother big time."

"Okay, I haven't even met him but his stock just went up."

"Listen, Lexi, I married a wealthy guy who was incredibly handsome, but I was young and stupid and had stars in my eyes. I'd gladly trade the house and money to have not gone through that. So take it from me, when you do settle on a guy, make sure it's for love. At the end of the day, looks and wealth don't mean a damn thing."

CHAPTER FIVE

Kyle was determined to make a good impression on the little redhead, as he was decked out in a dark blue windowpane three-piece suit. A haircut this morning, an old-fashioned shoe shine from a sidewalk guy. His red silk tie had a perfect dimple in the knot after three tries, and a matching pocket square. He looked at his watch as he leaned against his car. Ten till six.

He'd actually been there since five-thirty, having left extra time in case there was traffic. This was one date he didn't want to miss, and he sensed she wasn't kidding when she said she'd be gone if he was late.

Still, as he waited for his date, his mind wandered to the girl on the phone. Lexi Harlow was an amazing conversationalist, incredibly in tune with him, even though they'd never met. And with his crazy travel schedule he wondered when that would be possible.

The sight of the little redhead walking toward him knocked him back to reality.

The sweaty girl in a tee-shirt and shorts with her hair up didn't remotely resemble the vision heading in his direction. Red tangles dusting the shoulders of her knee-length turquoise dress, her hair bouncing from the energy in her walk. Spectacular eyes done up like an Egyptian princess.

And a pair of platform heels that had to be at least five inches high. He wouldn't be calling her Little Red.

The woman wasn't kidding about wanting to be the dominant

one in the relationship. He stood up to greet her, stretching as much as possible to his full height. *Don't say a word about her being taller.*

She smiled as she moved toward him. "You're off to a good start. I like a guy who's on time. I really like a guy who's early."

"I'm sorry, I don't believe we've met. I'm here to pick up a sweaty girl from the gym."

"Very funny. Though I thought I was glowing, not sweaty."

"Sorry. But right now you look terrific. As my friend from the South would say, you clean up good."

"Thank you." She ran one finger under the lapel of his suit jacket. "And you look much better in a suit. I'm impressed."

"Thanks. Oh, one more rule for tonight, along with the hundred-dollar limit. No shop talk. We're not allowed to talk about work."

"Why not?"

"Because if we do that we won't really get to know each other. People are very different away from the office."

She nodded. "Yeah, you're right about that. Okay, we won't even say what we do for a living."

He opened the car door and gestured inside. "Right, off we go."

She got in and looked up at him. "So where are we going?"

"A wedding."

"Huh?"

"Trust me. It's not just *any* wedding."

"So who's getting married?"

"Actually, no one."

"You're not making any sense."

"All will become clear shortly, young lady."

Lexi smiled as she saw the marquee above the dinner theater. *Angelo and Antoinette's Wedding.* "Oh, I read about this. I've always wanted to go."

"Me too. Dinner theater that's an Italian wedding beats the hell out of some depressing Ibsen play on Broadway."

"No kidding." They crossed the street and headed toward the box office. Lexi noted the price on the little sign in the window. "Hey, it's fifty-nine bucks each. Do the math. You're already over the limit. Gotta stay under a hundred bucks, remember?"

He pulled a slip of paper out of his pocket and held it up. "Not a problem. Two-for-one coupon."

She nodded. "Ah. Pretty slick."

"I've got one of those books with all sorts of two-fers in New York. Really pays for itself in no time."

"I admire a man who knows how to save a buck. Since I have to do it every day."

"I admire a woman who doesn't get pissed off that I use coupons." He paid for the tickets and led her inside, looking at the slip of paper the ticket seller had given him. "Hey, assigned seats."

"Yeah, I read they do that because they have actors at each table who are part of the show."

They found their table already occupied by a couple, who looked right out of Mafia central casting. A burly guy with slick black hair, wearing a black pinstripe suit with a white tie, and a woman with raven hair teased out to eighties standards wearing a ridiculous amount of cheap jewelry while smacking a wad of gum. The guy stood up and greeted them with a wicked Noo Yawk accent. "How youse guys doin'? I'm Carmine and dis is my ball and chain, Carmella."

The woman glared at him. "Real nice first impression, Carmine." She turned to them. "Youse friends of da bride or groom?"

"Uh, both," said Lexi. "We're Kasey and Alexandra."

"Nice to meetcha," said Carmine as he sat down. "Still don't believe these two are gettin' married. *Madonne*, tawk about a couple with nuthin' in common."

Carmella rolled her eyes. "Yeah, like we're a match made in heaven." She turned to Lexi. "We're like Bill and Hillary without the money or the politics."

Lexi sat down next to her date and lightly took his arm. "This is gonna be a hoot."

"No kidding."

The lights dimmed and a spotlight shone on the door as the bandleader on stage moved to the microphone. "And now, ladies and gentlemen, please welcome for the very first time… Mister and Mrs. Angelo Goombatz!"

Lexi patted her belly after her last bite of chocolate wedding cake. The food was actually excellent, unlike many dinner theater meals. She leaned back and watched the newlyweds finish their first dance together with a hilarious argument on the dance floor.

"Didn't take long," said Carmine.

His "wife" slapped the back of his head, mussing up his hair. "Ah, shaddup, Carmine. At least let them get to the honeymoon."

"Yeah, it'll be the undercard on the next pay-per-view heavyweight fight."

The song finished and the lead singer watched the newlyweds storm off the dance floor toward the kitchen, continuing their argument along the way. "Uh-oh, I think we need some damage control here. Why don't the rest of you dance while we put away all the breakables?" The sound of plates breaking filled the room. "Too late. Anyway, please enjoy the music. Ladies, please drag your dates to the dance floor since you know damn well they're not going to make the first move. Let's go back to the seventies with some classic disco!"

Carmella got up, grabbed Carmine by the ear and yanked him out of his seat. "Let's go, Fred Astaire."

Lexi laughed, then held out her hand toward her date. "This girl wants to dance. I mean, if you know how."

He stood up and took her hand. "I can do a box step."

She rolled her eyes. "Oh geez."

"Personally, I'm just hoping you'll let me lead."

"Very funny."

He led her to the dance floor and staked out an open space as the band played a Bee Gees' tune. He took her hands. "Relax your arms."

"Huh?"

"Let your arms go limp."

"Okay." She relaxed and within seconds he was whisking her around the floor like someone from *Dancing with the Stars*. The guy was incredible, even managing to twirl her despite the five-inch platforms that made him get on his toes and stretch. The other people on the floor backed up to give them more room and they suddenly found themselves bathed in a spotlight. He expertly led her through a series of slick moves, then dipped her as the song ended. The crowd cheered and applauded as he helped her up.

She was out of breath but amazed. "Sonofabitch! How the hell did you learn to dance like that?"

"My older sister. Prom queen who insisted on practicing every day after school before the big night."

Lexi nodded. "Well, I'm impressed. Box step, ha!"

The music started again, this time a slow dance. He gave her a look that seemed to be asking permission. "Care to go again?"

She smiled. "Absolutely. I wanna see what else you've got in your repertoire."

"Then we'll be dancing all night."

"Fine with me." He moved closer, taking one hand while placing his other lightly on her waist. He locked eyes with her and she felt a shiver as he began to lead her in a waltz.

An hour later the singer asked for all the single women to come to the dance floor as the bride was about to throw the bouquet.

Lexi didn't move.

Carmella looked at her hand. "Youse two aint married?"

Lexi shook her head. "First date."

"Well, youse look like a couple. Anyway, you're single, so getcha ass out there."

Her date patted her on the hand. "Go ahead, be part of the show."

She got up and headed to the dance floor, finding herself and a few other guests surrounded by all the "bridesmaids", who were busy shoving one another to get in position. The bride stood on the stage and turned her back to the group, as the singer started the countdown. "One, two, three!" The bridesmaids practically tackled one another as the bouquet flew on a line right into Lexi's arms. One of the bridesmaids got up and glared at her. "Look at that hair! She ain't even Italian!"

Lexi headed back to the table, laughing hysterically as she carried the bouquet.

"Nice catch," said her date.

She saw the groom take his place on the stage. "Hey, fair's fair, you gotta get out there and try for the garter."

"Well, okay." He got up and headed to the dance floor, was surrounded by the groomsmen and caught the garter with a leaping grab.

"Okay," said the singer. "Now this lucky guy gets to put the garter on the young lady who caught the bouquet. And I believe they're already together." Someone placed a chair in the middle of the dance floor and Carmella shoved Lexi out of her seat. She walked to the chair and sat while Kasey got down on one knee holding the garter.

Then the band played the old classic, *The Stripper*.

She widened her eyes at him as he slid the garter over her ankle, never breaking eye contact with her.

Okay, how far is he going with this?

She saw him blush while beads of sweat blossomed on his forehead. He gently slipped the garter up her calf and just over her knee, then stopped, got up, and extended his hand.

Hmmm. Gentleman.

"Last dance everyone, thank you all for coming on this very special day."

Just as the lead singer finished the announcement, the bride chased the groom across the dance floor, screaming all the way. "I saw you checkin' out the rack on my maid of honor! You shoulda married *her*!"

The crowd laughed as Lexi finished her glass of wine just as her date extended his hand. "One for the road?"

"Sure."

She followed him to the already-crowded dance floor as the band played a romantic oldie she recognized. He reached for her hands but she moved forward and wrapped her arms around his shoulders. He leaned back and smiled, looking up at her as he slid his arms around her waist, locking his fingers on the small of her back.

"This is that song from *Ghost*, right? The one when Patrick Swayze and Demi Moore are doing pottery."

He nodded. "Yep."

"What's it called?"

"*Unchained Melody*."

"That's an odd name for a song."

"That's because it's from the movie *Unchained*."

"How the hell did you know that?"

"I read a lot. And I never miss *Jeopardy*."

The wine and the music relaxed her. She pulled him a little closer, breathed in his earthy cologne as they swayed to the music. She rested her head on his shoulder.

Wearing ridiculous heels did have its benefits.

They stepped out into the cool night air. "I have to admit, that was a great experience," said Lexi. "I am willing to concede you're very good at planning a date."

"Oh, we're not done yet. It's only nine and I've got forty-one dollars left."

"There's more?"

"It's not even close to being over. One more stop. Right around the corner."

"If it's that cheesecake place I'm stuffed and couldn't eat another bite."

"It's a restaurant, but we're not going to eat anything."

"I don't understand. If we're not—"

"Patience, young lady. We'll be there shortly."

They turned the corner and she saw bright lights coming from inside the restaurant, so bright they lit up the sidewalk. "What's going on in there?"

He opened the door and ushered her inside. "Movie set. My buddy is an assistant director and he needed some well-dressed extras. You're about to be in a major motion picture."

She saw a tall man moving toward them she recognized as Jimbo from the basketball game. "Hey, buddy, I appreciate you coming by." He turned to her. "This can't be Little Red."

"It's me. My workout clothes are in the wash, so I threw on this old outfit."

"Well, you sure clean up good."

She couldn't help but laugh. "Second time I've heard that tonight. Thank you."

"You guys look perfect for this scene. Follow me." He led them over to a desk filled with a bunch of papers manned by a young woman. "If you'll each fill out one of these and then I'll get you situated."

"What's this for?" asked Lexi.

"Union rules for extras."

"Okay."

They filled out the forms, then followed Jimbo over to an empty table. The restaurant was filled with well-dressed couples while one table stood empty in the middle of the room. A woman with a light meter wandered around checking things. Jimbo gave a loud whistle. "Okay, everyone, listen up. In this scene our stars will be seated at this table. While they're talking I want you all focused on one another. Don't look at the actors or the camera. Remember, don't actually talk, just pretend by mouthing words. As soon as the actor gets down on one knee to propose, I want you all to turn and watch. It would be nice if all the women got a dreamy-eyed look. Then when the actress accepts and he puts the ring on her finger, I want everyone to cheer and applaud. Got it?"

Lexi turned back to her date. "So who's in this movie? Anyone famous?"

He pointed at the stunning couple heading toward the empty table. "You might recognize them."

She turned and spotted two of Hollywood's biggest stars. "Brad Fenwick and Jennie Dale? You gotta be kidding me!"

"We're about to be in a blockbuster rom-com."

She watched as the world-famous actors took their places and a man with a movie slate placed it between them and the camera. "*Proposal of a Lifetime*, scene thirty, take one."

The director moved behind the camera. "Okay, extras, eyes off the stars and on each other. Nice, looking good. And… action!"

Lexi started mouthing words as Kasey did the same. Not actually speaking forced more eye contact than normal.

And she felt it again. A shiver of… something.

A few seconds later she caught movement in her peripheral vision and saw the star get down on one knee. All the extras turned to watch the proposal, then applauded as the woman accepted.

"And cut! That was terrific. Let's do a few more takes."

Jimbo thanked them as the production team wrapped for the night. "I appreciate you coming by. It's not easy to get people to commit late on a Saturday night, even with the chance to be in a movie."

"Oh, thank *you*," said Lexi. "That was a really unique experience. And I guess we'll be memorialized on film."

"Yeah, this is one scene that absolutely won't get cut and you two were both in the shot. Well, I gotta go and lock things up. You can pick up your pay at the check-in table."

"We get paid?"

"Of course, this is a major production." Jimbo disappeared as her date led her toward the table where a woman was handing out cash to the extras.

Lexi's eyes went wide as the woman handed her a crisp hundred-dollar bill and did the same to her date. She turned to him. "So, we're actually making a profit on this evening?"

He shrugged. "Hey, what can I say? It pays to date me."

"You're amazing. This has really been an incredible evening."

"Oh, the date's not over yet. One more stop."

"You said that last time."

"Maybe there's more than one, maybe not. But there's at least one."

The full moon seemed to set her hair on fire as the boat moved through the water. They leaned against the rail and looked at the spectacular view of Manhattan. Kyle thought she looked like a little girl, wide-eyed with all the freckles. "So, you've never been on the Staten Island Ferry?"

"Nope. Never had any reason to go to Staten Island. This has to be the best free thing to do in New York. I mean, look at the view."

"I grew up on the island and our house didn't have air conditioning. So on really hot days we'd take the ferry to cool off." He noticed her hunch up her shoulders a bit. "Speaking of cooling off, are you cold?"

"Just a little chilly, I'll be fine."

He took off his suit jacket and draped it around her shoulders. "Better?"

"Now you'll be cold."

"I'm wearing a vest, I'm very comfortable."

"Well, thanks. Very chivalrous of you."

"My sister trained me well."

"Speaking of being comfortable, I wanted to ask you something. Are you shy around women?"

"Not really. Why?"

"You were very much a gentleman putting that garter on my leg. But you were blushing."

He smiled and looked to the side for a moment. "Well, I barely know you and you don't run your hands up a girl's thigh on the first date."

"Obviously you were raised right."

"You can thank my older sister again. She'd smack the hell out of me if I treated a woman badly."

"Sounds like I need to meet this sister of yours. By the way, what were you talking about during our movie scene? I couldn't read your lips."

"Ah, nuclear physics. And you?"

"Brain surgery. But that's a discussion for another day. She patted his hand. "Now I can't wait for the movie. Fifty years from now I can watch it and see myself. And you."

He looked at his watch as the ferry pulled into the Manhattan dock. "Listen, I get that you're being careful with someone you just met, but I'm not going to drop you off in front of the gym at this hour. It's not safe."

She smiled as she looked at him. "I think you've proven yourself enough to see where I live."

Lexi stared at the moon through the windshield as he found a space about a block from her building. He opened the door for her and she stepped out onto the sidewalk, still fairly busy at this hour. They started walking toward her apartment, passing a sidewalk fruit and flower stand, which was still doing business.

Suddenly he stopped. "Hang on a minute." He turned around, headed back to the stand, and bought a single rose. He returned with a smile and handed it to her.

"Thank you, kind sir." Lexi smelled the rose, breathing in its wonderful scent as they continued down the street. He'd been a perfect gentleman, not making a move on her, his hands never going where they weren't supposed to be, even on the dance floor or putting on the garter. She reached over and looped her hand around his elbow.

He turned and smiled at her. "So, was tonight creative enough for you?"

"I can honestly say this was the best first date ever. But I'm not sure if I can win this bet."

A bit of worry crept into his face. "But you're gonna try, right? I mean, surely a competitive woman like you doesn't just fold at the first sign of a challenge."

He thinks I don't want a second date with him. "Oh, I'm absolutely gonna try. You're way too much fun. But I have my work cut out for me to even come close to what you did tonight." She reached the front door of her building and stopped. "It just hit me… I'm not sure any girl who isn't a hooker has ever come home with a hundred bucks after a date."

He laughed uproariously. "Only you would look at it that way."

"*Only me?* You don't even know me."

"Yeah, but I've pretty much figured out you have a PhD in snark." He took her hands. "Anyway, I had a wonderful time. Thank you for coming."

"You're thanking *me?* After taking me out for an incredible evening? Uh, I think you've got it backwards."

He shrugged. "You could have turned me down."

"Yeah, and I would have missed the best first date ever." She studied his face for a moment, seeing something special in his eyes, a look that went right into her soul. She couldn't put her finger on it, but it was a look of hope that told her he was somehow different than any other man she'd ever met. He wanted her, but not like other guys, not just physically. "By the way, why are you using past tense?"

"Excuse me?"

"You said you *had* a wonderful time." She grabbed his tie, pulled him close, took his chin in her other hand, tilted it up and gave him a long, soft kiss. When their lips parted he wore a wide-eyed look of shock, his jaw slowly dropping. "I'm going to use one of your lines. The date's not over yet. One more stop."

She took his hand and led him up the stairs.

CHAPTER SIX

Kyle reclined his seat and took a look at the beautiful sunrise as the plane reached cruising altitude. He was tired, but as his mentor used to say, it was a *good kind of tired*.

Best. First. Date. Ever.

He agreed with her.

But she had surprised him, taking charge when they reached her building. Not just inviting him into her apartment but hauling his ass into it. She'd basically launched herself at him when she shut the door, pinning him against the wall and kissing him like she was trying to devour him. Then doing the same while straddling him on the couch for nearly an hour before he reluctantly told her he had an early Sunday plane to catch.

She'd blown his mind. Waiting two weeks to see her again would be torture.

She was unlike any woman he'd ever dated. A whip-smart, strong-willed, aggressive, cute as hell, competitive woman with an amazing personality who took what she wanted.

And last night she had wanted him. If only for a makeout session. Though he wondered how far things might have gone without a plane flight in the picture.

Kyle pulled out his tablet to read the Sunday edition of the *The Post* that he had downloaded while waiting to board. He'd already finished the sports section, so he turned to *Page Six*. Gossip was a guilty pleasure, and also the home of news about

New York's athletes. He'd actually picked up a client from a story on *Page Six.*

He clicked on "Pics of the Week" and his jaw dropped.

There she was, out on the town, with Jake Frost. The unidentified stunning redhead. Looking even more spectacular than she had last night.

His best date ever. Out with New York's most eligible bachelor. Rich. Famous. Male model handsome. Twice his size.

He bit his lower lip as his pulse quickened and his armpits grew damp. Suddenly he was back in high school, panicked as the members of the football team scooped up every girl he was interested in. Running home to the comfort of Donna's hugs. He had no shot back then.

He disgustedly shoved the tablet in the seat-back compartment, then stared out the window at the clouds, knowing that in a competition with someone like Jake Frost he had no shot with her.

Again.

***

Lexi breezed into the office Monday morning, head held high and hair bouncing, with a spring in her step. Chandler looked up and studied her face. "It appears someone had an excellent weekend."

"Damn right."

"Ah, I take it the gallivanting about town with the young man from the gymnasium went well. I assume he was not at all upset about what you referred to as the *ass kicking* you gave him on the basketball court."

She picked up the mail and started sorting through it. "Honestly, Chandler, it was the best first date ever. Actually, the best date I ever had."

"You didn't—"

"Now you know damn well I don't go jumping into bed on the first date."

"I was merely concerned, since you have, so to speak, *gotten back on the proverbial horse* so quickly after your relationship with Dave came to quite the incendiary end."

"The horse of which you speak is figurative. I didn't want to sit around brooding like the last time I got dumped and I wanted to see what the city has to offer as far as single men are concerned. I've never played the field before. In fact, I have another date with Jake tomorrow night."

"So, if I'm reading the situation correctly, you now have two gentlemen who have captured your interest."

She smiled as she put the mail back on his desk. "I prefer to look at it in another way; *I've* captured *their* interest. Nice problem to have."

"Does the young lady prefer one over the other?"

"The young lady thinks it is much too early to tell. But they're very different. One is a millionaire Greek god and the other is a seriously cute little thing who clips coupons."

Chandler gave her a quizzical look. "Would you like me to prepare a dossier on the gentleman you refer to as the more diminutive of the two?"

She shook her head. "Nah. He's not like a professional athlete with women hanging all over him. Although he is cute as hell, with an incredible personality, so you never know. But I get a really good feeling about him. I can tell right off he's not the type to break any rules or even play games with me. And what really impresses me is that he respects me as an equal, especially in light of said ass-kicking on the basketball court. He also didn't seem to mind me taking the initiative at the end of the date."

"Very well. But please be careful. You know what happens when you burn the candle at both ends."

"Yeah, you get burned."

"No, you run out of wax twice as fast. Then the light goes out and you're left in the dark."

***

A red flag had begun a slow ascent right after Jake's call. "Meet me in the lobby of my building."

What? He thinks I make out with him for ten minutes and I'm gonna spend the entire next date in his apartment? Ain't happenin'.

Lexi was apprehensive as she got out of the taxi and headed into Jake Frost's luxury building. A doorman held the door and greeted her as she entered the spectacular lobby. Jake was already there, dressed in a dark suit, talking with another doorman. He turned and shot her a smile while giving her outfit the once-over. "Hey there. You look great."

"So do you."

He stuck out his elbow. "C'mon, let's go."

But he headed to the elevator.

She grabbed his arm and pulled him to a stop. "Whoa, Mister. Uh, Jake, if we're just going to spend the night in your apartment, I can tell you right now—"

"We're not going to my apartment."

"We're not?"

He pressed the up button on the elevator. "We're going to the roof."

She furrowed her brow as the elevator door opened and he led her inside. "What? We're going hang gliding? I think Manhattan has laws against that. And, with my luck, I'd get impaled by the Chrysler building."

"No hang gliding, parachutes, or bungee jumping."

"So what's on the roof?"

"You'll see." He pressed a button, the door closed and the elevator quickly headed up.

She slowly started to nod. "Oh, I know what you're up to. You're recreating one of those movie scenes with a catered dinner on the roof."

"Nope. We're not eating up there. Besides, it's supposed to rain later."

"Now I'm confused."

"You won't be shortly."

The elevator slowly came to a stop, the door opened and a very loud noise filled the car. Lexi was greeted by a strong breeze and the sight of something she never expected to see.

A helicopter.

He led her toward it as the pilot cranked up the rotors. "You ever ridden in a helicopter, Lexi?"

"Nope. So, let me guess, you couldn't get an Uber car during rush hour?"

"A car wouldn't get us where we're going and back in time."

"So where are we going?"

"You'll see."

He held her hand as she stepped up into the chopper. He sat next to her and handed her a headset. "Otherwise we can't talk while we're flying. Hope it won't mess up your hair."

"Eh, no problem." She put it on as the chopper took off, giving her a spectacular look at the Manhattan skyline during sunset. "Wow, that's gorgeous." Then the chopper banked and headed out toward Long Island.

Dinner in the Hamptons.

A cool ocean breeze blew through her hair as the waiter placed the plate of lobster thermidor in front of her. "Oh, yeah."

"It's their signature dish," said Jake, who had ordered the same thing.

She took a bite, savoring the rich seafood. "Oh. My. God. This is better than sex."

"Geez, I hope not."

"Figure of speech. It's fantastic, Jake. This is a real treat."

"I thought you'd like this place. It's a little out of the way, but worth it."

"A little out of the way? *New Jersey* is a little out of the way. We had to take a helicopter to get here."

He shrugged. "Just basic transportation."

"Yeah, right. I don't know too many guys who would charter a helicopter to take a girl to dinner."

"Lexi, you ever see the movie *Wall Street*?"

"Sure, the one with Michael Douglas and Charlie Sheen. What about it?"

"Well, there's one point in the movie when Sheen says to Douglas, *How many yachts can you waterski behind?*"

"Not sure I understand where you're going with this. Unless you've got a yacht, too."

"The point, Lexi, is that I couldn't spend all the money I've made in ten lifetimes. What the hell good is it if you can't enjoy it doing stuff like this?"

She nodded as she took a sip of wine. "I guess so. But I'm sure this evening is costing you more than I make in a year."

"You seem like you're worth it."

She couldn't help but smile. "Thank you, kind sir. So do you."

"Speaking of money, I wanted to ask you for your advice."

"*You* want financial advice from *me*? About all I could tell you is not to play three-card monte in New York. And don't buy anything made in China."

"Not that. I fired my agency this morning. Since my agent went to jail."

"*That* was your agent? I read the story in *The Post*."

He nodded. "Yeah, I can't be associated with an agency that tries to cover up a crime of a client. They wanted to hook me up with another of their agents and I told them to get lost. So I need someone else, especially since I'm in the last year of my contract and will have to negotiate a new one after the season."

"Not sure how I can help you there."

"Actually you can. Noah Washington told me about his agent, the guy you work for, Kyle Caruso. Noah really likes him and I loved the way you guys got him out of a jam and turned around his reputation."

"Well, that was the first time I've ever worked for Kyle. He was out of town and needed someone to do damage control in a heartbeat. I haven't even met him yet, but I've talked with him a lot on the phone. He seems like an incredibly decent guy and I can tell he's very, very smart."

"Do you think he'd be the type to do what my former agency did?"

"Like I said, I've never met him but I get a good feeling about him. He has mentioned that he likes clients who stay out of the headlines. Right now he's on the road trying to sign that squeaky-clean running back out of Brigham Young."

"Well, that speaks volumes."

"So, yeah, give him a call."

"I think I will. Who knows, you and I might end up with a working relationship as well. You could do my public relations."

"You planning to get in trouble?"

He shot her a wicked grin. "Only if you let me."

***

Kyle couldn't get out of his funk as he moped around the budget hotel room. He knew he needed to focus on his next potential client, as his business needed the revenue.

But all he could think of was the photo of Alexandra on *Page Six*.

He had crashed and burned after the high of the best date of his life.

Still, he couldn't help but wonder; why would any woman

dating Jake Frost be interested in him, Kyle? Was Alexandra one of those women who hated spending Saturday night alone since he knew football players had an early curfew before a game? And if she was dating New York's most eligible bachelor, why had she been all over him in her apartment?

It didn't make any sense, but the demon dancing in his head told him that it was the same story as the one in high school. The best girls go for the football players. Money, fame, and looks trumped just about anything.

Meanwhile, he thought he'd give Lexi a call. She seemed like a sensible woman – perhaps she could help him figure things out. And maybe, just maybe, she might have girlfriend potential as well.

He was about to call her when his cell rang. He hoped it was her but the screen read "private number." He had no idea who it could be as he answered the call. "Kyle Caruso…"

"Kyle, this is Jake Frost of the New York Jets. I got your number from Noah Washington."

His eyes bugged out as he stood up straight. "Oh, uh, hi Mister Frost. What can I do for you?"

"Right off the bat you can stop calling me Mister Frost, for one. That was my father."

"Sure, Jake. How can I help you?"

"Well, I'm sure you heard my agent, make that *former* agent, went to jail for obstruction of justice."

"Yeah, I saw that. Not a good idea trying to cover up the crime of a client. Especially a crime like that."

"Anyway, even if he hadn't gone to the slammer, I don't need to be associated with an agency that participated in a cover-up like that. So I'm shopping for a new agent. My contract expires after this season and I'll need someone to negotiate a new deal. Meanwhile, I've got a few small endorsements I've been offered and that needs to be taken care of right now. Anyway, Noah said great things about you and I also got a glowing endorsement from your PR girl, Lexi Harlow."

"You know Lexi?"

"We met at the news conference for Noah. I loved what you guys did for him and she spoke highly of you."

"That's good to hear, but I cannot take credit for turning Noah's reputation around. That was all Lexi's idea."

"Still, if she's part of your team that tells me you have good judgment, and I can always use a great PR woman for some stuff. So I want to talk with you. When are you going to be in town?"

***

Lexi rubbed her temples as she entered the office and saw Chandler already behind his desk.

"Who knew Wednesdays could require a hangover remedy?"

"Oh, shut up, Chandler." Lexi pulled off her sunglasses, then took off her jacket and hung it up on the coat rack. "I didn't have any champagne."

He stood up and moved closer. "So why do your eyes look like the New York interstate system?"

"I had too much wine."

"Different incarnation of the grape, alas with the same result. I take it you had an enjoyable evening with…who was it last night? The mythologicial figure from Mount Olympus or the vertically challenged gentleman from the *Wizard of Oz*? I have so much trouble keeping your escapades straight."

She playfully slapped him on the shoulder. "They're not *escapades*, and I'm only dating *two* guys, smartass. I was with Jake last night, and by the way, the other guy is not a munchkin, he's just a little guy. Anyway, last night with Jake was amazing. He actually took me on a helicopter to this incredible restaurant in the Hamptons."

"And were you home by curfew?"

"Yes, Dad, I even finished my algebra homework. But, hey, get

70

this, Jake fired his agent and is looking for someone new. He's gonna consider Kyle Caruso and talked about maybe using me to do some PR." She studied Chandler's face. "We're not smiling. Why are we not smiling? This could be a huge client for us."

"Stop talking about me in the third person."

"Oh, so you don't like it either. Anyway, why are *you* not smiling?"

"Conflict of interest. And he may have ulterior motives."

"Huh?"

"You'd be dating someone who's also paying you. I'm not sure you can mix a business relationship with a romantic one. Generally there's a descriptive term for women who are paid for—"

"Oh, stop it. I'll be fine. I can keep my business and personal lives separate."

"That candle you're burning appears to have generated another wick."

CHAPTER SEVEN

Kyle rolled his eyes when he saw the flight time on his ride home change yet again, adding another thirty minutes to his layover. His mind still going off in several directions: an upcoming meeting with Jake Frost, a client who could catapult him onto the A-list of agents. A second date with a fantastic woman, who was also on Frost's arm in a New York tabloid. How he might deal with dating the same woman, who was also going out with his client.

And somehow, the thought of representing someone who would probably steal the woman he liked.

A lot.

Sure, it was just one date so far, but there was something very special about the spunky redhead.

His cell rang, jarring him out of his deep thoughts. "Kyle Caruso—"

"Hi, Kyle, it's Lexi."

He sat up straight, suddenly getting a surge of energy. "Well, hey there."

"Listen, I want to apologize for not getting back to you. I saw you called last night but I got home too late and didn't want to wake you. Hope it wasn't anything urgent."

"No. How you doing?"

"Pretty good. You got time to talk?"

"Stuck in an airport for a while."

"Ugh. So what's up?"

"Well, couple of things on the radar. I got a call from Jake Frost, the Jets' quarterback, who wants to meet with me next week since he's looking for a new agent."

"Yeah, he mentioned that he was going to touch base with you."

"How did you know?"

"I, uh, happened to run into him. I told him you were a good guy."

"We haven't even met."

"Yeah, but we've sure been burning up the cell minutes and a girl can tell. He was impressed you were out at BYU trying to sign Rob Norman. How'd that go, by the way?"

"Looks pretty good. Anyway, Jake also mentioned he was really impressed with what you did for Noah, so he might have some work for you as well."

"Nice to hear. So what was the other thing? Another of your clients in need of a bail bondsman?"

He laughed a bit. "No, most of my clients are straight arrows. I was looking for some advice about, well, about women. For a friend. I know I really don't know you, but—"

"Hey, I'm an expert on women. Been one all my life. You wanna know why we have so many shoes?"

"No, though that has puzzled me for years. By the way, are you single?"

"Yeah, so if this is a dating question, I might not be the best person as I haven't been very good at picking men in the past, though things have changed for the better of late. I guess you get smarter when you turn thirty."

"That's very true. The light bulb over your head goes on. Anyway, it's more of a general question. So, hypothetically, if a woman is dating two guys, one rich and incredibly good-looking and the other who is just average and doesn't have any money, does the rich guy have the advantage?"

"In most cases, yes. I know that sounds superficial, but that's the way a lot of people are. And it works the other way around too… guys chase rich, beautiful girls as well. Personally, it doesn't matter to me. And, you know, the guy without any money might be something special and the better guy. As long as the guy without any money has ambition and a plan to succeed and is smart, that's usually enough for me. Of course, he's gotta be a real old-fashioned sweetheart. Kind. And faithful. That last thing trumps all. But, then again, I'm not most girls. While you can't buy happiness, you can't live on love. Some women will overlook anything for money. And I've heard plenty of women say it's just as easy to marry a rich man as a poor one. Does that help?"

"Yeah. Anyway, I'll pass along your thoughts to my buddy."

"Sure thing. So, any chance you'll be in town long enough for us to meet?"

"Well, I'm getting together with Jake Frost on Monday at ten, so why don't you join us? Come by about an hour early and we can work out a plan to pitch him together."

***

Lexi had chosen an emerald green dress for her second date with Kasey, along with a pair of matching four-inch heels. She put her hair up on one side and did a little extra work on her eyes. A single strand of pearls was her old-school accessory.

And her plan for a creative date was damn clever. Not nearly as good as his, but she figured he'd appreciate the effort. And considering what he'd gone through on the first date, she owed him one.

She stepped off the elevator and found him chatting up the doorman, looking sharp in another dark suit that fit his slender frame perfectly. She felt a bit of a rush as she moved toward him. "And he's early again."

She saw his eyes widen as he turned to face her. "Wow."

74

"Wow, what?"

"You look fantastic. Still can't believe you're the girl on the basketball court. "

"I could go change into a pair of sweats if you like."

"No way. You realize you're doing wonders for my ego."

"Not sure I understand."

"Being able to take a woman like you out in public."

She narrowed her eyes. "What do you mean, *like me*?"

"You know. Gorgeous."

"I'm not, but thank you." She couldn't hold back a smile as she looped one hand around his elbow. "But it's a two-way street, Mister. You look damn good yourself and you're a wonderful accessory for my arm."

"Oh, I'm just an accessory to you?"

"Accessorizing is critical for a woman's overall look. You match the necklace with the earrings. Going out on the town with the wrong man as an accessory… well, it's just not proper. Worse than wearing white after Labor Day."

"Yeah, that's a major turnoff," he agreed.

"Well, shall we go?"

"Where are we going?"

She handed him a slip of paper with an address. "We have dinner reservations here."

"Nice restaurant. I've been there. But I think you're gonna blow the budget on this place."

"Hey, you're not the only one who can find a bargain. Trust me, I'm not going over the limit."

Lexi smiled as she finished her last bite of cheesecake and leaned back in her chair. "Damn, that was good."

"No kidding. Great choice. So I'm assuming you're doing the buy-one-get-one-free coupon thing?"

She shook her head. "Nope. Don't even have to buy *one*."

"So, what, we're gonna skip on the check? Dine and dash?"

"This girl doesn't break the law. And I'm betting you don't either. But your answer is on the way." She looked up as a man in an expensive dark suit arrived at their table.

"Good evening, I understand from the name on your reservation that you're our mystery couple tonight."

She nodded. "That's us."

Kasey furrowed his brow. "Mystery couple?"

The gentleman smiled at him as he put a pad on the table. "I guess your companion didn't tell you that you were dining undercover. From time to time I like to get objective opinions on our service and food, so I use a secret shopper service to send people in to test things." He turned back to her. "I'm the owner of the restaurant, and I want to thank you for participating in our survey. If it's all right, I'd like to get your opinions while they're fresh in your mind."

"Sure," said Lexi.

They both answered questions for about ten minutes on the food, service, decor, atmosphere, and valet parking service. When they were done the owner grabbed his notes, stood up, pulled an envelope from his jacket, and handed it to her. "I'm so glad you enjoyed your experience here and I hope to see you again."

"Absolutely," she said. "Though I guess we've gotta pay next time."

He pointed to the envelope. "That should cover some of it. Enjoy the rest of your evening." He turned and headed toward the kitchen.

Her date nodded in approval. "Secret shopper, huh? Very clever."

"I thought you'd appreciate the frugality. And not only did we get a free dinner, which does beat a two-for-one coupon, but we also got paid." She opened the envelope, took out two fifty-dollar bills and handed one to him.

His eyes widened. "Impressive. You are definitely off to a good start."

"Glad you think so." She looked at her watch. "Okay, as is the custom, I must say the date's not over yet. One more stop."

"Where are we going?"

"To the coolest apartment in town."

"Back to your place already?" He tried to hold back a smile, but couldn't.

"I appreciate the compliment from the look on your face."

"What look?"

"The same one you had the last time a redhead was on your lap."

He scratched his chin. "Hmmmm… which redhead was that?"

"Smartass. Anyway, you'll like our next stop. This one involves a time machine."

***

He looked up at the sign. "There's an apartment in Grand Central Station?"

"Not anymore, but this used to be the office and saloon of a tycoon in the roaring twenties named John Campbell. Hence, the name Campbell Apartment."

He held the door for her and she led him inside to a refurbished bar right out of a history book. His smile widened as he took in the surroundings. "Wow, this is seriously cool. We really are back in time."

"Yep, I love this period. And of course, 1920 was the year the nineteeth amendment became law."

"Which one was the nineteeth amendment?"

"Women got the right to vote." She wrapped an arm around his shoulders and pulled him close. "Since then, you guys haven't been able to control us."

"No argument here, though I believe that thing started with a woman in a garden who gave her significant other an apple."

"Anyway, let's get a vintage drink and then I'll give you a tour." She led him to the bar and got the attention of the bartender, who was dressed in vintage clothes, with a bow tie. "Two Prohibition Punches, please."

He laughed. "Seriously?"

"Vintage names for vintage drinks. People had to endure the worst decision Congress ever made."

"I'll drink to that."

"But at least they repealed it. Much to the dismay of the rum runners." The bartender slid two drinks in front of them. Lexi paid the bill, lifted her glass and clinked his. "To old-fashioned guys."

"And old-fashioned girls."

They raised their glasses and each took a sip. "C'mon, let this flapper show you around."

***

Kyle couldn't find a parking space closer than two blocks away, so they had a short walk back to her apartment. She wrapped one arm around his shoulders so he slid his around her waist. He wished the walk were actually a little longer, enjoying the ego boost of being out in public with a pretty redhead on his arm. And he didn't want the date to end, though he assumed she would haul his ass into her apartment again. "Alexandra, you certainly did exceptionally well tonight. I must say, that was one of the best haunted houses I've ever seen."

"Well, I love Halloween and it was for a good cause."

"Comparing our two dates, I'm honestly not sure who won. We don't exactly have an objective observer to judge."

She shook her head. "Nah, you won fair and square. I think being in the movie put your date at the top."

"You might just be saying that to get out of a third date.

Remember, if you won I had to buy you dinner. If my date was the better one, you said I was already the winner since I had the pleasure of your company for two nights."

They came to a stop in front of her building and she turned to face him, then put her hands on her hips. "You must think I'm a complete idiot."

"Huh? What'd I say?"

"Why in the world would I be trying to get out of a third date with you? Damn, Kasey, for a smart guy you sure are slow to catch on when it comes to women." She grabbed his tie again, pulled him close, tilted his chin up with one hand and gave him a long kiss, wrapping one arm around his back. Their lips parted and she leaned back a bit. "That clear it up for you?"

If this woman was hung up on a millionaire football player, she sure didn't act like it. "Uh, yeah."

"You got a plane to catch tomorrow morning?"

"Nope. Not going anywhere till Tuesday."

She flashed a big smile and gave his tie a gentle tug, then took his hand and led him inside.

***

Lexi handed him a glass of wine in the kitchen, picked up hers, then took his hand and led him to the couch. "I want to talk to you about something."

He studied her face. "Okay…" She sat on the couch and patted the seat next to her. He sat and placed his wine on the coffee table. "So what's up?"

"Since I like you a lot and want to continue seeing you, I want to be totally upfront about my situation. You're a terrific guy—"

"Oh, hell. Here comes the *but* in the discussion."

She noted his face tightened a bit, eyes tinged with disappointment. She shook her head and smiled at him as she took his face lightly in her hands. "No, sweetie, there's no *but* at all. I just believe in being totally honest in relationships and wanted you to know I am dating someone else I recently met. That's all."

His face relaxed. "Oh. I thought I was about to get the *you'll make someone else a wonderful husband* speech."

"No. For one thing it's too early for me to tell what you'd be like as a husband. You could be the perfect man or a slug who becomes one with a reclining chair. But considering we seem to have a connection, I intend to find out if you have spousal potential." She saw him begin to smile.

"That's nice to hear. And an interesting term."

"My college roommate came up with that."

"So, what qualities must a man have for the proper level of spousal potential?"

"Well, you've already checked the boxes on a few. You're a gentleman, you're old-fashioned, you actually listen when I talk instead of giving me the bobblehead."

"The what?"

"That stupid head-bob men do when they pretend they're listening to women. *Yes, dear. You had sex with an alien today? That's nice.*"

"Oh."

"And you don't check out other women while we're together."

"Why the hell would I do that when I've got you on my arm?"

"And you're damn good at compliments. Forgot to check that box."

"Surely there must be more boxes to check."

"There are many. The biggest one is fidelity."

"Yeah, that's a deal-breaker for me too."

"I figured as much. Anyway, just wanted to make sure you were okay with me dating someone else."

He shrugged. "Hey, we just met and I don't own you."

She patted his hand. "Thank you for saying that. I appreciate it." Lexi hoped he might mention something about other women he was dating, but he said nothing.

"So, that was all you wanted to tell me?"

"Yeah. Oh, and I want you to continue to plan creative dates. I really get a kick out of the fact we can go out for an amazing night in New York City without spending hardly anything."

"So, you don't think I'm cheap?"

"Hell, no. I know what it's like to make ends meet in this city. And I don't come from a rich family. We clipped coupons and I got a job when I turned sixteen."

"Thanks, I have to watch my money. So, I'll get cracking on planning our next date."

She put her wine on the table, slid closer, locked eyes with him and slid her fingers through his hair. "Later. *This* date's not over yet."

CHAPTER EIGHT

Chandler looked up from his desk. "You're in early. Did you drink Red Bull instead of coffee?"

Lexi shot him a sarcastic look. "Very funny. I've got that meeting upstairs with Jake Frost. And I'm finally gonna meet Kyle Caruso."

"Ah, the mysterious man who you refer to as the one who enhances your libido via a cellular network."

"Yeah, he gives good phone. Been dying to see what he looks like."

"May I remind the young lady that she only has two hands so she does not have any pinkies available around which to wrap additional suitors?"

"I don't have them wrapped around my little finger. It's more like I'm wrapped around them, though they can't ever know that. Not that I mind after what you refer to as my *incendiary breakup* with Dave."

"Ah, so we had another pleasant evening with bachelor number two."

She nodded and smiled. "Yeah, you could say that. He seems really special. Then again, so does Jake. Nice problem for a girl to have."

"And in this duel of equine accomplishment, does one have the advantage over the other?"

"If you mean it's a two-horse race, they're neck and neck. Though perhaps not in the height department."

"Does the young lady have a plan should she find Mister Caruso attractive?"

"She does not. And stop referring to me in the third person. In any event, that will take a back seat to signing Jake Frost as a client."

"Tread carefully. Mixing business with pleasure can be a dangerous thing. I believe there's a metaphor regarding casting one's line from a corporate structure."

"Chandler, this ain't fishin' off the company pier. Anyway, gotta go. Wish me luck."

"With the business or pleasure aspect?"

"Hell, how about both?"

***

Lexi started to take the stairs but saw yellow tape across the door with a "wet paint" sign, so she was forced to take the elevator up one floor. And she knew damn well with her luck the car would be full of people who would roll their eyes at the young woman too lazy to walk up one flight of stairs. She hit the button and waited, bouncing on her heels, wired about the possibilities the day held. The elevator door opened and what she saw made her eyes widen.

Only one person was in the car.

Her Saturday-night date. Kasey.

She flashed a smile. "Hey, didn't expect to see you here."

"I work here. What are you doing here?"

"I'm also a tenant in the squalor arms. Wow, small world." She got into the elevator, started to hit the button for the next floor and saw it was the only one lit up. "And apparently we're going to the same floor."

"How about that?" The door closed and the car headed up for a few seconds. The door opened and he gestured toward the hallway. "After you."

"Thank you." She got out and headed toward Kyle's office and noticed he was right behind her as she grabbed the doorknob. "You following me?"

"No. You sure you're going to the right office?"

Lexi looked at the sign on the door to double check. "Yep." She opened the door and entered the office, seeing Donna at her desk.

He followed her in and shut the door.

Donna got up and smiled. "Ah, I guess I don't have to introduce you two."

Lexi furrowed her brow. "Huh?" She turned to Kasey. "And what are you doing here?"

Donna shook her head as she put her hands on her hips and glared at him. "Sweetie, you know I love you but you left the cap off the toothpaste this morning... *again*... and it ran all over the counter. So you're gonna clean it up."

"Sorry, babe." He moved toward Donna, wrapped an arm around her and kissed her on the cheek.

Donna slapped him on the ass, then turned to Lexi. "He's a bad boy. You think I'd have him trained by now." She rolled her eyes. "Men."

Lexi stood there, jaw hanging open. "I'm... uh... confused. About a bunch of stuff. You two live together?"

Donna smiled. "Yeah. Remember?"

He turned to Lexi. "So what are you doing here?"

"I have an appointment. I could ask you the same thing."

"I work here."

She waved her hands. "Hold on, now I'm *really* confused. So you work with Kyle?"

"I *am* Kyle."

"Whoa, wait a minute. I thought your name was Kasey."

"My nickname from my initials. Kyle Caruso. K. C. My friends have called me Kasey for years." He moved closer. "I still don't know why *you're* here."

84

Donna took his forearm. "Geez, Kyle, I thought you met Lexi in the hallway."

Now it was his turn for the jaw to drop. "*You're* Lexi?"

"Last time I checked, yeah."

"I thought your name was Alexandra."

"That's my real name, but I go by Lexi. You told me you liked the name Alexandra, so I let you call me that."

Donna waved her hands. "Hold on a minute. You two have actually been going out for a few weeks and didn't know your real names?"

"I guess so," said Lexi. She moved closer to Kyle, folded her arms and looked him in the eye. "And *you* apparently forgot to mention you were living with another woman."

"I told you that at lunch," said Donna.

"Huh?"

She wrapped her arm around Kyle. "I told you my brother moved in with me. Remember?"

"Whoa. You're brother and sister?"

"Yeah," said Donna. "You don't think I'd swat my boss on the ass if we weren't related, do you? Well, damn, here I was wanting to fix you guys up and you were already dating. This is some big-time serendipity going on here. It just shows I've got some serious chops as a matchmaker."

Lexi smiled at Kyle. "So you're the one I've been talking to for hours when you were out of town."

He nodded and smiled back. "Yeah."

Donna leaned against her desk. "How the hell did you two go out twice and not know… didn't the last names give you a clue? Or what you guys do for a living?"

Lexi shrugged. "I guess we forgot about last names. Or occupations."

Kyle developed a sheepish grin. "We were, uh, having too much fun."

Donna moved to the coffee machine. "See, Lexi, I told you

85

that you were perfect for him. Well, this really makes my day. I'm gonna make coffee so you two go get ready for that star quarterback."

Kyle cocked his head at an open door. "C'mon, I'll give you a tour of my office."

"I'm right below you, remember? We've got the same layout."

"Oh, yes." He moved into his office and sat behind his desk, while she took the chair opposite it. It was appropriately decorated for a sports agent, with photos of athletes and various bits of autographed paraphernalia. Balls, jerseys, pennants. He smiled as he folded his hands in his lap and leaned back. "Well, this is certainly interesting. The plot has definitely thickened."

"A very pleasant surprise. I've been wondering what the man on the phone looked like, and figured, with my luck, you were a four-hundred-pound bald guy."

"I thought the same thing."

"You thought I was an obese man with no hair?"

He laughed. "No, just the obese part. This is funny… I was thinking when you finally let me go home the other night—"

"When I *let you* go home?"

"I would say that was a pretty accurate description since you were on top of me and had me pinned to the couch."

The image flashed through her mind and made her blush a bit. "Uh, right. Point taken. Though I didn't exactly hear you complaining."

"Anyway, I was thinking how I'd come across two lovely women recently, even though I didn't know what one looked liked. And thought it would be nice if I could combine both into one person."

"I was imagining the same thing. So we both get two for the price of one."

And then it hit her.

I'm about to be in a room with two men I'm dating, both of whom are about to pay me.

Oh, shit.

86

Damn, this company pier is pretty long and here I am covered in bait.

***

Kyle looked at the page of ideas she'd brought, but couldn't get one thing out of his head.

I hired this woman, who I really like, to take care of a client and she ends up in The Post *dating Jake Frost, the most eligible bachelor in New York, who will be here in a few minutes. Why are the romance gods conspiring against me?*

He looked up at Lexi, who seemed to be staring into space, with his page of ideas on her lap. "Earth to Lexi."

"Huh?"

"You're awfully quiet. You don't like my ideas?"

"No, they're excellent. I was trying to picture how they would play out. Sometimes I get deep in thought and it looks like I'm zoned out. But we definitely have to use these."

"Great. I like your ideas as well." He leaned back in his chair, studying her face.

She's nervous because two guys she's dating are about to be in the same room and have to work together. But she doesn't know that I know she's dating Jake.

Don't look jealous, don't look jealous…

He heard the office door open and Donna's voice. "Good morning, you must be Mister Frost."

He turned to Lexi. "Looks like our prospective client is here." He noted her eyes went wide with a bit of fear.

"Yeah."

"Well, let's do this."

They both got up and headed into the reception area. What Kyle saw surprised him.

The quarterback was even more handsome in person. Dressed

in a black suit with a starched white shirt that was open at the collar, perfect hair and the smile of a soap opera star, he looked like a male model. Kyle moved forward and extended his hand. "Jake, nice to meet you. Kyle Caruso."

The man shook his hand and smiled. "Pleasure, Kyle. Thanks for seeing me on short notice."

Kyle had to crane his neck to look up at the man, who was possibly a foot taller and nearly twice his size. "Not a problem." He gestured toward Lexi. "And I believe you already know this talented young lady."

"Hi, Lexi, I didn't know you'd be here."

She still looked like she had itching powder in her clothes. "Uh, yeah, I work in the building and Kyle thought we'd put our heads together to come up with some proposals for you."

"Sounds great."

Donna moved forward and lightly put her hand on his forearm. "Mister Frost—"

"Jake, please."

"Sure. Can I get you anything? Coffee? Soda? Kyle's unattached sister?"

The quarterback laughed. "You're Kyle's sister?"

"Somebody has to keep him in line."

"Okay, then. Cup of coffee would be great. Black."

"I'll bring it in." Donna turned, head on a swivel as she kept looking at Jake, and walked straight into her desk. She turned beet-red and moved to the coffee machine as Jake bit his lip, obviously trying not to laugh.

Kyle gestured toward his office. "Jake, c'mon in and tell us how we can help you."

Jake Frost headed into the office, lightly putting his hand on Lexi's shoulder on the way. She went rigid as Kyle tried his best to keep a poker face.

Though his heart rate spiked like never before.

Ninety minutes later Kyle got up and shook hands with Jake. "I hope this is the start of a great relationship."

The quarterback smiled and nodded. "I have a good feeling about you two handling things. I think letting you guys take care of these upcoming endorsements will be a good test to see if we're the right fit for each other. If things go well, I'll let you handle my contract after the season."

Lexi cocked her head at Kyle. "He's the one who knows the legalese."

"Yeah," said Jake, "but there's a lot of PR that goes into it as well. You don't want to be seen as too greedy or someone who puts himself ahead of the team. It's a fine line to walk and, Lexi, I'm sure you know there's a certain way to feed stuff to the media. I held out for more money in my rookie year and it was a huge mistake. The fans really let me have it on talk radio."

Kyle nodded. "I remember that, but the fans are behind you now. I'm sure the Jets will make a generous offer."

"They'd better. I'm thirty-three and this will be my last contract, more than likely."

They all headed for the door. Donna got up and, obviously smitten, shot Jake a big grin. "So nice to meet you."

"You too, Donna."

The phone rang, she answered it, and put it on hold. "Kyle, it's Noah Washington for you. He said he just needs a minute for a quick question."

"Let me take this. Jake, we'll see you at the endorsement announcement."

He moved toward the phone as he saw Jake put his hand on Lexi's shoulder again.

Her eyes widened in fright. "Uh, let me walk you out." He watched her quickly usher Jake out of the office as he took the call, trying his best to focus on the client who was on the phone instead of what might be happening behind that door.

And he was laser-locked on that door.

But one thing was for sure… even though she had been up-front with him about the fact she was dating another man, Lexi didn't want him to know it was Jake she was dating.

**

The phone call ended quickly and the minute he hung up, Donna grabbed his arm. "Dear Lord, Kyle, that man was chiseled out of granite by Michelangelo. And he seems like a good guy. Please invite him back to the office."

"Huh?"

She took his face and turned it so he was facing her. "Hey, your single-and-available sister, who has been spending Saturday nights with a bottle of wine and a book, is talking to you and you're in some sort of trance."

"Sorry."

"Anyway, if you can find a way to get me involved—"

"He's dating Lexi."

"Whuh… what the hell are you talking about? I thought she was the girl *you're* dating."

"We're not exclusive. Remember that photo on *Page Six* I told you about? How I saw the girl I was dating out with Jake?"

"That girl and Lexi are the same person? Damn, I'm gonna need a scorecard by the end of the day. And no wonder she had that deer-in-the-headlights look when he walked in." She shook her head and smiled. "This is a woman's worst nightmare. The two guys you're dating in the same room, working together."

"I think it's more my nightmare at this point, Donna."

"Why?"

"Oh, come on. You just referred to him as something created

by Michelangelo. You really think I've got a shot at her with him in the picture?"

"Why not? You're a terrific guy."

"You're biased, you're my sister."

"Bullshit. You're still a terrific guy. And you said the woman basically ravished you the two times you've been out."

He shook his head. "I dunno. It's gonna be hard working for the guy knowing she's dating him… and then having her handle his PR. Talk about a love triangle." He heard the doorknob turn. "Don't say anything to her!"

"You think I'm a friggin' idiot?"

Lexi walked back in. "Well, I guess we've got a chance at a big client long-term."

Kyle held up a check. "Hey, I'm just happy with the retainer. Of which you get half."

"Don't be ridiculous, Kyle. You'll be doing more for him as his agent."

"And you'll be doing more for him with the endorsements. We're a team, Lexi." He locked eyes with her. "As long as we work together, we're a team of equal partners."

"Well, I appreciate that. God knows I can use the money."

Donna took his elbow and pulled him toward Lexi. "You two should go out for a nice lunch and celebrate. Something more upscale than a hot dog cart."

Kyle shook his head. "Love to but can't. I'm meeting Jeff Anders for lunch."

"Oh, right, I forgot." She turned toward Lexi. "How about a girls' lunch then?"

Lexi nodded. "Sounds good."

Donna smiled, turned to Kyle, and gave him a wink.

***

Lexi stared at her pastrami sandwich but her mind was far away.

So Kasey is really Kyle and Kyle hired me, which resulted in my meeting Jake and I'm dating both men while they're working together and both are paying me and if they find out I'm dating both—

"Hey, you're out to lunch while we're out to lunch."

She looked up and saw Donna smiling. "Sorry. I was deep in thought."

"Yeah, that happens to me when I eat Häagen Dazs. I get so deep I eat the whole container."

Lexi relaxed a bit. "I don't mean to be rude. Just trying to process everything that's happened in the last few hours."

"Yeah, the stars seem to be aligning in more than one way. A new client for you and my brother… and you two were actually going out before I had the chance to fix you up. Still funny as hell you guys didn't know your real identities."

"Yeah, hard to believe."

"You know, he's been all upbeat lately. He hadn't dated anyone in a while and all of a sudden he's been going out with you and talking to this great girl on the phone, and you turn out to be the same person."

"Same deal for me."

"Well, I'm loving seeing my brother happy." She took a sip of her soda. "Now I need someone for me. But the only men I meet are athletes who come by the office, and there's no way I'd go there."

"I noted that Jake turned your head."

"I can look at the menu without going to the restaurant." Donna rolled her eyes. "I mean, talk about men you can't trust. A girl would have to be nuts to hook up with a pro athlete."

"I'm sure some of them are faithful."

"Yeah, right. One of the reasons Kyle went out on his own was his old agency always looked the other way on that stuff. He had one client who had seven children by six women. Talk about confusion on Father's Day."

Lexi laughed. "True, they don't have the best reputation. But anyway, I'll keep an eye out for someone for you. What's your type?"

"Breathing."

"No, seriously."

"The opposite of my ex-husband. And someone just like my brother. A decent human being. Seriously, that's all I want, Lexi. That's really all any woman needs, doncha think?"

CHAPTER NINE

Chandler looked up from his desk and studied Lexi's face as she returned. "You were gone so long I assume it went well. Afternoon delight?"

"Oh, stop it. I went to lunch with Kyle's assistant – and sister – Donna, but yeah, the meeting with Jake went very well. Oh, you'll love this. She's the woman we hear through the air duct with the accent. Anyway, Jake is going to let us handle a few upcoming endorsements and if we do a good job on those, he'll let Kyle take care of his contract and I'll do his PR. He gave us a retainer and Kyle generously split it with me, so we're out of the woods financially for a while."

"Excellent. But for some reason I detect a sense of worry."

"You're not going to believe this, but Kyle is actually Kasey."

"Not sure I follow."

"The guy I've been dating, the one who I've been referring to as Kasey, is actually Kyle. They are the same person. Kasey is his nickname from his initials. So the guy I've been going out with is also the one I've been talking to for hours on the phone."

"How did you not know this?"

"Real names never came up in conversation. He thought my name was Alexandra."

"Did you tell him your name was Alexandra?"

"No, he saw my monogrammed jacket with the letter A on it and guessed."

"And he didn't know Alexandra and Lexi were the same person either?"

"Nope."

Chandler suddenly sat up straight. "Ah, I've realized the reason for your facial expression. You just spent a few hours in the same room with both of your suitors."

"Bingo."

"And you'll be working for both as well."

"Bingo again."

"And accepting money from both."

"Don't go there, Chandler."

"Do they know you are dating both of them?"

"Dear God, no."

"I imagine you were in a rather uncomfortable situation."

"That's putting it mildly."

"Ah, you now have the dual challenge of not only separating business from pleasure but also separating the gentlemen from each other."

She rubbed her temples. "Don't remind me. It makes my head hurt."

"Does the lady have what she refers to as a *game plan*?"

"She does not. She is worried this will blow up in her face and the two men will end up having a duel. And that proverbial candle now has so many wicks I won't have to pay for a waxing. Does her humble assistant have any advice?"

"He does not. However, he would advise the lady to tread carefully and keep in mind that things usually sort themselves out."

"Problem is, things could sort themselves out to the point where the lady ends up losing both of them."

"She is a strong, independent woman and would do fine. But, as the lady likes to say about entertaining two suitors, 'tis a nice problem to have.'"

"She used to think so. Now she's not so sure. And it's a lot less stressful talking about her in the third person."

Donna stood up to greet Kyle as he returned to the office. "So, how'd it go with Anders?"

Kyle shook his head. "Eh, not great. We're really not on the same page at all. He's kind of a sleazeball and wanted to know if I could put him in touch with someone to help him beat a drug test."

"Not our kind of client."

"Nope, not at all. I told him he'd be better off with someone else. Then I dropped a dime on my contact with the league that the guy was using steroids."

"But, hey, at least we got a client with deep pockets this morning."

"Yeah, it really helps. Especially with that big expense coming up." His face tightened. "Speaking of the man you refer to as a block of granite—"

"Stop it, little brother. Don't you dare bring yourself down worrying about how you two measure up."

"I know exactly how we measure up. He's twice my size—"

"Stop it!" She moved forward and took his shoulders. "You're the best man I know, and I'm not saying that because you're my brother. And speaking of worrying about the other guy, I put a few bugs in Lexi's ear about the dangers of dating a pro athlete."

"Oh, really?"

"Yes, really. You know your sister has always been your *corner girl*. C'mon, lemme hear it…"

Kyle smiled, dropped his voice and did his best Sylvester Stallone as Rocky Balboa impression. "I can't see. Cut me, Mick."

"There's the fighter I know and love. Anyway, I pretty much dragged athletes through the gutter and gave her some stuff to think about. Meanwhile, I can tell she really likes you."

"And I really like her."

"By the way, I told her about how you wiped the floor with

my ex and she was really impressed. Anyway, play it smart, Kyle. Be yourself. Don't try too hard, like you always do. You're not in a competition. Let the other guy punch himself out trying too hard. Rope-a-dope. Then you come in for the knockout. And in this case you'd win the knockout."

"But I *am* competing with him."

"Love is not a competition, Kyle. It's something magical that either happens or doesn't. You can't force it, like I tried to do with that scumbag I married." She ran her fingers through his hair. "And you've got magic in your soul. If Lexi is the woman I think she is, she'll see it. Then again…"

His face tightened. "Then again what?"

Donna shrugged. "*She* might not be good enough for *you*. After all, you've only been out twice. You need time to get to know each other. And I need to get to know her better."

He folded his arms and smiled. "Oh, so I need to get your blessing in this relationship?"

"Damn straight. Our parents are gone and I'm older, so I'm in charge. So we both need to get to know the woman. And I'll let you know if she's worthy of you."

"I see. You have a right of first refusal."

"Yep. Don't want my brother to end up like me."

"Well, I appreciate you looking after me. By the way…"

"Yeah?"

"In reference to the man you referred to as a block—"

"Oh, geez, will you stop!"

"No, I was going to ask if you wanna get fixed up with him?"

Donna shook her head. "Nope."

"I thought you were smitten."

"I was. I am. But I'm not going to try and steal a guy from Lexi to help your cause. She has to choose you on her own. It's my non-interference directive."

"It always comes down to *Star Trek*, doesn't it?"

"Yep. Everything I need to know in life I learned from Captain

Kirk. Of course, if you *want* me to try and steal Jake to get him out of the running—"

"No. Please don't. You were right the first time. If I'm going to win her, it has to be fair and square."

"Okay, then. But if she dumps him, I want the leftovers."

***

Jake was waiting for Lexi for their now-regular Tuesday night date when she arrived in the lobby of his building. He moved forward to meet her and began ushering her back out the door. "You look great, as usual, Lexi."

"Thank you, so do you. So I take it we're not taking the chopper tonight?"

"Nope, but it's still not the traditional form of transportation." He stepped onto the sidewalk and waved at the corner.

"Is your limo driver down there?"

"No limo tonight. Non-traditional, remember?"

"For me a limo and a helicopter *are* non-traditional."

Then she heard it.

The familiar clip-clop of hoofbeats on a New York City street. Her face lit up as she saw the hansom cab headed in their direction, driven by a man in a top hat and tails. He pulled to a stop in front of them, then tipped his hat at her. "Good evening, young lady. Mister Frost."

She nodded at him. "Good evening." Then she turned to Jake. "I've always wanted to ride in one of these."

Jake took her hand and led her to the carriage, then helped her into it. "Well, a limo is not terribly romantic."

"It ain't exactly chopped liver." She sat on the red-leather seat as he slid in next to her. "This is really nice, Jake. So where are we going?"

"Just out to dinner."

"Yeah, right. Like last time was just out to dinner. But I'm not complaining."

Jake wrapped his arm around her shoulders as the carriage started moving. She leaned toward him, taking in his earthy cologne, while enjoying being treated like royalty.

The carriage came to a stop at a marina. Lexi's eyes went wide. "We going on a boat ride?"

"Nope."

"Swimming?"

"In this water? Not a chance." Jake handed the driver two hundred dollars as he got out and extended his arms toward her. She started to step down but he placed his hands on her waist and easily lifted her out of the carriage and set her on the ground. The horse-drawn carriage moved on as he took her hand and led her onto the marina dock.

"I thought we weren't going on a boat ride."

"If it's under twenty feet it's a boat. This is a little bigger."

She was a bit unsteady as they walked to the end of the pier, her heels making things difficult on the uneven surface. He noticed and wrapped an arm around her waist. Her jaw dropped as she took in the large yacht in front of her. "You chartered a yacht?"

"Nope."

"So, what's the deal, it's called a ship?"

"No, it's a yacht. It's called *mine*."

Her eyes bugged out. "You *own* this thing?"

"It gets me from point A to point B."

"Yeah, right." She walked toward the yacht and saw a man in a white captain's uniform headed toward the side. "So this is our transportation to some restaurant."

"Not exactly. This *is* the restaurant."

The yacht slowed down and came to a stop, offering them a perfect view of the Statue of Liberty and the skyline of Manhattan.

Lexi shook her head in amazement. "Beats the hell out of a table next to the kitchen."

"I thought you might be a girl who enjoyed the water."

"Looking at it, yeah. Dining on it – never happened before."

"Well, trust me, you'll get hooked. Nothing has better atmosphere than the actual atmosphere."

"No argument here."

A chef headed toward their table wheeling a cart with two plates covered by sterling-silver domes. "Good evening. I hope you will enjoy what I've prepared for you tonight."

Lexi laughed. "Not like we can send it back if we don't like it."

The chef gave her a worried look.

She put her hand on his forearm. "I'm kidding! I'm sure it's wonderful."

He placed the two plates on the table and removed the domes, revealing a sizzling filet mignon topped with crab next to a few huge grilled shrimp. "I hope this meets with your approval."

Lexi grabbed her knife and fork. "Looks delicious, thank you."

The chef then popped the cork on a bottle of champagne, filled their glasses, and bowed. "Bon appetit." He headed back below deck.

"This looks amazing," said Lexi.

"Thought you might be a surf-and-turf girl."

"For me that's usually a hot dog and a can of tuna." She sliced off a bit of the beef and savored the taste. "Oh. My. God. This is, without a doubt, the best steak I've ever tasted."

"It's Kobe beef."

"You spoil me, Jake. You're gonna turn me into a diva."

"Fine with me. A girl like you deserves to be spoiled."

She hated to admit it, but this kind of life was very tempting.

Lexi sipped coffee after her last bite of the best cheesecake she'd ever had. She leaned back in her chair and took in the view.

The Statue of Liberty and Manhattan skyline didn't look bad, either.

Jake sat there smiling at her, studying her face like no one ever had.

Her trance was broken by the sound of a boat motor. She looked to the side and saw a small boat coming up to the yacht. "Looks like we've got company."

"Nope. Just a ride for the help."

"Excuse me?"

The chef and captain walked up to the table. "Excuse me," said the chef. "If you are no longer in need of our services—"

"Take the rest of the night off," said Jake, as he slipped each one a hundred-dollar bill. "And thank you for making this a terrific evening."

"Have a good night," said the chef, as he and the captain headed toward the other boat, which had pulled up alongside. They pulled the boats together using a rope, then hopped onto the other one.

Lexi turned back to Jake. "Uh, where are they going?"

"Home for the night."

"And… how are we supposed to get home? You know how to drive this thing?"

"Of course. I just didn't want to be preoccupied getting us out here, and I wanted some privacy after dinner. Don't worry, I take the yacht out all the time by myself."

"So what made you buy this?"

"Great place to hide from the media. They can camp out by the limo or outside your building, but lotsa luck cornering me out here!"

She looked at her watch. "Hey, it's eleven. Don't we need to get going if you need your beauty sleep?"

"Not really."

"Breaking curfew?"

He shrugged. "The yacht has a bedroom."

Her eyes widened and jaw clenched as a touch of fear ran through her veins.

I'm all alone out here on the water with a guy twice my size who wants to sleep with me. I can't exactly yell help if I need to.

"Lexi, you okay?"

"Uh, yeah."

"Most women don't look terrified when I ask them to spend the night."

Most women? File that for future reference.

"Look, Jake, I like you a lot, you've been a perfect gentleman and our dates have been incredible, but you need to know I'm also dating someone else I just met."

His face dropped a bit. "Oh, sorry. I didn't know. I just figured since we get along so well and this is our third date—"

"Even if I wasn't dating someone else it would take a lot more than three dates before I spend the night with a guy. I'm a tad old-fashioned."

"Damn, Lexi, I apologize. I've obviously made you uncomfortable. I'm really sorry."

"It's okay, Jake. Really. It just takes me a while to get to know someone. And after my last breakup I'm being very cautious. I hope you can understand that because I really do enjoy spending time with you and want to continue our relationship."

"Sure, no problem. I guess we'll need to get going soon." He tossed his napkin on the table. "You wanna drive it in?"

"Are you out of your mind? I've never driven a boat. I wouldn't even know how."

"Not a boat, it's a yacht. C'mon. I'll keep my hands on the wheel."

She detected a touch of hurt in his eyes. Obviously he wasn't used to being turned down and his confidence had taken a hit. Still, she didn't want him to think she was a total prude, and she sure didn't want him to give up on her. She got up, moved around the table and climbed on his lap, straddling him. She took his face in her hands. "Listen, you very nice man who has taken me out for a wonderful evening. Why don't you keep your hands on me instead of that wheel for a few minutes?"

He locked eyes with her as his hands slid up on her waist. "You sure?"

"Hey, just because I'm not spending the night with you doesn't mean I don't want a goodnight kiss. Or two. Or several. So pucker up, big boy."

"Demanding little redhead, aren't you?"

"Part of my charm. So, you gonna kiss me or what? Clock's running. Tick tock."

She got lost in his kiss, not noticing another boat sitting still in the water a few hundred feet away.

CHAPTER TEN

Upbeat after picking up enough work to keep her business afloat for the foreseeable future along with the afterglow from a great date with Jake, Lexi energetically wheeled her cart through the supermarket toward the checkout line on a busy Saturday afternoon. She wanted to get her ton of errands out of the way and relax a bit before Kyle picked her up for what promised to be another unique night out on the town.

Meanwhile, Jake's comment had been weighing on her for the past few days.

"Most women don't look terrified when I ask them to spend the night."

How many constituted "most" anyway? What was the number? Five? One hundred? While she realized pro athletes had hot-and-cold running women at their beck and call, Jake seemed different. Had he truly grown up since his days chasing women from bikini magazines? And while expecting sex after three dates wasn't out of the ordinary in this day and age, it was a little fast for her. Making out was one thing, and she enjoyed the hell out of that with a man who had a body to die for, but spending the night was the point of no return, especially when you're dating two guys. Once she reached that point, it was decision time one way or the other. She'd never sleep with both.

She waited in line behind a woman with a ton of groceries and scanned the rack of tabloids with headlines that were always entertaining.

Michael Jackson's body exhumed by aliens!
Hollywood star's sex change shocker!
New Jersey invaded by ten-foot bats!

She laughed as the woman in front of her moved forward and created room on the conveyor belt. Lexi began to put her groceries on the belt when the photo on the front page of one tabloid made her drop her last item, a dozen eggs. A grainy photo, taken at night, of her straddling Jake Frost on his yacht while he kissed her neck, her head thrown back, mouth open in ecstasy, the pair looking like the cover of the proverbial bodice-ripper romance novel.

Jake Frost's Midnight Ride!

"Sonofabitch!"

The young checkout guy stopped scanning groceries and turned to her. "Excuse me?"

"Uh, I, uh, dropped my eggs." Lexi quickly opened the carton. "Whew, they didn't break. Sorry for the foul language."

The woman in front of her smiled. "Shit, honey, don't worry about it."

The checkout guy went back to scanning as Lexi grabbed the tabloid from the rack and practically ripped the thing looking for the page with the article.

It got worse.

Four more grainy photos of her and Jake in various stages of ecstasy sat atop the story.

New York City's most eligible bachelor, Jake Frost, may have been caught by a redhead seductress, who apparently had her way with him during a midnight ride on Frost's million-dollar yacht. The New York Jets star quarterback, who has a long, torrid history of dating supermodels, was captured in

a steamy exchange with an unidentified date. Since he had also been spotted at one of the city's trendiest restaurants with the same flame-haired babe, we can only assume Frost (once known as "one-nighter Jake") may actually be in a serious relationship after going through bimbos like Kleenex early in his career.

After dinner on the yacht, the crew left the boat, giving the couple privacy. Within seconds the redhead pounced on her prey, straddling the quarterback and seducing him with a vengeance. Afterward the woman piloted the ship back to a private marina, driving the boat with Frost's arms around her, presumably re-enacting a scene from the movie *Titanic*.

The yacht, named "Wet Dream" and referred to as "Jake's water bed" by teammates, was purchased by Frost five years ago and is fully equipped, with two bedrooms. Frost has been known to use the craft to escape the media and often spends the night on it. Usually in the company of a stunning woman.

"You gotta be kiddin' me!"

The checkout guy stopped again. "Miss, you okay? Your face is all red."

"Uh, just the sale prices in this place are amazing."

"Must say, I've never seen anyone get so excited in a grocery store." He scanned her last item, the eggs, then pointed at the tabloid. "Did you want that magazine?"

"Oh, yeah. Guilty pleasure. They sure can make up funny stuff, huh? Of course, none of it's true."

She handed it to him. He scanned it, then stopped a moment to look at the cover. Then looked at her, studying her face. "Hey, this woman really looks like you."

Her face tightened. "Her? Pffft. No way."

He looked at the photo again. "Yeah, I guess not. And you don't look like that type."

"What do you mean by that?"

"I mean, uh, you know, the woman on Jake Frost's lap looks like… well… like he paid for her."

***

Donna's eyes filled with fear as she spotted the tabloid in the department store checkout line. She grabbed Kyle's arm just as he started to put the items on the conveyor belt.

Right in front of the magazine with Lexi's photo.

"Little brother, go get some lottery tickets, I'll check out and meet you at the car."

He glanced at the full cart. "I'll get 'em later. There's a lot of heavy stuff in here."

"I'll get it. I need the exercise."

"Donna, the bag of kitty litter weighs more than you do."

She yanked on his arm and swapped places with him. "Lottery tickets. I feel lucky. The computer is going to spit out the winning quick-pick right now."

"What the hell has gotten into you?"

She started putting the items on the conveyor belt. "Nothing." She reached for the bag of cat litter and winced at the weight of the thing.

He noticed. "See? I told you that you can't lift it." He reached for it, scooped it up, placed it on the belt—

And stopped.

Damn, he's seen it.

"What the hell?" He grabbed the magazine and started to open it.

Donna snatched it from his hands. "You don't need to see this."

"Too late. I can't un-see it. Still want lottery tickets?"

She gave him a soulful look. "I was just being a good big sister and trying to protect you because I know this will be kicking around in your head all night, and you've got a date with her in a few hours."

He grabbed the magazine back from her and opened it.

"Kyle, please—"

He put up his hand. Then bit his lower lip as he read, his eyes becoming deep pools of hurt.

Donna lightly touched his arm. "Hey."

He finished reading and put the magazine back on the rack. "What?"

"She does the same thing with you, right?"

"From the expression on her face it looks like they probably did a little more after the pictures were taken. What's your point?"

"That she does the same thing with you. Got it?"

He slowly nodded. "Yeah, but—"

"Yeah but nothing. Get that damn image out of your head. And tonight I want you to be as confident as possible."

"You think Lexi has seen this?"

"I'm sure she has. But she doesn't know *you* have. Just make sure she doesn't suspect anything."

He shook his head. "After seeing that I almost wish we weren't going out tonight."

"Bullshit. You've been counting the hours till you can see her again."

***

Lexi stormed into her apartment, then started jamming the perishable groceries into the fridge like she was stabbing it. She practically threw the ice cream into the freezer. The second she finished she grabbed her phone and called Jake. He answered on the first ring. "Hey, sexy Lexi, how's it going with—?"

"Good God, Jake, have you seen it?"

Long pause, followed by an audible sigh. "I was, uh, hoping you hadn't."

"Geez, Jake, I thought we were safe from that kind of stuff out on the boat. You told me that's why you bought the thing."

"Like I said, there's that Twitter hashtag. Someone must have spotted us in the hansom cab and then saw us get on the yacht."

"Well, the time we were in *Page Six* wasn't bad, but this makes me look like a cheap slut!"

"Oh, it does not, Lexi. People probably think it's photoshopped. Nobody takes those magazines seriously. And your name's not in there."

"Yeah, but my face sure is, front and center in every checkout line at Stop 'n' Shop. And the expression on my face looks like something out of a porn movie."

"Lexi, other than saying I'm sorry it happened, I'm not sure what you want me to do. I can't un-ring that bell."

She finally exhaled a bit of her anger. "I know, Jake, and I'm sorry to take it out on you, but I've been really upset since I saw it."

"I'll make it up to you. Promise. Even if I have to wear a wig and a fake beard."

She laughed a bit. "I think I might be the one who needs a wig."

"Maybe, but you wouldn't look good with a beard."

"Very funny. Again, sorry for unloading on you, I know it wasn't your fault. You have a good game tomorrow."

"Thanks. And cheer up, Lexi, Tuesday's coming. Bye."

"Bye." She ended the call and looked at the clock. She had one hour to get ready for Kyle.

And one hour to pray he hadn't seen that tabloid.

***

Lexi studied Kyle's face as he entered the lobby, searching for any indication he might be upset.

She saw nothing.

Just a wide smile as he spotted her and headed her way. She stood up to greet him. "You said dress very casual. This casual enough?" She pointed at her outfit: skinny jeans, stacked-heel boots and a gathered red top under a light jacket.

"Perfect. And that's the right color considering where we are going for dinner."

"Red... what, we're gonna slaughter our own cow?"

"Not quite. But things might get a little messy."

"Where the hell are you taking me?"

"You're such an impatient little thing. Wait for the big reveal."

"Okay. But only because your surprises are so spectacular." They started heading for the door. Lexi's heart downshifted as she was now convinced he hadn't seen the tabloid. She reached out and wrapped one arm around his waist, holding on a bit tighter than normal.

He rested his arm across her shoulders and shot her a wide smile.

"We're gonna make our own pizza?"

Kyle smiled as the cook handed each of them an apron. "We're going to try like hell."

The cook looked at her. "You ever throw a pie crust before?"

"What, you mean like toss dough in the air and catch it?"

"Yeah."

"Are you kidding?"

"I will teach you. Follow me." He led them back to the huge kitchen filled with patrons trying to throw dough in the air, most of them unsuccessfully. Most were laughing hysterically. One blob of dough fell from the ceiling.

She grew a worried look. "Oh, this isn't going to be pretty."

"You might be good at it," said Kyle, who suddenly waved at

someone behind her. She turned and saw a photographer headed their way.

"Oh no, you are *not* going to take pictures of me doing this."

"It's included in the price of admission. You have to experience the entire pizza-making experience. If you don't see yourself from another point of view, you'll never get better."

"And I assume I have no choice in the matter."

"You do not."

"I will get even for this."

"Hey, you're the one who insists on creative dates. I took it literally. We're going to create a pizza."

The cook grabbed a big blob of dough and stood in front of her. "Righty or lefty?"

"Righty."

"Okay, your right hand stays flat and you control the dough with it. But when you catch it, you do so with your fists. Watch." The guy started tossing the dough in the air, effortlessly catching it before sending it up a split second later. Within a minute he placed a perfect crust on a tin. "Now you try."

"Oh, I can't do that."

He handed her some dough. "Try. Remember, right palm flat, catch with your fists. It's all in the fists, not all in the wrists. It ain't rocket science."

"Got it. You guys might wanna stand back." She took the dough and tossed it up, just a few inches, then caught it.

"You gotta go higher and spin it, use the centrifugal force to create a crust."

"So there's physics involved in pizza?"

"Along with sauce and cheese, yeah. Da Vinci came up with the concept."

"Yeah, right." She tossed it up a little higher and caught it again, then kept throwing it up as the photographer snapped a few pictures.

"Much higher," said the cook. "You're getting the hang of it."

"Okay, here goes." Lexi, bent her knees a bit and sent the dough four feet in the air, then realized her aim was way off. The dough came down right on her head, covering her. She heard the photographer's auto-winder and Kyle's laugh as she pulled the dough from her hair. "I'm glad you're all enjoying this."

Kyle and the cook helped her get the dough out of her hair, then tossed it in the trash. The cook handed her another blob of dough. "You were very close. Try again."

"Seriously?"

"Go ahead," said Kyle.

Five minutes later she had the makings of a decent-looking crust. The cook nodded his approval as he took it from her and spread it on the pan, stretching the dough a bit more. "Not bad."

"And not round."

"Doesn't matter when it gets to your stomach. Now we do the toppings." He led them over to a table filled with all kinds of cheeses, meats and veggies.

Her eyes lit up. "Now this I can do." She ladled sauce on the crust, then Kyle reached for the toppings.

"You want sausage, pepperoni, olives, onions, mushrooms?"

"Yes."

"Which ones?"

"Yes means everything. And make sure you carpet-bomb it with so much cheese you can't see the toppings."

He loaded up the pizza with the goodies and then covered everything with mozzarella.

The cook backed up and looked at it. "Might need a forklift to get it in the oven. But looks good. I'll bring it to your table when it's done. You can turn in your aprons."

After twenty minutes and two glasses of red wine, which went right to her head on an empty stomach Lexi licked her lips as a waiter slid the steaming pizza onto their table. "That is one ugly pizza, but I don't care." She quickly grabbed a slice and took a bite, savoring the crisp crust and spicy toppings. "Oh. My. God. This is seriously the best pizza ever."

Kyle took a bite. "Damn, you're right. And you made it."

"*We* made it."

"I was just the sous chef. You were in charge."

"Well, it may look like something from geometry class, but it's fantastic."

"They've got some secret spices in the dough, that's why the crust is off the charts. And they make their own mozzarella fresh every day. You can't buy cheese like this in a grocery store."

"I take it you eat here often."

"I try. You don't have to make your own, I just thought you'd enjoy that option."

"That was really fun, Kyle, thank you. Once again, you managed to come up with some unique stuff."

"I'm glad you're enjoying yourself."

She took another bite, then talked through the pizza. "So, can I ask you something?"

"Since when do you need permission to ask anything?"

"True. Anyway… I have this friend dating someone new. They've been out a few times, get along great, and he asked her to spend the night. She didn't. She's a little old-fashioned. Anyway, she was wondering… what's the general number of dates before a guy expects you to sleep with him?"

"What the hell kind of question is that?"

"Like I said, my friend wants to wait but worries the guy might lose interest. So, ya know, at what point does the guy give up and move on? I'm just collecting male points of view from single guys."

"Uh-*huh*."

"So, what's your take on the dating protocols today?"

"You really wanna know how many dates before a guy expects a woman to have sex with him?"

"And how many before he leaves skid marks if she doesn't. I basically need the over and under."

He sipped his wine, took a bite of pizza and leaned back. "Well, depends on the guy. Some guys want a one-nighter and if that doesn't happen they move on. Others can be very patient. As for a specific number, who knows?"

"What about you, Kyle? You got a number?"

"Seriously? You're asking me this?"

"Yeah."

"I guess you've had too much wine before the pizza got here. What the hell. This is, what, our third date?"

"Yeah."

"We're about two dates overdue."

Her eyes went wide.

"Lexi, I'm kidding!"

"Oh." She relaxed.

"But if we're talking about me and you, well, much as I love spending time with you and feel a certain chemistry, there's no way I'd sleep with you right now even if you hauled my ass into your bedroom tonight."

"Really? I got the impression we had a physical connection."

"We do, very much so. I find you extremely attractive and you're incredibly affectionate. But…"

"Yeah?"

"You said you were dating someone else. I can't go down that road. Sex is a big commitment for me, and I couldn't have that kind of relationship with a woman who was going out with someone else. I'm just an old-fashioned, monogamous guy."

"Old-fashioned is good. So is monogamy."

"Glad you think so." He leaned forward again and attacked the pizza. "So, what's this… *friend of yours*… going to do about the guy she's dating?"

Lexi shrugged. "I think she's going to let things play out."

"I see. If I were her, I wouldn't worry about the guy leaving if she makes him wait too long. Any guy who does that isn't worth having."

Lexi dimmed the lights in the apartment, slid onto Kyle's lap and wrapped her arms around his neck. "Again, you have outdone yourself, young man."

"Glad you enjoyed the evening. I was afraid you would think the date was too… cheesy."

"Very funny. In this case, cheesy was good. So, you ever gonna run out of amazing things to do?"

"In New York City? No way."

She leaned forward and kissed him, still feeling guilty and wondering if she had to make it up to him, even though he hadn't seen the magazine. Kyle ran his fingers through her hair—

Then stopped kissing her and leaned back with a tightened face.

Lexi studied his look. "What? I've got onion breath?"

He started to smile. "No." He pulled his hands back and showed them to her. "You've still got dough in your hair."

"Oh my God!" She started to laugh. "Well, you're responsible for getting it there, you get it out."

She turned around and let him get the dough out of her tangles. "It's not much. Though if it was hot outside it might have baked and you would have a crust on your head. We could have enjoyed a late-night snack. Okay, your flour highlights are all gone."

"Thank you." She turned back around and they shared a laugh. Lexi wrapped her arms around him and lay her head on his shoulder. Suddenly she just wanted to be held.

He gently stroked her back and kissed the top of her head. "You okay, tonight, Lexi? You seem a little different. Like you've got something on your mind."

"You will soon come to realize the wheels are always turning under the red tangles. But right now I don't want to think. I just want you to hold me. Would that be okay?"

"Happy to oblige."

CHAPTER ELEVEN

"Well, well, well, if it isn't the redheaded seductress reporting for work."

Lexi narrowed her eyes and glared at Chandler. "Bite me."

"Glad to see you are walking normally after *pouncing on your prey*. I was surprised to learn a woman of such conservative values had that move in her repertoire."

"I didn't *pounce* on him and I didn't seduce him! And Jake is not my *prey*! I'm not a friggin' black widow! And I don't have a damn *repertoire*! Sitting on a guy's lap and kissing him does not constitute a *repertoire*."

"Fine. Though you must admit that being referred to as a *flame-haired babe* inflated your ego just a tad."

"Whatever. At least Kyle didn't see the damn thing. Wish I had enough money to buy up every copy in town."

"Ah, so your weekend suitor did not exhibit any evidence of jealousy."

"No, but if he'd seen it he probably would have stood me up. Honestly, Chandler, I never expected to be involved in a situation where I was being stalked by the paparazzi."

"Such is the life of a *Wag*."

"A what?"

"*Wag*. Acronym meaning *wives and girlfriends*. Term for the women who date or marry athletes."

"Eh, *wag this*."

"So, after discovering your escapades in print, how did your evening with Kyle go?"

She smiled. "Really well. Damn, Chandler, I like both of these guys. And they're so different. I really hate the thought of hurting one of them. Kinda hoping things shake out by themselves so the choice is made for me." She grabbed the morning mail from his desk and flipped through it. "Oh, by the way, is there a costume shop in the neighborhood?"

"Why?"

"Well, I won't have to worry about the paparazzi tomorrow night thanks to Halloween. Jake is taking me to a restaurant where costumes are required this week."

***

Even if a tabloid photographer was lurking outside the restaurant, Lexi wasn't worried. Her Cleopatra costume, complete with black wig and a ton of eye makeup, rendered her unrecognizable. And Jake's face was nearly covered by his Batman cowl, though he turned every female head in the place thanks to him filling out the rest of his costume perfectly. "So, we going home in the Batmobile tonight?"

"I didn't think of it, but that can probably be arranged. I love your costume, by the way."

"Thank you. And you certainly make a good superhero."

"Had to go to three costume shops to find one that would fit. Apparently most of the guys who dress as Batman are little. I guess they can dream."

The waiter arrived and took their order. Lexi handed her menu to him and grabbed her glass of wine. "This was a great idea. I was really wondering how we were ever going to go out in public again."

"Well, we can't use Halloween all the time, but I have some other ideas for the upcoming weeks." He leaned forward and dropped his voice. "Lexi, I'm really sorry about last week. I mean, between my asking you to stay the night and the pictures ending up in the tabloids—"

"Pffft." She waved it away. "I'm over it. My name wasn't in it, and, like you said, that was the important thing. Besides, I was in the grocery store this morning and the new issue is out. Front page says one of the Kardashians had an ass transplant."

He laughed. "Well, glad that thing is outta here. Oh, I do have another place where no one knows who I am, or cares, for that matter." He reached in his pocket, pulled out a business card and handed it to her.

She looked at it and furrowed her brow. "A travel agent? What? Is this guy going to send us to a private island or something?"

"Not exactly. More like someplace I'm not a household name. You know how the NFL schedules a game or two in London every year?"

"Yeah."

"Well, this is our year. Anyway, my travel agent has a charter going across the pond and since we have the week off after the game I'm going to stay on a couple of days and see the sights. I was wondering if maybe you'd like a seat on the charter and then we could spend some time in London after the game."

She couldn't hold back a smile or the bug eyes. "You wanna take me to London?"

"Well, you're dressed like a queen, may as well treat you like one. But look, I've gotta go anyway. And you'd be helping out my travel agent to fill the seats on the plane."

"Something tells me you have an ulterior motive to helping out your travel agent."

"Fine, I'd like to take you. It's an amazing place. Have you ever been there?"

"No, I've only been out of the country once, on a cheap

Caribbean cruise, where the locals hounded me and wanted to braid my damn hair every time we got off the ship."

"Well, London is a lot classier and the people are incredibly polite."

"I'm sure. How much is the ticket?"

"The charter is already paid for. So, nothing."

"Bullshit."

"Fine, I'll buy you a seat. Seven hundred bucks. I already have a hotel booked for me after the game. And I don't want you to feel any pressure, so I can, you know, get you your own room. So if you have a passport and would like to join me in jolly old London, I'd love to show you around. And we wouldn't have to worry about being spotted. To them football means soccer and nobody knows me."

"Jake, this is really tempting."

"Perhaps you can ask your boss for some time off?" he teased.

She knew damn well she could be away from the office for a few days, but she needed to think about it. A helicopter ride to the Hamptons was one thing. A little vacation together in London was quite something else.

A big step.

"Can I get back to you on this? It sounds wonderful, but I need to check with my assistant."

"Sure, no problem. But let me know by Thursday if you can."

***

Chandler looked closely at her eyes as he handed her the morning messages. "Ah, I see you are now partaking of the grape in moderation."

"If you mean I had less than a whole bottle of wine, yeah. Stopped at two glasses. And we had a nice evening, since I know that was your next question."

"I am becoming too predictable. I need to work on that."

"Oh, stop it. But an interesting proposition did present itself."

"Ah, he asked you to spend the night with him again."

Her face tightened. "No. Where did you get that idea?"

"You said he propositioned you."

"I did not. I said an *interesting proposition* presented itself."

"Ah. Do tell."

"Well, the Jets are playing in London next week, Jake has the week off after that and asked me to come along for a few days."

He didn't smile. "Curious."

"That's your reaction? *Curious*?"

"Well, you did tell him you were being escorted by someone else, did you not?"

"I did."

"From my perspective, it appears he is, as they say, upping the ante. London is quite the romantic locale and a trip to Europe is a rather large step in a relationship."

"Yeah, I know. But London! I've never even been to Europe."

"So you accepted his invitation?"

"Told him I'd think about it. I'm on the fence. I'd have my own room and everything, but still… anyway, I've got a couple days to think about it." She flipped through her messages.

"Oh, Mister Caruso's executive assistant Donna related that she has a check for you if you'd like to stop by."

She didn't see a message from Donna among the slips. "When did she call?"

"She didn't. She banged on the ceiling, presumably with either a broom handle or stiletto heel, then yelled through the air duct. Her exact words were, *Yo, Lexi, I got your check ready.* That was followed by, *cha-ching.*"

"That woman's a pistol. Let me run upstairs and get it. Or our bank account will be running on fumes. Maybe soon we can afford an office where we don't have to listen to conversations coming from other businesses."

***

Lexi entered Kyle's office and found Donna on the phone. Kyle's sister shot her a smile, then pointed at the end of her desk and put her hand over the mouthpiece. "Your check's in that batch," she whispered.

Lexi gave her the thumbs-up and moved to the end of the desk, where she saw five checks lined up. She looked for one with her name on it and found it, but not before noticing the one next to it for six hundred dollars.

Marked "child support."

Her eyes went wide as she quickly took note of the name and address on the check and picked up her own. Donna finished up her call and looked up at her. "Got it?"

"Uh… yeah. Thanks, I really need this one. Very nice of your brother to split Jake's fee with me."

"He's a fair guy, Lexi. Honest as the day is long."

We'll see about that…

The phone rang again and Donna reached for it. "Lunch later?"

"Yeah. Sure. Gotta run."

Donna answered the call as Lexi left the office. She ran down the stairs, taking them two at a time and flew into her own office.

"The banks are open till five, you know," said Chandler.

"Not why I'm in a hurry. I need your computer-snooping skills." She grabbed a pen and wrote a name on it. "Find this person for me. I'm looking for a woman with at least one child."

He furrowed his brow. "Is there some reason—"

"Find it, then I'll tell you. Oh, the woman has a Staten Island address."

"Very well. Should not be too hard. And those with young tykes do so like to overshare on social media." He tapped a few keys on the keyboard and got a few hits. "Let's try Facebook first." He clicked on the name and a photo popped up.

What Lexi saw made her jaw drop.

A redhead who could be her sister.

Holding a small boy who was a dead ringer for Kyle.

She read aloud the paragraph under the woman's photo. *"Lucky to be part of a wonderful family. Life's often a struggle, but we have each other. Our futures are tied together."* Lexi pointed at the screen. "Click on the photos."

Chandler did so and a few dozen pictures popped up. Her face dropped. He turned to look up at her. "Do you want—"

"I've seen what I needed to see. Why the hell didn't he tell me he had a kid?"

Chandler reached up and placed his hand lightly on her forearm. "I'm sorry, Lexi. I know you prefer gentlemen without those sorts of ties."

She shook her head. "I know it sounds shallow but I just can't deal with that kind of situation. Ex-wives, or ex-girlfriends… tied to him forever. Shuttling kids back and forth every two weeks. The mother of his child hating me. The kid hating me. I've never even considered getting into that sort of relationship. I always wanted a guy with a clean slate."

"So, what are you going to do?"

"About Kyle? I don't know. I sure can't confront him about it or he'll know I was snooping. Dammit, why the hell do I have to like him so much?"

"And what are you going to do about the other man in your life?"

"This." She pulled out her cell phone and called Jake. It went right to voice mail. "Hey, it's Lexi. I'm going to London with you."

CHAPTER TWELVE

The bellman opened the door to her hotel room and Lexi was greeted by the scent of flowers. She smiled as she saw a huge bouquet in a vase on a table in the middle of the room, which was the biggest hotel room she'd ever stayed in. The bellman opened the drapes, offering a spectacular view of London. "Wow."

"Yes, our views are quite brilliant." He handed her a key. "If there's anything you need from the bell stand, just press nine on the phone. Have a pleasant stay, Miss."

"Thank you." She tipped him and moved toward the table, which also held a bottle of wine in an ice bucket and a box of chocolates. Lexi leaned toward the bouquet, breathing in the fragrance, then noticed an envelope next to the vase. She opened it, finding a note along with some British currency and a ticket to the game.

Lexi, so glad you came along. A driver will come by to take you to and from the game. Here's some pocket money as well to get you through the day. If you want anything to eat and don't feel like going out, just order room service. The gift shop has anything you may have forgotten. I assume you are jet-lagged so I have booked a massage for you in the spa. I will see you later tonight after the game.
-Jake

"So this is how the other half lives." She opened the box of chocolates, bringing it with her to the window, to take in the view. She was indeed jet-lagged, so the chocolate gave her a sugar rush she needed. Alcohol would put her down for the count before the game, which would start in a couple hours, so she figured she'd save it for later.

A first-class flight, fabulous hotel room, a massage, flowers and candy waiting for her. "Yeah, I could get used to this."

***

The game had just started and Lexi was feeling incredibly relaxed after the massage. The usher pointed her toward a group of seats occupied by what looked to be a Barbie doll convention. "You're in the section with the players' wives."

"Oh, I'm not married to a player. I simply handle the public relations for one."

"Well, if you don't wish to sit there you may take any seat you wish. We're not exactly full up."

"Thank you." She pulled her wide-brimmed hat tighter on her head and adjusted her sunglasses, taking an empty seat a few rows back from the wives' section and across the aisle. But near enough to hear the loud chatter coming from the group.

By the second quarter both the Jets and Jake were getting pummeled, already losing 28-0. She turned her attention to the field just as Jake got leveled by a defender for about the sixth time, the hit making her cringe. Then the comments from the Barbie contingent made it even worse.

"Ow, that one left a mark!" said one of the wives.

"Yeah, looks like it'll be girl on top for Jake tonight."

"I think that redheaded tramp on the cover of the tabloid already has that position covered."

"Aw, hell, she's long gone by now."

"Yeah, she looks like one of his Kleenex girls. One blow and thrown away!"

"Haven't you heard? Jake is settling down. He's down to one penicillin prescription a month."

"Well, thankfully he'll never get married. I would miss these conversations too much."

Lexi's eyes widened as her fists clenched. She heard a cheer and saw another touchdown, putting the Jets down 35-0. Jake remained on the bench, the coach mercifully taking the first team out of the game. "Hell, I'm outta here."

***

The gentle tap on the door woke her from a deep sleep. Lexi looked at the clock and saw it was only eight in the evening, but her body clock was all out of whack from the jet lag. She got up and staggered to the door, opened it, and found no one.

The tapping continued from behind her.

She realized it was the connecting door to Jake's room, opened it and found him standing there. "Hey, Lexi, hope I didn't wake you up."

"I confess I was taking a nap, but I'm glad you did." She moved forward to hug him and he grimaced as she did.

"Ow."

"Sorry. I guess you got beat up pretty bad today."

"Thank goodness the coach got me outta there. Anyway, come on in."

He ushered her into his room, a spectacular suite. "Damn. I thought my room was nice, but wow."

"Well, I always get a suite with a whirlpool when we're on the road. And I'm gonna need it tomorrow."

"Yeah, that game wasn't pretty. Sorry you lost."

"That's why they won the Super Bowl last year. Did you have dinner?"

"No."

"I'm too sore to go out. Room service okay?"

"Fine with me. You look like you need to take it easy anyway. We can be tourists tomorrow."

"Thanks, Lexi, appreciate you being so understanding."

"I appreciate you bringing me here. This is incredible. Can't wait to get out and explore."

After a fabulous room-service dinner of steak and champagne Lexi found herself covering a yawn. "I'm sorry. I've never flown overseas or gone through so many time zones."

"I have the same problem. That's why we came over on Wednesday. Probably best if we both turn in."

"Yeah."

"Hey, before you go, can I ask you a favor?"

"What do you need?"

"Just rub some Ben-Gay on my back. I really took some shots there."

"Sure." She pointed to the bed. "Take your shirt off and lie on your stomach."

"Thanks, Lexi." He handed her a bottle of the muscle rub and began to unbutton his shirt. He removed it, revealing perhaps the most perfectly chiseled torso she'd ever seen in person. He moved to the bed and lay face down. She sat on the edge and squeezed some of the stuff on his back, then began to massage it in. The sensation of rubbing his huge, hard muscles sent a bolt of electricity through her body. "Oh. My. God."

"What?

"Just, uh, that you've got so many bruises."

"Comes with the territory. I've gotta ice my elbow later. And my knee. They hurt like hell. I'm just falling apart in my old age."

She laughed and tried to put some muscle into her massage,

126

but his body was like steel. She licked her lips, locked in on his massive shoulder muscles. "So is all this worth it? I mean, playing football when you feel like this after the game?"

"Absolutely. It's a rush like you couldn't believe. It's like being a gladiator. The bigger and stronger survive."

"Sometimes the faster and smarter win."

"But for the most part it's a game of pure physical strength. You know the best part of the game?"

"What?"

"When I have to scramble out of the pocket and I can run right over someone who's smaller, I mean just crush the guy. It's a great feeling to be able to physically dominate another man. I love the feeling of being bigger and stronger than my opponent."

"Well, you are a big boy. How am I doing on the back rub?"

"Damn, Lexi, you've got a future as a masseuse."

"I was wondering if I'm strong enough to make a difference. You're so, uh, firm."

"Feels great, Lexi."

She finished covering his back with the rub, working it into his muscles with her thumbs. Though he didn't ask her to massage his arms, his biceps were too much to resist, so she ran her hands down to the elbow.

"Ow!" Jake jumped.

"Geez, sorry. Did I hit a tender spot?"

"My right elbow."

"Sorry. You gonna be okay? What does the team doctor say?"

"It's always sore after a game. To be honest, I had another doctor look at it and I'll need major surgery on it after the season."

"Oh, no. Will you be able to play afterwards?"

"Oh sure. But if the Jets know about that they'll drop their offer. Besides, I don't trust the team doctor, so I went to the best specialist in the country. Anyway, keep it under your hat."

"Sure, no problem." She went back to rubbing his back. Lexi didn't want to stop, but knew she had to. "Okay, I've got you covered." She put the cap on the bottle, placed it on the nightstand and moved to the kitchen to wash her hands. By the time she returned he was lying on his back, smiling at her. "You feel better?"

"Yeah, thank you. By morning I'll be able to move around."

She sat on the edge of the bed, not able to take her eyes off his chest and washboard abs. "Glad I could help."

"Lexi, my eyes are up here."

Busted. "Funny. I'm not built to use that line and I hear it from a man." She blushed as she turned to face him. "Sorry, I can't help myself. You've got an amazing body."

"All yours if you want it."

"Not quite yet."

"You're perfectly built, Lexi. And while I love the feeling of crushing my opponent on the football field, somehow I feel powerless against you."

"Oh, so the tower of muscle known as Jake Frost could be dominated by a hundred-and-ten-pound woman?"

"Absolutely. You could do whatever you want with me and I couldn't resist. I'm ready to be taken."

"Again, not quite yet."

"Anyway, one more favor, if you don't mind."

"Sure. What do you need?"

"One of your fabulous goodnight kisses."

She sat up straight, hands on hips. "Just one? That's all you need?"

"I'll take all I can get, but I need at least one.'

She leaned forward, taking his head in her hands and kissed him. He reached for her and pulled her on top of him, running his hands over her back and through her hair. After a while she slid off to the side, lay her head on his chest and began to run one hand over his abs, savoring the touch as he wrapped one arm around her waist. Then she yawned again. "Damn, Jake, I'm sorry I'm so tired. I've never flown overseas. The jet lag is off the charts."

"You're too tired and I'm too sore. We sound like an old retired couple in Florida."

"Yeah, no kidding. But this is really nice, Jake. Just being held." She closed her eyes, just for a while, wanting to savor the moment, the touch of his body.

And she instantly fell asleep.

***

"Well, look who finally woke up."

Lexi cracked open one eye and saw the fuzzy vision of Jake wearing nothing but a towel around his waist. "What the hell— oh my God, I fell asleep!"

"That's what people generally do at the end of the day when they're tired."

Her heart kicked into overdrive and she sat up. "I slept here! In your bed! With you!"

"Yeah, you were exhausted and so was I. We both nodded off." He rubbed another towel through his wet hair. "You looked so peaceful I didn't wake you. I already hit the hot tub and feel a lot better."

"Jake, I'm so sorry."

"Sorry about what?"

"I don't want to lead you on by sleeping with you."

He sat on the edge of the bed and laughed. "You know, the image I had of you spending the night was not one with you fully clothed and me with my pants on. But that's how we fell asleep. Nothing happened, Lexi. Stop beating yourself up."

"Still, I…"

"You hungry?"

Her stomach made an audible growl. Suddenly hunger trumped guilt. "Starving."

"Good, me too. Go get ready and we'll go grab some breakfast. And then, London awaits."

129

"So, Lexi, any reason you wanted to see the Tower of London first?"

"I'm a woman. I want to see the Crown Jewels."

"The female fascination with shiny rocks never ceases to amaze me."

"They're *jewels*, not rocks." She led him toward the display that had a large crowd around it, then stopped behind a slightly built young man who had his head close to the glass. She squeezed Jake's hand. "This is exciting for me."

"Whatever turns you on." After a few minutes with no one getting out of the way he looked at his watch, then around the room. The guy in front of them wasn't moving. "Hey, little buddy, you've had your turn. Let someone else have a look." The guy didn't respond.

"That's okay, Jake, I don't mind waiting."

"Girl like you waits for no one." He reached under the guy's arms, picked him up and dropped him a few feet away.

"What the hell?" The guy turned around and found himself face to chest with Jake, who towered over the man.

Jake looked down his nose at the guy. "There a problem?"

The guy backed off. "No, not at all." He turned and quickly walked away.

Lexi put her hand on Jake's arm. "That wasn't very nice."

"He wouldn't get out of the way. So I got him out of the way for you." He gestured toward the jewels. "Well, the point is moot now, it's your turn."

"Go apologize to him."

Jake looked around. "He's long gone. I guess I'll just apologize to you."

"You shouldn't do stuff like that."

"Sorry. I'm used to pushing people out of the way in my job. Like I said, I need a woman to fix me. Am I forgiven?" He gave her a hangdog look, which seemed to drain the anger from her.

"Yes, but don't let it happen again." She exhaled and shook her head, then turned back to the display. The sheer beauty of the jewels distracted her. About a minute later she left the display. She spotted a television camera following some large men, one of whom she recognized as one of Jake's teammates. "Uh, I thought nobody knew who you were over here?"

Jake turned and nodded. "Oh, one of the New York stations is still here. I guess they're doing a story on some of the guys sightseeing."

"Jake, I don't need any more publicity."

"Tell you what, I'll go give them a soundbite and you go look at your rocks. Once they've got enough video of the guys looking around they'll take off. I'll meet up with you later in the gift shop."

"Sounds good." Lexi turned and headed toward another exhibit while Jake walked over to the camera.

Damn, that was close.

Lexi leaned her head against his shoulder as he led her to his suite. "Jake, thank you for a fabulous day. I mean, wow... the Tower of London, Buckingham Palace, the incredible dinner and that giant Ferris wheel... what do they call it?"

He unlocked the door and led her inside. "The London Eye."

"Damn, that view was spectacular. But I think you bribed the operator to stop the thing when we were at the top."

He held out his wrists as if waiting to be handcuffed. "Guilty as charged."

"Seriously? I was kidding."

"I don't kid around when it comes to someone special. Like I said when you were dressed as Cleopatra, you deserve to be treated like a queen."

"You're so sweet to me."

"You know what I could use right now?"

"Champagne?"

"Yes, but after all we did today a half hour in that hot tub would really be relaxing. And it's right next to the window. We could turn out the lights and look at the skyline."

"That does sound wonderful and my back could use it, but I didn't pack a bathing suit. Didn't think I'd need one in London this time of year."

"Well… I'm sure the hotel gift shop sells bathing suits."

"I'm sure they do, Jake. Ten-dollar suits for two hundred bucks."

"So go get one. They're open twenty-four hours."

"It's a waste of money."

"My money, and you're not a waste. Go get one." He gestured toward the floor-to-ceiling window. "When will you ever get to use a hot tub with a view like this?"

"You've got a point. Well, okay, you twisted my arm. Be right back."

He was already in the bubbling hot tub, steam rising from the water, his glistening back to her as he faced the window. She headed toward him wearing a bathrobe over the swimsuit she'd bought, moved around to the other side of the hot tub. "They only had one in my size."

"Good. Come on in, the water and the view are wonderful." She stood there for a moment. "Well, what?"

"The suit isn't something I would normally wear. It's a bit, well, skimpy."

"Your problem being?"

"Very funny."

"Get in here."

She spun her finger in a circle. "Turn around."

"Not happenin'." He folded his arms and stared at her. "I should at least be able to see if you spent my money in a worthwhile fashion."

"I'm worried I don't measure up to what you're used to."

"I'm sure you do. Now get in the water."

"Okay." She slowly removed the robe and let it drop to the floor, revealing a red string bikini.

His eyes went wide. "Wow."

"Wow?"

"If they only had one in your size, I'm glad it's that one."

She quickly stepped into the tub. "I'm going to assume you're being polite since you have been in the company of women who graced the covers of swimsuit magazines."

"Oh stop it, you've got a great body. And unlike those other women you won't let me forget about, you've got a brain too."

"Well, thank you."

"Besides, you take a model out to eat and all she has for dinner is Diet Coke and cigarettes."

Lexi laughed as she leaned against the tub, letting the hot jets of water massage her muscles. "Oh, this is nice."

"What are you doing over there, Spin Girl? View's over here, and we've got a full moon."

She turned around and saw the spectacular skyline as the moon was rising in the background. "Now *that* deserves a *wow*." She slid over to his side of the hot tub. He grabbed a remote and turned out the lights in the suite, the only illumination coming from the skyline and the moon.

He slipped his arm around her waist and pulled her close. "How's that?"

"Amazing."

"Relaxing, huh."

"Very." She leaned in to him, molding herself to his body. "You sure know how to treat a girl, Jake."

"So, I guess I'm forgiven for that incident at the Tower of London?"

"Yeah, I'll cut you some slack on that. But you were a bad boy and might need a spanking."

"So you like bad boys?"

"They have their good points. As long as they're only bad in private."

"Now *that* I can do." He reached to the side with his free hand, grabbed two glasses of champagne, and handed one to her. "To redheads in string bikinis."

"Hmmm. How about… to one redhead in a string bikini."

"More than enough for me. As long as the one is you." He clinked her glass and they downed the champagne.

"Enjoy it while it lasts, Mister, because I'll probably never wear it again."

"That would be an incredible waste of my money and your great body."

She took his empty glass and set it aside with her own, then turned back to him and gave him a soulful look while taking his head in her hands.

"Lexi, you're missing the view."

"I like this view better." She kissed him and began to run her hands across his chest and shoulders as the jets of hot water bubbled around them. He pulled her onto his lap, his hands gently resting on her back. His touch, his kiss, the feel of his muscles in the hot, bubbling water, the spectacular, romantic setting, sent electricity rocketing through her entire body like never before. Lexi was having her way with a Greek god and was about to take him.

Which meant quickly reaching the point of no return with Jake. But for some reason she wasn't quite ready. Something was holding her back.

So she stopped. "It's getting really hot."

"I can turn the water temperature down."

She slid over to the other side of the tub and got out, then wrapped the robe around her. "I wasn't referring to the temperature."

He gave her a sly look. "Is it something you *shouldn't* do, or something you don't *want* to do?"

"Oh, the *want* part is off the charts. I want, I really want. But I shouldn't. Not yet."

He nodded and smiled. "Sure, I understand. I'm not happy about it, but I understand. You're worth the wait."

"Thank you for being incredibly patient with me. I'm sorry if I'm so old-fashioned."

"That, young lady, is part of your attraction." He reached out with his arms. "C'mon, at least come back in and enjoy the view with me. I promise I won't try anything. Unless you start."

"Not sure I can trust myself, but okay." She nodded and got back in the hot tub, sliding over to him. He wrapped one arm around her shoulders. "Thank you for putting up with me."

"You're welcome, but it's no big deal. And do me one favor. Next time you buy a bathing suit, get the most unflattering one-piece you can find. The thing you're almost wearing right now makes me wanna do a little more than hold hands."

"I'll wear a burlap sack next time." She leaned back and took in the view as the moon continued to rise. "By the way, what time is our plane tomorrow?"

He shrugged. "How about we leave after lunch?"

"Uh, don't you need to check the plane tickets to see what time our flight is scheduled?"

"Oh, we're not flying commercial. We can leave whenever we want."

***

"I know it sounds clichéd to say this, but it's the only way to fly." Jake raised a glass of champagne to Lexi, seated next to him.

"No argument here." She settled back in the huge seat, while running her hand across the tan leather that was soft as butter. "I've never been in a private jet before. You didn't have to do this for me."

"I didn't. I basically share the jet. It's one of those deals where I get so many hours per year. I figured this was the perfect opportunity to avoid flying commercial. I can't fit in those seats anyway."

She took a sip of the champagne. "You could have gone home on the Jets charter."

"Then who would have shown you around London?"

"Good point. Again, this is a real treat, Jake. You're really spoiling me."

"I enjoy spoiling you. I was thinking of commissioning a pedestal for Christmas so I can put you up there."

"Now *that* is something I never want. Being spoiled is enough."

The limo dropped her off at her apartment. With the time change it was still the middle of the day, though it was dinner time in London. It would take her a while to get back to normal.

She carried a batch of mail as she opened the door to her apartment. She dropped her suitcase near the door, vowing to unpack later. Right now she needed another nap.

Lexi turned on her cell phone for the first time in days. Her carrier didn't have international service and if Chandler needed anything he could have reached her by email. The phone screen cleared and showed four messages.

All from Kyle.

Her face dropped as she bit her lower lip.

Sonofabitch. I forgot all about him.

***

Kyle stretched out on the lumpy mattress in the budget hotel, which happened to be the only hotel in Podunk, Montana. He unwrapped a fast-food burger from the one restaurant in town, then turned on the ancient tube television and tuned to a sports network, which was about to wrap up its daily recap.

He took a bite of the dry, tasteless burger as he watched the final story, a feature report on some of the New York Jets who had stayed behind in London to do the tourist thing. An interview with Jake Frost at the Tower of London filled the screen, the quarterback talking about the great things to do in the United Kingdom.

And then he saw her.

Lexi, in the background, touring the Tower of London.

He slowly nodded. "So, that's why you haven't returned my calls. He took you to London."

Kyle turned off the TV, shoved the burger back in the bag and tossed it in the trash, no longer hungry.

Then he called Donna.

CHAPTER THIRTEEN

Three weeks later the picture had cleared.

Lexi hadn't seen Kyle, who had been on the road. Their phone calls were less frequent and not as long as they used to be. The conversation, on her end at least, seemed a bit strained.

The fact that he had an ex and a child was always lurking in the back of her mind. She knew she had to be strong and probably break things off.

Still, she missed him. His fantastic dates, his quick wit, which gave her a run for her money, his incredible kisses.

Meanwhile, Jake had continued their whirlwind courtship, taking her on elaborate dates. The world of limousines, private planes, helicopters, restaurants that opened just for them, and all that came with dating a celebrity, was intoxicating. She knew she had to remove the rose-colored glasses, that money shouldn't be a factor in how she felt about him. But the lifestyle he offered was something out of a fairy tale. It was very hard to overlook.

However, today was Thanksgiving. Jake was playing in Dallas while Kyle had invited her a month ago to a family dinner.

It would be the perfect time to find out once and for all what he'd been hiding from her. And if she couldn't find out by the end of the day, she'd confront him with it.

And if it was true, she'd say goodbye. Not being able to trust someone was a deal breaker.

She headed up the walk to their Staten Island home, already looking festive with colorful arrangements of gourds, maize, and a large ceramic turkey on the front porch. She heard loud conversation as she stepped on the front porch and rang the bell. She saw someone moving toward her through the beveled glass and realized it was Donna. Kyle's sister opened the door and smiled. "Lexi, you made it! So happy to have you join us this year. Come on in."

Lexi stepped inside as Donna closed the door. "Thanks for inviting me. I picked up a cheesecake in case you didn't have enough desserts."

"This is an Italian family, Lexi. We're never short of food. But thank you, and I know it won't go to waste."

Donna led her down the hall just as Kyle turned the corner. He spotted her, smiled and quickly moved forward, giving her a strong hug that lifted her off the ground. "Damn, I missed you." His embrace brought back all the wonderful memories for a moment, seeming to drain any negative feelings from her.

He put her down and she kissed him on the cheek. "Missed you too. You've been out of town too long."

"I'm home for a while. We can catch up. I'm really glad you could come today. Hopefully my very loud family won't scare you away." He led her into a huge, beautifully decorated living room filled with a lot of people and loud conversation. "Everyone, this is Lexi. Lexi, everyone."

They all yelled hello.

And then a statuesque redhead, who had to be six-foot-two in her heels headed in her direction.

His ex. The mother of his child.

Lexi tried to keep her eyes from bugging out. He invited *her*?

The woman came forward and took her hands. "So, this is the woman I've been hearing so much about. Hi, I'm Joanne."

"Lexi."

"So glad you came. It's nice to have another redhead here in this sea of Italian black."

And then it got worse.

The little boy walked up to her side. She wrapped one arm around him. "And this is our pride and joy, Brian. Brian, say hello to Lexi."

"Hi, Lexi."

He stuck out his hand and she shook it. "Hi, Brian, nice to meet you." *Damn, talk about a dead ringer for Kyle. The kid could be a clone.*

Joanne turned toward Kyle and wrapped one arm around his shoulder, towering over him in her stacked-heel boots. "Well, she's exactly as I pictured. You two look good together. I approve."

She *approves*? You gotta be kidding me.

She pulled him close and gave him a kiss on the top of his head. "I'm tellin' ya, Lexi, this one's a keeper. Anyway, I gotta get back to the kitchen and we'll catch up later. I wanna hear about that other life you lead as Spin Girl. I hear you can seriously kick ass when it comes to damage control."

"I sure try."

The woman headed toward the kitchen with her son. Lexi grabbed Kyle's hand and pulled him into the hallway. "Can we talk in private for a minute?"

"Sure. It's nice outside. C'mon, we can sit on the porch." He studied her face. "You okay, Lexi?"

"I'll explain in a minute."

They headed out to the porch and sat on a wicker bench. The air was crisp but the sun was strong, so she wasn't cold.

"So what did you wanna talk about?"

She shook her head, staring at the street. "I cannot *believe* you invited me, knowing she was coming."

"Who? Joanne?"

"Of course, Joanne."

"Why, do you two know each other?"

She turned to face him. "Kyle, I *know* about her and Brian."

He furrowed his brow "Lexi, you have totally lost me."

140

"You know, we've been honest with each other all along. At least I thought so. It would have been nice if you hadn't left out that little detail about having a child and an ex who looks just like me."

"Lexi, what in the hell are you talking about?"

"I know Brian's your son. And don't deny it, he looks just like you."

"Huh? Where the hell did you get that idea?"

"Child support checks ring a bell? I saw one on Donna's desk when I went to pick up my own check."

He started to laugh.

"What the hell is so funny?"

"Lexi, Joanne is my sister-in-law. Brian is my nephew. Donna and I send them money because my brother is disabled and can't work anymore. He got hurt serving in Afghanistan."

The blood drained from her face. She buried her head in her hands. "Oh my God, I am such a damn idiot. I am so embarrassed."

"Don't be. I think it's kinda funny."

"Please get me the biggest shoehorn you can find so I can get my foot out of my mouth. Or a shovel, so I can dig a hole to China. Then bury my sorry ass. Dear God, Kyle, I must seem like a nosy bitch. Oh, I am so, so sorry. I probably should go." She started to get up but he grabbed her by the waist and sat her back down.

"Whoa." Then he wrapped one arm around her and pulled her close. "You're not going anywhere and if you try to leave I'll throw you over my shoulder and carry you back inside. I haven't seen you in three weeks and I need my Lexi fix."

She looked up at him, eyes wet. "You're not mad at me?" Her voice cracked.

"For what?"

"For not trusting you when you have never given me any reason to *distrust* you. I... I... got the name and address off the check and looked up Joanne on social media and saw the photo of the kid and he looks just like you and she looks like me and I thought you just wanted a replacement redhead—"

He kissed her to shut her up. Then leaned back and wiped the tears from her cheeks. "I don't need a replacement redhead because you're the original redhead. Is this why you've sounded so distant on the phone lately?"

She nodded. "I thought you were lying to me. Keeping a huge secret... and thought I couldn't trust you. I know this is going to sound really selfish, but I just don't want a relationship with someone who has an ex-wife and kids. I know that seems shallow—"

"I'm the same way, Lexi. If you're selfish and shallow, so am I."

She bit her lower lip. "How can you forgive me after being so judgmental?"

"You were being careful, Lexi. Trust me, I would have done the same thing. If you'd like to be fair I could go on the Internet and check out your past."

Her pulse shot up at the thought of him seeing her on *Page Six* and the cover of the tabloid. "I, uh, think for this to be fair I need to be in charge of about the next six dates and pick up the check at every one."

"Fine with me. So how about we go back inside?"

She leaned over and rested her head on his shoulder. "In a minute, Kyle."

He leaned back and kissed her on the forehead as he took her hand, entwining his fingers with hers. "By the way, if you want full disclosure, I do have an ex-girlfriend but she's a blonde and you look nothing like her. Thank God."

She started to laugh.

"Along with four wives and about a dozen kids. I'm part of a polygamy cult."

She laughed out loud.

He tilted her chin up and gave her a soulful look. "Aw, I made her smile."

"You always make me smile."

Lexi sat on the porch as she watched Kyle's family play touch football on the lawn while the turkey was cooking. His brother Anthony sitting in a wheelchair, smiling as Kyle threw a pass to Brian.

Joanne sat next to her and handed her a glass of wine. "You don't wanna play?"

Lexi stuck out one leg. "Normally I would, but not in these heels."

"Yeah, same here." She looked out at the game. "God, Anthony and I don't know what we'd do without Kyle. He's so good with our son."

"So, if this isn't too personal, what's the prognosis for your husband?"

"I don't mind talking about it. He's got one more surgery that'll cost a fortune and the doctor is confident he'll walk again, but he'll never be completely normal. His hands will always shake from time to time. And of course he'll never be able to work. Financially, it's gonna be tough. This country really doesn't take care of veterans very well. Without help from Donna and Kyle and the Wounded Warrior Foundation we'd be in the poor house."

"Yeah, I understand they send you money."

"And set up a charitable foundation in his name as well. They do fundraisers and stuff. Donna got a lot from her ex but gave most of it to me. And I don't really believe that story about Kyle having to move in with Donna so he could start his own business. He did it so he could give us more money. I know Kyle can't really afford it but he loves his brother. And you can see he has a bond with Brian. My son adores his uncle."

"Yeah, he seems good with kids."

Joanne turned to her. "Look, he told me about your situation,

143

that you're dating someone else. This is going to sound like I'm lobbying for my brother-in-law, but you won't find a better guy."

"I'm beginning to see that. The thing is, the other guy I'm dating is nice too."

"Good problem to have, I guess."

"Actually, it's not."

"Don't like playing the field?"

"I thought I would but… well, it's confusing when you like two guys at the same time."

"Well, things will sort themselves out. People are always on their best behavior when they start dating, but eventually they reveal their true selves. Stick with him and you'll see." She patted Lexi on the hand. "Anyway, I can tell you'd be good for him."

"How so?"

"He lights up around you like I've never seen. And you're all he talks about. Lexi, Lexi, Lexi… that's all I hear. He never shuts up about you."

Lexi was seated between Kyle and his brother, whose hands trembled a bit as he worked through dinner. Anthony was a much bigger version of Kyle, with very broad shoulders, though she had no idea how tall he was. His arms were thick and sinewy, probably from pushing himself around in the wheelchair. But his facial expressions were a carbon copy of Kyle's, and he had the same great eyes.

Joanne tapped her glass with a spoon, bringing everyone to attention. "Okay, since we're in the middle of this feeding frenzy, let's go around the table and say what we're thankful for. I'll start. I'm very thankful that I have a very generous brother-in-law and sister-in-law who have been incredibly supportive."

The comments went around the table until they reached Kyle. He reached over and patted Lexi's hand. "I'm thankful that my brother is going to get out of that chair soon… and that I've met a terrific woman this year."

"Who would that be?" asked his brother.

Everyone laughed. "Smartass." He looked at Lexi. "Your turn."

She locked eyes with him. "I'm grateful that I met a terrific guy this year, who is Kyle, by the way, who might be the most understanding man I've ever met. And quite possibly the sweetest."

"Damn, I'm gonna get a cavity," said Anthony. "Make it stop."

"Oh, shut up," said Kyle. "Your turn, Anthony. Wrap it up."

"Thankful that my brother *finally* met someone nice."

Lexi folded her arms and looked at him. "And who would that be?"

"Yeah, she's a keeper," said Joanne with a smile.

Everyone went back to eating. Lexi saw Anthony's hand shake as he tried to raise a glass to his lips. She reached over and put her hand over his, steadying his hand as she helped him. He shot her a soulful look as he took a drink, then put the glass down. "Thank you, Lexi."

Lexi patted him on the back. "No problem."

"My wife is right. You're a keeper."

Lexi helped Joanne clear the table and bring the dishes into the kitchen. "That was one of the best Thanksgivings I've ever had."

"Oh, honey, it ain't over."

"What, we're gonna watch football?"

"No. We're gonna play cards. And have the Venetian hour while we do that."

"What's a Venetian hour?"

"Italian tradition. An endless parade of desserts."

"More? I thought we already had dessert."

"Sweetie, if you're gonna be part of this family, you'll need to get with the program. And maybe get a pair of stretch pants for the holidays."

***

Lexi stepped out into the crisp night air as Kyle held the car door for her. "Damn, I ate so much I can barely move. You might have to carry me inside."

"Well, okay." He reached over and easily scooped her into his arms, then headed for the door.

"I was kidding! Put me down, you're gonna hurt yourself."

"Oh, please, you don't weigh anything."

"Well, I'm about ten pounds heavier than when I left."

"You're light as a feather." He carried her through the empty lobby, save for a doorman, who shot them a smile. "Hit the elevator button, will ya?"

"Seriously, you don't have to carry me up to my apartment."

"Sorry ma'am, we provide door-to-door service. Besides, do I look like I'm breathing hard?"

"No, actually you don't. You're awfully strong for— I mean—"

"For a little guy?" He smiled at her.

"Not what I meant to say."

"It's okay, Lexi. You know what they say. Good things come in small packages."

She ran one hand through his hair. "Right now you're the biggest man I know."

The elevator door opened and he carried her inside.

The second the door closed she took his head in her hands and kissed him, long and hard. "Been waiting all day to do that."

"Wow. What was that for?"

"For still wanting to be with me after I was such an idiot."

"Well, if that's the case you should be an idiot more often."

"Honestly, Kyle, most guys would have dumped me after what I did."

"Most guys would be idiots to dump a girl like you."

"Well, as you get to know me you will realize that sometimes I can do really stupid stuff. So keep forgiving me and you'll be rewarded." She wrapped her arms around his neck and lay her head on his shoulder.

The elevator arrived at her floor and he carried her to her apartment, then set her down. "I'm really glad you came, Lexi. Hope you enjoyed it."

She put the key in the door, opened it, took his hand and pulled him inside. "Day's not over. I haven't seen you in three weeks and I want my Kyle fix. And I need to give thanks."

CHAPTER FOURTEEN

"Yo, Frankie."

Lexi smiled at the diminutive paparazzo as she spotted him in the lobby on Monday morning. "Lexi, how's it going?"

"Okay. You have a good Thanksgiving?"

The slender photographer with the black hair and eyes that nearly matched nodded. "Yep. Y'know, I been meaning to stop by and talk to you about something. I, uh, saw you in the tabloids—"

She cringed. "Yeah, I've been trying to forget it. But what about it?"

He shook his head. "Something funny about the whole thing. And with you ending up on *Page Six* as well."

"Well, I am dating a celebrity. I assume it goes with the territory."

"Something isn't right, Lexi."

"How do you mean?"

He leaned against the wall and folded his arms. "Well, if you're gonna make a living at what I do, chasing a shot of a pro quarterback making out with a girl isn't exactly going to pay the rent. Especially a guy with his reputation."

Her face tightened.

"Sorry, Lexi, I didn't mean it that way."

"Well, he admits he was immature when he was younger."

"Well, in his defense, if I was a millionaire quarterback at twenty-two with bikini models throwing themselves at me, I'd be immature too."

"Nice save, Mister."

"Anyway, back to my point... a photo of him... gets you a hundred bucks, maybe one-fifty, tops. I got two grand for that stuff you tipped me off about when you torched your boyfriend's clothes. Now that I think about it, I owe you a kickback. You are apparently someone I don't want on my bad side. You know, since you like to play with matches."

"Hey, forget it. It was worth it to see him and his bimbo in the papers."

"No, no, I always take care of my tipsters. I'll slide something under your door. But anyway... that stuff with you and Jake Frost... not really a big 'get' if you know what I mean. And certainly not worth the time and expense of a stakeout."

"Maybe it's some rookie paparazzo making a few bucks on the side to pay the light bill."

He shook his head. "Nah, that one of you on the boat took a special lens and they had to be on another boat. No way that was shot from shore. Lexi, someone went to a lot of time and trouble to get that shot, and I know damn well the payoff wasn't worth it monetarily. And that was not a story worthy of a front page on a tabloid."

"So what are you saying?"

"Just that the whole thing is very curious. I don't mean to scare you, but to me this sounds like someone is following Jake Frost, and not for the usual paparazzi reasons. That tabloid stuff doesn't do his supposedly cleaned-up reputation any good. Someone pulled some strings to get that shot on the cover of that tabloid because that's not the kind of stuff that sells. Someone paid them off."

"Hmmm. Frankie, is there any way you can find out who took those shots?"

"I'll check around. But I know none of the regulars would waste their time following him. We have bigger fish to shoot."

"Thanks, Frankie. Let me know."

"Sure thing."

The paparazzo went up to his apartment while Lexi headed out the door.

Then she remembered something.

The Twitter hashtag about Jake Frost's location.

She stopped, pulled out her cell phone, and did a Twitter search on #WhereIsJakeFrost.

There were several posts. She scrolled back, looking for anything about their dinner date or the ride on the yacht.

Nothing.

Frankie was right.

Jake was being followed.

***

"I'm coming with you today."

Lexi smiled at Chandler as she entered the office. "And good morning to you, too. Any particular reason you wish to accompany me to a basic announcement of an endorsement?"

"It is time I observed the two suitors who have been courting you."

"Bullshit. You wanna see me squirm with both of them in the same room."

"I will admit, that prospect sounds terribly entertaining. However, as the lady knows, her choices of significant others has not been terribly successful in the past and I do fancy myself as a protector of her."

"Fine, the lady has had bad taste in men. Past tense. Now she's seeing two good ones. However, she does appreciate your concern and welcomes your input. You do look at things objectively, Chandler. And you did warn the lady about her last boyfriend."

"Glad you approve. I will have a detailed list of observations on your desk by the end of the business day."

"Chandler, all you've gotta do is tell me what you think of them when we get back."

"I prefer to do it in writing. Then beat a hasty retreat in case you find my comments distasteful."

"That won't happen. Trust me, you'll like both of them."

"You hope."

***

Lexi and Chandler entered the crowded ballroom to find Kyle leading Jake around the room as they worked the crowd. "Damn, Chandler, I can't believe so many people showed up for a guy announcing he's going to endorse shirts."

"Tis a celebrity nation. And it is America's best-selling line of shirts."

"True. Well, I know you're here to meet these guys, so let's go." She headed toward Jake and Kyle, who were busy shaking hands with various corporate bigwigs.

They both spotted her at the same time, both smiled, and both said, "Hi, Lexi" in stereo.

Chandler leaned down and whispered in her ear. "So far they're even."

"Very funny." They arrived and Lexi handled the introductions, then felt a tap on her shoulder. She turned and found Donna smiling at her. "Hey, didn't know you were coming."

"I like to get out of the office once in a while."

"Well, great. Oh, this is your counterpart, Chandler. Chandler, this is Donna, who is also Kyle's sister."

She stepped aside a bit as Chandler's eyes went wide. He took Donna's hands. "The voice I frequently hear through the air vent belongs to this lovely creature?"

Donna beamed as she looked up at him. "That's me. And, speaking of voices, I love that accent."

151

"I'm from Brooklyn."

Donna laughed. "Fuhgeddaboudit."

"Chandler is from London," said Lexi, noting they were totally locked in on each other. Cupid's arrow had struck both of them like a thunderbolt.

"Ooooh, London," said Donna, "I hear it's fabulous. I'd love to know more about it. I've never been there."

"I would be happy to share a few stories."

"I'd love to hear them. Perhaps you're free for lunch after this?"

"I would be honored to escort you for a midday meal. If my boss can spare me."

"You're overdue for a long lunch. Knock yourself out."

Donna turned to Lexi, playfully biting her tongue as her eyebrows did a little jump. "Where have you been hiding this one?"

"Right below you."

She leaned forward and whispered in her ear. "Sounds like something I'd enjoy."

***

Lexi wrapped up her remarks about the endorsement at the podium. "I know both Jake and the Torano Shirts people are very happy to enter into this partnership, so I'll turn things over to them."

She stepped aside as Jake and a middle-aged woman in a red business suit from the shirt company moved in front of the microphone, greeted by applause. "Thank you," said Jake. "I've actually been wearing Torano shirts for years, so it's nice to finally get them for free." The crowd laughed as Lexi took her seat between Kyle and Chandler at a table in the front. "By the way, we have a gift for everyone, so don't forget on your way out today, pick up a shirt in your size... we've got every size you can imagine; stuff that fits guys like me or little guys."

152

The corporate woman leaned toward the microphone. "And we're happy to have a spokesman who fills out our shirts so well." She squeezed his biceps and smiled. "That said, we'd like to give you a preview of the TV campaign, which will start airing soon in prime time on all the major networks."

Kyle leaned over. "Have you seen the commercial?"

Lexi shook her head as she grabbed her glass. "I was tied up while they were shooting it and I understand they were racing the clock to finish editing the thing late last night."

Jake and the woman moved off to the side as the lights dimmed. The giant screen behind them lit up with the logo for Torano Shirts, went to black, then dissolved to the commercial.

It started with Jake in a player's meeting, wearing a dress shirt, raising his hand. "Coach, can we get to the new plays—?"

"Ah, keep your shirt on," said the coach.

Cut to a shot of Jake in a restaurant flagging down a waiter with an empty glass. "Excuse me, can I get some more water—?"

"Yo, keep your shirt on," said the waiter.

The crowd snickered.

"Cute," said Kyle.

Cut to a shot of Jake in an emergency room. "Excuse me, will I be able to see the doctor soon?"

"Hey, buddy, keep your shirt on," said a nurse.

Cut to video of Jake tying a necktie in front of a mirror as a sultry woman's voice filled the air. "Torano shirts... so comfortable you won't want to take them off."

Cut to video of Jake in an embrace with a towering buxom blonde in a revealing top and very short skirt. "I know," he said. "Keep my shirt on."

The blonde shook her head. "Not this time."

The blonde quickly unbuttoned his shirt and removed it, a tight shot revealing Jake's amazing torso. All the women in the audience gasped, their mouths hanging open like a school of trophy bass. "At the end of the day," said the narrator, "there's only one reason to take off a Turano shirt." The blonde started to run her hands across Jake's chest as the commercial faded to black.

Chandler leaned over and whispered as the crowd applauded. "You're going to shatter that glass if you don't relax your death grip on it."

Lexi looked at the white knuckles on her hand, then put the glass down.

The lights in the room went up as Jake moved back to the podium. "Did you like our first commercial?" The crowd shouted approval. "Great. Oh, and I know the men in the audience want to meet my co-star." He looked around the room. "Where's the guy who played the waiter?" That got a big laugh. "Seriously, meet the Torano shirt girl, who will be my sidekick in all the commercials." He gestured to a table off to the side. "C'mon up, Brittany." The woman bounded up the steps, wearing the same outfit from the commercial, gave him a hug, then started to unbutton his shirt.

Jake pushed her back and wagged a finger at her. "It's not the end of the day, young lady."

The crowd laughed as they hugged again.

Lexi stared daggers at the woman.

"So, what'd you think?" Kyle lightly touched her arm.

"Huh?"

"The commercial. Kinda cute, huh?"

She turned to him. "I guess. What'd you think of the girl?"

He shrugged. "If you like that type, I guess she's okay."

"That type?"

"Plastic Amazonian top-heavy blondes who look like they'll tip over."

"You think it's too sexy for a shirt commercial?"

He shook his head and whispered. "Nah. I think it's a very effective spot. It makes me wanna go buy one so you'll do that to me."

Lexi smiled and looked at her watch as Chandler returned to the office. "Well, well, well… I'm going to assume that due to the hour your lunch with Donna went well."

He hastily took off his coat and moved behind his desk. "Sorry, I lost track of time. I'll stay late to catch up on things."

"No you won't, you work too hard for me already." She sat on the edge of his desk. "So… details. What do you think of Donna? You looked, as you might say, positively smitten."

He couldn't hold back a smile. "She is… rather enchanting."

"Enchanting, huh?"

"How is it you never sought to introduce us before? Did you consider me, as you Yanks like to say, chopped liver?"

"Of course not. I didn't think you'd have anything in common even though you're both very nice people. And between your British accent and her Noo Yawk, I figured you'd need a translator."

His eyes took on a dreamy look. "I do so find her manner of speech somehow endearing."

"Seriously? *Youse wanna go tawk ovuh a cuppa cawfee* is endearing to you?"

"It is."

"This isn't one of those *My Fair Lady* fantasies you've got going with you playing Henry Higgins trying to take Eliza Doolittle to charm school, is it?"

"I wouldn't change a hair on her rather exotic head."

"Yeah, Donna is a looker, all right." She reached over and patted his hand. "So, youse gotta date wit the goil, or what?"

"She will be accompanying me to dinner and a show Saturday night."

"Well, I'm happy for you, Chandler. Donna is a terrific woman. Meanwhile, back to your original mission today."

"What mission?"

"You met both the men I'm dating. So, whaja think? And I don't wanna wait for you to type out a bunch of notes."

He leaned back and folded his hands in his lap. "Fine. These are first impressions, mind you. I found Jake to be very friendly and comfortable in his own skin. He worked the crowd like a pro. Of course he is used to being in the public eye and dealing with the media. But…"

She sat up straight. "But…"

"Too early to tell. But he does sort of remind me of one of our political clients. Telling people what they want to hear. Rather… I don't know… scripted."

"So you didn't like him."

"I didn't say that. I simply think you need to peel back a few more layers to discover his true nature."

"I think that blonde peeled back a layer in the commercial. It was disguised as a shirt."

"Ah, yes, I did note the arrival of the green-eyed monster at our table coincided with her appearance."

"Fine, I get jealous when a twenty-year-old six-foot blonde with legs up to her neck rubs her hands all over a guy I'm dating. Moving on. What about Kyle?"

"Ah, Miss Donna's sibling. Yes, quite the amiable chap."

"And…"

"He's quite the contrast to Jake, isn't he?"

"And…"

Chandler shrugged. "He may not be what you want, but he's what you need."

"Maybe Jake is what I need. Maybe I need the rich guy to treat me like a queen."

"Perhaps. Does not Kyle treat you like royalty?"

"You got me there."

"Alas, there were no red flags in evidence that would lead me to believe you should provide an exit visa to one or the other. I am still of the belief that things will sort themselves out."

"Well, I hope they sort themselves out soon. I can't take much more of this. I'm about to explode. By the way, did you and Donna discuss me and Kyle?"

"It did come up in conversation."

"And…"

"Suffice it to say, she thinks you would make a great sister-in-law." Chandler leaned forward. "Let me ask you a hypothetical question. Assuming you choose one over the other eventually, which one would be hurt more should he be the runner-up?"

"That's easy. I don't think any relationship ending could hurt Jake. I mean, let's be honest, he could have any woman he wanted in a heartbeat. You saw the women at the event. I shoulda sent him over to the police station to have him dusted for prints."

"And Kyle?"

"He, uh, can't. Have any woman he wants, that is. He's a great guy but women don't fall all over themselves for him. What's your point?"

"My point is that it doesn't matter. Kyle doesn't want *any* woman. He only wants a *certain* one."

Now she leaned forward, eyes wide. "Why? Did he say something?"

"He didn't have to, Lexi."

***

Kyle noted Donna practically floated back into the office wearing a huge smile and a dreamy-eyed look. "Well, someone certainly looks happy."

She hung up her coat, moved behind her desk and sat down. "He's really different."

"Who?"

She rolled her eyes. "Who? Ya friggin' blind? Chandler, of course."

"Just yankin' your chain, sis. So I take it you like him."

"You might say that. He's so charming. And that accent."

"Oh, you and your obsession with British accents. Half the time I think you watch BBC America just to hear them talk."

"Actually I don't watch the channel, I just listen. Anyway, it's what he *says* that goes along with the accent. He's really smart and old-school classy. Very proper. It was just lunch and he made me feel special."

"So I take it he asked you out?"

"No."

"No?"

"I asked him."

"You were afraid he wouldn't ask you?"

"Hell, no, I'm sure he would have asked me. I just took the initiative. Besides, I'm the New Yorker showing the foreigner around town. Anyway, dinner and a show Saturday night."

"Well, I'm happy for you."

"Meanwhile, dear brother, I got a little intel for you regarding a certain redhead."

He moved forward and pulled up a chair. "Oh, really?"

"Yep. Let's put it this way. Jake Frost doesn't have an advantage over you. You guys are dead even. And she really likes our family."

"Interesting."

"Meanwhile, did you catch the look on Lexi's face when that blonde bimbo had her paws all over Jake in the commercial? It spoke volumes."

"And if this look could speak it would say…?"

"She's worried she can't trust him. Look, women may want a guy who looks like Jake, but not many would be able to sleep at night wondering what sort of skanks are throwing themselves at him while he's on the road. Factor in his reputation and the fact athletes are a bunch of bed-hoppers. While he may be totally trustworthy, temptation will always be there right in front of him. And that will always be lurking in the back of her mind."

158

CHAPTER FIFTEEN

Chandler stuck his head in the door to Lexi's office. "Your ten o'clock is here, Mister Jonathan Egan."

"Send him in."

He lowered his voice. "Watch your language."

She shot him a smirk as Chandler stepped aside. Lexi got up to greet one of the NFL's most squeaky-clean players, who was well known as a devout Christian. "Jonathan, pleasure to meet you."

"You too. I've heard a lot about you from my teammates."

"Hope it's all good."

"Very much so. Especially the part about you dunking a six-hundred-dollar cell phone in a glass of water. Pretty darned funny."

"Yeah, that was expensive, but it worked." She gestured toward the chair in front of her desk. "Have a seat and tell me how I can help you."

"Well, I'm not sure how big a fan you are—"

"I go into an NFL coma every Sunday."

"Then you probably know I'm Jake Frost's backup."

"Right, I've seen you in pre-season. And watched you in college. You've got a ton of talent."

"That's why I'm here. That talent of which you speak is rotting on the bench. I've been here three years and rarely gotten into a regular season game. The only time I play is when we're way ahead or way behind."

"Not sure I can influence the coaching staff."

"Well, my contract will be up this year and I'll be a free agent. Since Jake already told me he has no intention of retiring anytime soon, I have no desire to sit on the bench any longer. I want to sign with a team that will let me play."

"I don't blame you. But I still don't know how I can help with that. I'm not an agent."

"I realize that, but I need you to help get me on the radar of other teams. Get them thinking about me. At least that's what my teammates say. They tell me I need to be in the papers more, maybe get an endorsement, do some high-profile charity work. Be more outspoken in a good way."

"I can pitch you for a few endorsements with some ad agency people I know. Meanwhile, have you ever done any charity work?"

"My wife and I are involved in a few. But I'm a Christian, and the Bible says it should be done in private. You know, not let the left hand know what the right is doing."

"Right, I remember that from Catholic school. So I guess since you're here you wouldn't have any problem with people knowing you do good deeds."

"I'm not wild about it, but image is important. And I look at it this way… the more money I make on my next contract, the more I can give to charity."

"Good way to look at things. And it's very true about image. Outta sight, outta mind. And you can be very marketable to your next team. Look, Jonathan, these days owners are fed up with players who get in trouble with the law and would want a guy like you to be the face of the franchise. Let's put it this way… suppose a team had a choice between you and a guy like Michael Vick, and you were both equal in talent and salary demands. They'd pick you every time."

"I suppose so."

"Do you have your own charitable organization?"

"No, mostly we just volunteer or write a check."

"You need to start your own. Every high-profile player has his own charity. What sorts of causes are important to you?"

"Domestic violence would be number one. My mother was a victim, and my wife is passionate about helping women who have nowhere to go."

Lexi nodded. "Okay, how much do you want to spend?"

"I was thinking a quarter million to start, Miss Harlow."

"Call me Lexi, please. And that's very generous."

"I'm very blessed and enjoy helping others. And, to be honest, if I don't give it away, the IRS and New York State will take most of it anyway."

"Very true. Hey, I just got an idea that plays on your current role... how about calling your charity something like the Jonathan Egan Backup Foundation."

"Not sure I understand."

"Well, you're Jake's backup, and you'll have the backs of women who need help."

He flashed a wide smile. "I really like it. How did you come up with that so fast?"

"It's my job to be creative. In this case, it will be even better because we're doing something for a good cause. And hopefully, with a little more notoriety, you won't be a real backup for long. More money for you and the charity."

"Excellent."

"Okay, let me work up some stuff, make some calls, and I'll get back to you in a couple days."

He stood up and reached out to shake her hand. "Sounds good. Oh, how much do I owe you?"

"For setting up a charity, nothing. I couldn't in good conscience take money for that. But I will charge you for work if I get you some endorsements."

"Fair enough. At least let me give you a retainer."

"Tell you what... in lieu of that, I personally know of another charity case you could help. A wounded veteran."

The light tap on the door made Kyle look up. "Oh, Jake, didn't know you were coming by."

"I was in the neighborhood. Thought I'd take the chance you'd be in. You got a few minutes?"

He gestured toward the chair in front of his desk. "About thirty, then I have a meeting. What's up?"

Jake sat down and leaned back. "Well, as you know I'm in the final year of my contract and the Jets have yet to make me an offer."

"Surely they will. Is this their usual policy?"

"In the past it depends on the player. But the common denominator in the past has been to wait until the contract ends to make an offer for players over thirty. Since we have a short shelf life, I can't exactly blame them."

"But you're the face of the franchise."

"True, but they always look to the future. Anyway, lately there have been a lot of speculative articles in the papers about how many years the Jets should offer, and there always seems to be one of those charts showing how quarterbacks break down in their thirties."

"Yeah, I've seen those lately. I can't exactly control what columnists write."

"Not asking you to. But I had an idea… and maybe you and Lexi could put your heads together on this. I think an endorsement of some sort of health product, like exercise equipment, would show the team and the media that I'm in top physical condition."

Kyle chuckled. "I think the shirt commercial served that purpose."

"Well, it's one thing to *look* fit, but I need to *show* everyone I'm in better shape than I was in my twenties. Maybe something that lets the world know I intend to play till I'm forty."

Kyle nodded. "That's a decent strategy."

Jake reached in his pocket, pulled out a slip of paper and handed it to Kyle. "Here's the name of a company that makes the exercise equipment I actually use. They're new and cutting edge but they don't have any publicity. Nobody other than a few pro athletes has heard of them. Perhaps you might contact them and work out some sort of endorsement deal. And the money isn't at all important. I'd actually be their spokesperson in return for new equipment every year. It's more about the publicity that I'm healthy. And since I know you work on commission and no money would be changing hands, I'd give you a flat fee. If that works for you."

"Sure, I can live with that. And I agree this sort of publicity will help when we go to contract negotiations."

"Great." Jake stood up. "Appreciate your help."

"Not a problem. I'm on it."

***

Lexi grabbed a chair in the restaurant opposite her prospective new client. "Eric, nice to meet you."

The author, who looked like he moonlighted as a middle-aged lawn gnome, stood up and shook her hand. "You too. I've heard a lot about you."

They both sat down. "Oh really?"

"Well, check that, I *heard* you. That podcast from the PR thing you did a while back."

"Yeah, that thing has certainly made the rounds. So, you've got a new book coming out and you need a publicist. Don't publishers usually handle all that in-house?"

"The bigger ones do, but this is a small company and while they're doing some ads and social media, I personally think that venue is saturated. I really want to get my name out there."

"Okay, so tell me about your book."

"It's called *Spotlight Dating*."

"Oh, it's a how-to book."

"No, not at all. It's about people dating in the media spotlight. I've gotten lots of interviews with celebrities, people who date celebs. What it's like to be famous and try to get some privacy, have a normal dating life. I got a lot of juicy tales about some pretty famous people. So it's marketed to people who like Hollywood gossip, only this isn't gossip. Everything in the book is true."

"Wow, there's a switch. Well, we are a celebrity nation, so it certainly has a good hook."

"And I figured you'd be the perfect person for this, since you're in a similar situation."

She sat up straight and furrowed her brow. "Excuse me?"

"I thought you were dating Jake Frost."

Oh, shit. "I, uh, handle his public relations."

"Oh, I saw those photos in the tabloid and on *Page Six* while I was collecting stuff for the book. If that's not you, then you've got a twin out there."

"Well, it's not me. Though I have seen the photos and there is a resemblance, I must admit."

"Look, if you want to keep things quiet, I certainly understand. I mean, I heard that a lot while doing research for this book."

"Sorry to burst your bubble, but it ain't me. I just handle the guy's PR. Jake's a client, that's it."

"Okay. Anyway, have you worked with authors before?"

"A couple. One had a political book, the other wrote a thriller. While authors are kind of a tough sell to get on TV, your topic is something that's marketable. I've got some good contacts with local talk shows, so if I play the celebrity angle I'm sure I can get some buzz going." She went over her rates and he agreed.

"Great. I'll email a copy of the manuscript and book cover to you." He took an envelope out of his pocket and slid it across the table. "That's a down payment."

She opened the envelope and saw several hundred-dollar bills. "Cash? Seriously?"

"My checking account got hacked a few years ago so I try to be as off the grid as possible. Hope that's okay."

"It's fine. I'll send you a receipt."

"By the way, there's more in my other pocket should you agree to be included in the book. I could add a few pages on your relationship with—"

She put up her hand. "Hey, I told you, he's just a client."

***

Chandler looked up as she returned to the office. "How did your lunch with the scribe go?"

"Odd."

"Excuse me?"

She tossed the envelope at him. "Check out the retainer he gave me."

Chandler opened it and his eyes widened. "Cash?"

"Yeah, for PR work. Something's not right. And get this, the guy wrote a celebrity dating book and pressed me for information about Jake, wanting to know if I was dating him, since he'd seen the photos. Then offered me more money if I would give him details."

"Did you acknowledge him?"

"Of course not." She handed him a slip of paper. "Here's his name, the newspaper he worked for, the title of the book and the publisher. He said he was a reporter for years, so please check him out."

"If that's the case, there should be plenty of articles online." Chandler spun his seat around to face the computer and began to search.

Ten minutes later Chandler walked into Lexi's office with a concerned look. "You're not going to like this."

"Uh-oh. What? He's a sleaze bag?"

"No. He doesn't exist. Neither does the paper he supposedly worked for. Neither does the publisher."

Her eyes went wide. "So what the hell is going on, Chandler?"

"It would appear someone is checking into the background of Mister Frost."

"Why pay me, then?"

"Perhaps to show you he was serious about getting information. Checkbook journalism isn't exactly rare."

"Very true. I'm thinking that Frankie was right."

"Who is Frankie?"

"Paparazzo who lives in my building. Said someone is tailing Jake because all the photos of the two of us really weren't worth the time or money to someone who takes pictures of celebrities."

"So who would be investigating your suitor?"

"There's only one possible answer. The team. His contract runs out at the end of the season and I'll bet they're looking for leverage. Maybe some sort of morals clause thing."

"The National Football League cares about morals?"

"Yeah, I know. But maybe the Jets think they'll dig up something serious about him. Still, they're not known for doing this kind of stuff."

"So what do we do?"

"Right now the only thing *to* do is warn Jake."

CHAPTER SIXTEEN

"Jake, we need to talk. And I wanted to do this face to face."

He put his fork down on his plate and looked up at Lexi. "Uh-oh. That doesn't sound good."

"It's not about you and me… well, it sorta is."

"You're not making sense."

"Jake, I'm pretty sure someone is investigating you."

His face tightened. "Huh?"

She told him the story of the phony author trying to pump her for information, and Frankie's theory. Her own theory of why the team might be trying to dig up some dirt on him. "This all happened last week, but I didn't want to get into it on the phone… just in case."

He slowly nodded. "Y'know, you're probably right about the team."

"Seriously? The team would tail you after all you've done for them?"

"Look, bottom line, it's still a business. There's no loyalty. Football players are basically interchangeable parts. When we wear out, they replace us. And I'm over thirty."

"But you're in great physical shape." The image of Jake in the London hotel hot tub flashed through her mind.

"I know, but when it comes to contract negotiations, they'll do anything to knock the dollar amount down."

"Why would they care who you date?"

"They wouldn't, unless you were a hooker. What they care

about is *what I do* on my dates. Or on my free time. Specifically, if there's anything illegal or against league rules going on. Let's say they got a photo or video of us doing drugs or me hitting you, or something like that. They could use it against me when it came time to negotiate." He shook his head. "Damn."

"So, what are you going to do?"

"You know what? Nothing. Bore them to death. I've got nothing to hide, so let them waste time and money stalking me. But I'm gonna make them pay when we sit down to talk dollars and cents. As for us, trust me, the minute I sign a new contract, all of this will disappear."

"So we gotta hide for two months?"

"Lexi, if being associated with me in public bothers you—"

"I didn't mean it that way, Jake. It's just that… I'm a very private person and those photos in the tabloids were extremely embarrassing."

"And again, I'm sorry that happened. But as long as we keep things innocent in public no one's going to care. I'm simply out with my public-relations person. In fact, you might wanna start wearing business clothes when we go out and carry a briefcase. We'll keep the not-so-innocent things private."

She began to blush. "Ah, the *old lady in public, whore in bed* thing. Every man's dream."

"Well, first, there's no way that last term would ever apply to you."

"You haven't slept with me yet, so you don't know. I might be full of surprises."

"Well, that's certainly intriguing. Though I have slept with you."

"Right, fully clothed. With your pants on."

"Now if *that* got out it would be a scandal."

She couldn't help laugh.

"Anyway, Lexi, I consider you a lady both in public and in private. But if you want to morph into something else in the bedroom, I certainly wouldn't complain."

***

Kyle took Donna's arm as he led her across the street toward the production studio for the exercise equipment shoot. "I think you're only here because you wanna see Jake in workout clothes."

"No, dear brother, you are incorrect. After Saturday night my eyes are only for a British gentleman right now."

"Just your eyes?"

She playfully slapped his arm. "Leave me alone. I was a good girl. Sorta."

"You got home at three-thirty."

"You checkin' up on me?"

"Just looking out for my sister."

"Your sister is older and she wants you in bed by ten. So what were you doing up at that hour?"

"It doesn't matter. I was up. Why did you wanna come along today?"

"He's just eye candy, Kyle. I can work up my appetite looking at the menu as long as I have dinner at home."

"I see."

"Besides, I wanna see how Lexi reacts again, especially considering there's also a supposedly hot woman in this ad campaign."

They arrived at the studio, already set up with lights, cameras and a ton of exercise equipment. Jake was in a bathrobe, talking to the director, while a blonde hardbody was getting her hair teased out in a makeup chair. Kyle looked around for Lexi, but didn't see her.

Donna grabbed his arm and smiled. "Hey, Chandler's here."

Lexi's assistant spotted them and headed in their direction, laser-locked on Donna. He flashed a wide smile. "Ah, I didn't know you'd be here. A pleasant surprise."

She took his hands. "Absolutely."

Kyle cleared his throat to break their trance. "Uh, Chandler, where's Lexi?"

"Ah, my compatriot is under the weather today so she is working from home for a few days."

"She okay?"

"Either a bad cold or a touch of the flu. She asked that I come in her place." He pulled a camera from his pocket. "She instructed me to take some photos of the production, so off I go."

"Sure, catch you later."

Chandler moved off as Kyle turned to his sister. "Well, this is interesting. You came here to see Lexi's reaction and now I get to watch yours."

"Reaction to what?"

"A guy you're hot for and a guy you think is hot in the same room."

"Very funny. This is not a love triangle."

"No, it's a lust triangle."

"Different kind of geometry."

"Common Core has nothing on you."

They headed toward Jake, who was in a conversation with a man from the equipment company. "Right, and I can't do any exercises that would put a strain on my right elbow right now," said Jake. "Too sore from the game." He spotted them and smiled. "Hey, my agent's here." He did the introductions as the blonde headed in their direction. "Oh, and this is Jennifer, who's going to demonstrate the exercises for women. We know each other from another photoshoot so I thought she'd be perfect for this one."

Kyle shook hands and looked up at the incredibly buffed woman, a solid tower of muscle in a sports bra and shorts who had to be six feet tall and looked like she could break him in half. "Hi, Jennifer. I'm Kyle and this is my sister Donna."

"Hi, there."

"Okay, we're about ready to get rolling," yelled the director.

Jake took off his bathrobe, clad only in a pair of tight workout shorts. He suddenly wrapped one arm around Kyle's shoulders, then turned to the equipment company man. "Hey, can you fix up my little buddy with some equipment?"

The guy nodded. "Sure."

"Great." He squeezed Kyle's shoulder hard. "You can get some meat on those bones. Right now you probably couldn't beat Jennifer at arm wrestling." He laughed and Kyle forced a smile as he turned to the model. "Whaddaya say, Jen, you think he could take you?"

"No way." She flexed her biceps in front of him. "Wanna go?"

Before he could say anything Donna cleared her throat. "Uh, Jake…"

"Yeah?"

She pointed at his face. "You might want to ask the makeup gal to cover up those wrinkles before you get started."

His smile vanished. "Oh. Uh, yeah. Thanks." Jake headed over to the equipment as the director went over the shots with a photographer.

Donna lightly took Kyle's forearm. "You okay, sweetie?"

"Yeah."

Donna took his hands, clenched in fists, and turned him to face her. "Hey."

"What?"

She worked her hands into his, trying to relax him. "Stop it. You know the type."

"I don't have to like it."

"No, you don't. But I took him down a notch."

"Thanks, but in the grand scheme of things—"

"Listen, an interesting opportunity has just presented itself. One I know you can take advantage of."

***

The knock on the door stirred Lexi from her nap. "Who the hell is that?" She threw back the blanket, got off the couch and shuffled to the door, rubbing her forehead with one hand and bracing the small of her aching back with the other. Her head weighed a ton, she couldn't breathe and every muscle felt sore. She opened the door and found Kyle smiling at her, holding a couple of grocery bags. "Kyle? What are you doing here?"

"Heard you were sick."

"So you did my grocery shopping?"

He moved into the apartment. "Look, I know you live alone and if you're sick you need someone to take care of you."

She closed the door. "I appreciate that, but I can take care of myself."

"Very true. On any given day, you're the toughest girl I know. But you're sick."

"So, what, you wanna get infected with this crap?"

"No, I'm cooking dinner for you to help you get well."

Her stomach made an audible growl.

He pointed at her belly. "And obviously you're starving."

"I was gonna order a pizza. And you really don't want to catch what I've got."

"Listen, young lady, tonight I'm taking care of you whether you like it or not, so sit down, shut up and let me make dinner." He moved closer and locked eyes with her. "Do I make myself clear?"

"Yes, Sir." She gestured toward the kitchen "Well, I'm in no mood to argue if you're hell bent on doing this. You really know how to cook?"

"My last name ends in a vowel. All Italians are born with the cooking chromosome." He placed his hand on her forehead. "Meanwhile, go lie down. You're hot as hell."

"You already told me you find me attractive."

"Apparently the snark in you is immune to anything."

Lexi pulled her chair up to the dinner table, smiling as he placed a plate in front of her. "Kyle, this looks fantastic. What is it?"

172

"Fresh fettuccine with shrimp, diced tomatoes, sautéed garlic in olive oil and a ton of spices. I call it *pasta la vista* cause it makes any illness go away." He picked up a cheese grater. "Parmesan?"

"You know what I like." Her eyes widened as he covered her plate with cheese, then she grabbed a fork, speared a shrimp and twirled some pasta around it. She popped it in her mouth and closed her eyes as she savored it. "Oh. My. God."

"Too spicy?"

"Hell no. That's incredible. This is the best pasta dish I've ever had."

"Glad you like it. It will clear up your sinuses."

She shoved another forkful in her mouth, then talked through it. "Beats the hell out of a pizza. Really, Kyle, this is very sweet of you."

He simply smiled at her, locking eyes for a moment.

Then she stopped. "Oh no!"

"What?"

"I just realized I look terrible."

"So what? You're sick. Besides, right now you look better than ninety percent of women out there."

"Yeah, I styled my hair with an eggbeater and I'm sure my breath would knock the proverbial buzzard off the proverbial shitwagon."

"Shut up and eat. I'm not exactly Prince Charming when I'm sick."

"No. But you're acting like him now." She took a sip of water. "So, how'd the commercial shoot go today?"

His face tightened and he looked down at his plate. "Y'know, okay. Nothing special. The ad guy was happy, the client was happy, Jake was happy. We got paid."

"You've got a look on your face that says *you* weren't happy."

He looked back at her. "No it was fine. Just not terribly exciting. Oh, Chandler showed up and took some shots for you."

"Speaking of Chandler, if I can trust you with this information, he's quite smitten with your sister."

"Yeah, she's been hit with Cupid's arrow as well."

"That's nice. He's a great guy and I already think the world of Donna. They'll make a cute couple."

"We should double-date sometime."

"Yeah. That would be nice."

She leaned back and patted her full belly. "Damn, I ate two plates of that. I didn't realize I was that hungry."

"Feed a cold."

"I have a fever. Aren't you supposed to starve a fever?"

"Italians feed everything. By the way, there's plenty more, so you have leftovers."

"Thank you. I must admit, it cleared up my head a bit. Though every muscle still aches. My back is killing me. You got any recipe for that?"

"Yep."

"If it's tiramisu, I'm game."

"No, it's not food. Let me give you a back rub."

She studied his face, not picking up anything sexual. The man was honestly trying to make her feel better. "Well, I am a sucker for a massage. And I sure could use it." She tossed her napkin on the table and got up.

"Okay, take off your sweatshirt and lie on your stomach." He pointed to the bed.

"Is this some trick to get my top off?"

"Absolutely. I'm not stupid. Though I'm sure your other side is much more interesting. If this is a chest cold…"

"Typical man." She spun her finger in a circle. "Turn around." He turned away from the bed as she took off her sweatshirt, tossed it on a chair and lay down on her bed. "Okay. Rub me, big boy."

174

"You got it." She felt him straddle the small of her back. "Am I too heavy?"

"No. Shut up and start rubbing."

"Yes, Ma'am. So, you're giving the orders now."

"Damn straight." She felt his hands rub her shoulders, working the knots out of the tight muscles. "Oh, God, that feels so good."

"That where it hurts?"

"Everything hurts, Kyle. My entire back and neck are one big knot." He continued to work his hands on her shoulders, then moved down to the middle of her back, pressing his thumbs into her muscles. She closed her eyes and savored his touch. "Between this and your cooking, you wanna move in?"

"If you were being serious, the answer would be yes."

He finished working her back, then ran his fingers through her hair and massaged her scalp. "Oh, that's amazing. Oh yeah. Don't stop."

"Y'know, if you have thin walls, your neighbors will get the wrong idea about what's going on in here."

"Who cares? Just keep doing… that. God, you're incredible."

He turned away from the bed again as she put her sweatshirt back on. "Kyle, I feel so much better. I don't know how to thank you."

"Something tells me you'd do it for me."

"Well, considering I could burn a salad, I'd probably make you feel worse if I made dinner for you."

He laughed as he helped her up. "You need anything else?"

"Yeah, a bunch of your kisses, but I don't want to infect you. I'll keep them on account."

"I'll hold you to that. Well, you get some sleep and I'll check on you tomorrow morning."

"Kyle, you don't have to—"

He put one finger on her lips. "You just don't know when to shut up and take orders, do you?"

"No, I don't. Part of my charm." She talked with his finger still on her lips. They both laughed as they headed for the door. "I won't hug you either. But trust me, when I get well, I'll make it up to you."

CHAPTER SEVENTEEN

Kyle stood up and shook Jake's hand as the quarterback entered his office carrying a bunch of newspapers. "Jake, good game on Sunday."

"Thanks. But I'm still sore. Six sacks doesn't feel too good."

"I can imagine. Hey, I saw the edits from the exercise commercial. Looked great."

"Yeah, thanks for putting that together. Listen, I got another favor that really isn't in your job description, but I'm thinking you might be able to help."

"Sure. What do you need?"

Jake placed the stack of newspapers and magazines on the desk. Kyle's eyes widened as he saw the supermarket tabloid with Lexi on the cover. "I think the team is following me. Lately I've been in the tabloids and on *Page Six*. I think they're trying to paint me in a bad light before the contract negotiations. Anyway, while I'm used to publicity I think this is something different. Apparently a paparazzo I know says photos of me aren't really worth the trouble." He pointed at the stack. "Anyway, in case you hadn't seen those, I figured you could check out each photo, maybe figure out who took them, trace it back to the team, you know? Give us some more leverage. Frankly, Kyle, I'm surprised they would stoop this low after all I've done for them."

Kyle noted his fists were clenched, so he put his hands in his lap. "I'll, uh, look into it."

Jake stood up and smiled. "Great. Just add whatever time you spend on this to my bill."

***

Chandler looked surprised as Lexi entered the office. "Ah, I didn't expect you back so soon."

"Feeling a lot better. Kyle basically came over and took care of me for two days."

"How nice. Both your suitors missed you at the exercise equipment shoot." He tapped his computer and the screen filled with photos.

Lexi leaned forward and looked at them. "Those are great, Chandler, thanks. Did the shoot go okay? Kyle didn't seem terribly impressed."

"The shoot went fine, but I think he's not terribly impressed with the competition."

"He doesn't like Jake?"

"Jake was a bit, shall we say, insensitive toward Kyle."

"How so?"

He pointed at the photos. "Note the blonde Amazon sharing the photo with Jake."

"Damn. She looks like she could bench-press a Toyota. What about her?"

"Well, Jake apparently knows her from a previous commercial endeavor. I overheard everyone talking while I was taking pictures. Jake asked the corporate person to provide Kyle with some free equipment, implying that Kyle was too weak, and then suggested he would be unable to defeat the towering young lady in an arm-wrestling match. Jake's rather old to act as a bully. I found his comments quite condescending."

"Yeah, that certainly isn't very polite. And it speaks volumes."

"You weren't there to keep him on his best behavior. Alas, Kyle did not seem pleased with the developments but managed to hold his tongue." Chandler leaned back and folded his hands in his lap. "Since you asked for my thoughts on your two suitors a

178

while ago and I gave you my first impression, would you like my updated opinion?"

"Don't hold back, Chandler, but I have a feeling I know what you're gonna say. And I have a very strong feeling I'm going to agree with you."

"Kyle is the better man."

"I know."

"He possesses a certain basic kindness the other gentleman does not. Let me ask you this… since both men knew you were ill, did Jake contact you to see if you needed anything?"

She shook her head. "No."

"Flowers?"

"Nope."

"And yet the other gentleman took care of you on his own accord for two days."

"Okay, you've made your point. Two points, actually."

"Have I?"

"Well, I've been leaning in Kyle's direction for a while now, but all this really tips the scales. Time to make a decision."

"It's *been* time, young lady."

CHAPTER EIGHTEEN

Kyle got out of the cab into the cold night air and headed toward the luxury apartment building. He honestly wasn't in the mood for a Christmas party, or to be in the same room with Jake and Lexi, but most of Jake's teammates would be there and it would be a great opportunity to hand out business cards and make contacts. Besides, Jake had insisted they both come. He entered the spectacular lobby and found Lexi signing in at the doorman's stand. "Hey, good timing."

She turned and smiled at him as she took off her coat and draped it over one arm, revealing a stunning emerald green knee-length cocktail dress with matching four-inch heels. "Hi there."

"Wow."

She looked around the lobby. "Yeah, quite a place, huh?"

"I was referring to your dress."

She blushed a bit. "You're always so sweet to me."

"I'm always so honest with you. So the *wow* is well deserved."

"Well, thank you."

"By the way, thanks for meeting me. Sorry I couldn't pick you up but I had that late meeting."

"Not a problem. But I'm having second thoughts, Kyle. I really don't think I wanna do this."

"Me neither, but we could both use some new business, and there will be a bunch of millionaire players here."

"I guess. But let's not stay long, okay? Make an appearance and then go do something fun."

"Fine with me."

"So you wanna hit up prospective clients as a team?" She took his hand as they started to head to the elevator.

"I think football players might be more inclined to talk to someone who looks like you if I weren't around."

"Yeah, that's the problem. I won't have you to protect me," she said.

"As you once said, you can take care of yourself."

"Good point. Okay, we divide and conquer. By the way, later tonight I have a big surprise for you."

"Ooooh, I love surprises. Give me a hint?" he begged.

"Nope. You'll have to be patient. But trust me, you'll be very, very happy. I sure am."

Lexi's heart rate went up as they rode up on the elevator. She didn't want to be here, really didn't want to see Jake any longer. Kyle was the one for her and she would tell him as soon as they got home. She couldn't wait for their first night together. But right now she didn't want to do anything that might make Kyle lose Jake as a client since Jake had insisted she be part of the team. He needed the commission, which would pay for his brother's surgery.

The elevator door opened. Loud conversation, and even louder music, spilled in. Lexi did her best to pretend she'd never seen the place. She practically had to yell. "Wow, I guess this is how the other half lives."

Kyle took a look around the crowded apartment, which looked like a full-blown frat party. "All this for playing a game."

"Apparently maturity is not a requirement." She noted most of the players were accompanied by scantily clad women. A few couples were making out on the couch while some of the younger players were chugging beer near a keg. Others were shooting champagne corks across the room while one was shirtless doing push-ups with a girl sitting on his back. "I think I'm overdressed for this."

"You look great, Lexi."

"I meant there's way too much fabric in my outfit. I don't exactly fit in. These women look like they need a bail bondsman and a public defender."

He leaned toward her ear. "Well, cheap bimbos do go for rich athletes."

Ouch. "Well, let's mingle. You think anyone's drunk enough to sign a contract?"

"I don't think we're gonna pick up any real clients in an environment like this. Shouldn't take much time to find out." He pointed at the couch. "I think it's about to turn into Caligula's palace."

A player wandered by with a leggy blonde thrown over his shoulder and disappeared into a room. "That barn door has sailed, apparently. Anyway, let's make an appearance and get outta here. Meetcha back here at the elevator in a half hour."

"Sounds like a plan. You sure you're okay flying solo?"

"Honestly, I feel like a virgin at an Aztec sacrifice, so keep a close eye on me."

"I always keep both eyes on you. It's very enjoyable. Especially considering what you're wearing."

"You sure know how to boost a girl's ego. Anyway, see you shortly. And then you get your surprise." They split up and headed in opposite directions.

She was right, there was no business to be had from the drunken jocks at the party. The only good thing was the food. Lexi had already been groped a few times when she felt two hands on her shoulders while she was eating hors d'oeuvres. She spun around, expecting to tell another player to get lost and found herself face to face with Jake, who was holding a beer and looking like he was feeling no pain. "Well, hey there, Jake. I was wondering if you were actually here or this wild bunch of hooligans had taken over your apartment."

"Just the guys blowing off steam. I've been tending bar for a while. Actually I think I drank more than I served." She backed up, the alcohol from his breath pretty strong. He brought the full bottle of beer to his lips, tilted his head back and drained it in one gulp.

"Hey. Slow down."

He placed the bottle on a table. "Oh, don't worry. A bottle of beer for a guy my size is like a shotglass for the average person. Anyway, glad you could make it."

She noted he was wearing a very tight, short-sleeved shirt, which showed off his massive biceps. She slid her finger under one sleeve. "You know, it's December. Little cold for this shirt, doncha think?"

"I like it warm in here at all times. Gotta keep the muscles loose during the season."

Uh-huh. Right. "Anyway, thanks for inviting me. I've made a few good contacts." *Liar. More like your teammates have contacted me.*

"Good, though I must confess that's not why I invited you. I like showing you off. But I'm glad you're getting some more business."

She licked her fingers. "And I'm about to get some more of these bacon-wrapped shrimp. They're fabulous."

He looked around the room. "Speaking of shrimp, is Kyle here?"

Her face tightened. "What do you mean by that?"

"Y'know, he's so short."

"That's not very nice, Jake. And he's not short, he's average height."

"Look, Lexi, nothing is sacred to football players. Anyway, he's a sports agent, I'm sure he's used to the way athletes talk."

"Right, I'm beginning to get the picture." She pointed across the room. "Anyway, he's over there near the kitchen."

"Oh, I see him." He waved and Kyle nodded back. Then Jake

pointed to the ceiling directly above them. "Well, how about that. Look where we are."

She looked up and saw the mistletoe just as he quickly ran his hands down her back and onto her hips, then lifted her up and started kissing her. She pushed hard against his shoulders and leaned her head back. "Put me down!"

"Something wrong, Lexi?"

"Jake, I'm not like these other girls who want to be carried away by a caveman. Now put me down right this minute."

He set her on the floor. "Geez, lighten up, Lexi. It's just the guys on the team, their girlfriends and wives. There aren't any photographers here. Don't worry about it. We can go to another room if you want some privacy."

"Yeah, I want some privacy all right." She spun around and walked away.

Five minutes after seeing their kiss, Kyle was still steaming.

Sure, it obviously wasn't her idea, and she'd pushed him away. But still.

Jake picked her up like he owned her and was ready to carry her away.

Kyle had quickly turned away, not wanting Lexi to spot him looking in their direction. She was currently heading for the elevator, trying to get through the crowd, so he started to do the same. It was time to leave. Suddenly he felt a hand on his shoulder. He turned and found Jake holding a beer.

"Finally, I find my agent. I was wondering if you were still here."

He backed up a bit, the liquor on Jake's breath incredibly strong. "Thanks for inviting me."

"Guess you were kinda hard to spot under all the big guys in here. You making some contacts with my teammates?"

"Yeah, I've talked to a few."

"Well, *everyone* needs to know you're an agent." He put the beer down, waved at the disc jockey, made a slashing motion across his throat and the music stopped. "Hey, can I have everyone's attention?" The crowd all turned to him. "First, I wanna thank you all for coming to my annual Christmas party. You rookies should know you've gotta clean up." Everyone laughed as he put one arm around Kyle's shoulders. "Anyway, most of you know my previous agent is now on an incarceration vacation, so I wanted you to meet the agent who's been handling things for me of late, Kyle Caruso." He looked at Kyle, then back at the crowd. "Oh, hang on a minute." He moved behind Kyle. Then Kyle felt Jake's hands under his arms and suddenly he was lifted a foot off the ground. "Just in case you can't see the little guy!"

Kyle watched everyone laugh as Jake effortlessly held him in the air for what seemed like an eternity and then started to carry him across the room. "C'mon, little one, I'll give you a ride and introduce you to everybody." He saw Lexi elbowing her way through the crowd, coming toward them, not looking happy.

She stopped right next to Jake and glared at him. "Put him down, Jake."

"Hey, Kyle, look. Lexi's here." He turned, still holding Kyle in the air so that he was facing Lexi. "Kyle, this is what Lexi looks like from a grown man's point of view."

She looked past Kyle right at Jake. "Put. Him. Down."

"I think he's okay up here." He extended his arms, lifting Kyle even higher. "You're not afraid of heights, are you, little one?"

She folded her arms. "Right. Now."

"Well, okay." He set him down on the floor. "He's too small to be much of a workout anyway."

Kyle turned and quickly headed for the elevator.

Jake was laughing with his drunken teammates, one of whom handed him a beer and gave him a high five. She grabbed his arm. "I need to talk to you. Right now."

He smiled at her, put an arm around her shoulders and pulled her close. "Guys, you met Lexi yet?"

She pushed him away. "We really need to talk, Jake. In private."

"Fine." He turned to his teammates. "I've obviously done something wrong." He excused himself and led her to the kitchen. "What's up?"

Her blood boiled. "What you did to Kyle was really uncalled for, Jake. I'm surprised at you."

He furrowed his brow. "What'd I do?"

"You embarrassed the hell out of him, picking him up like that in front of everyone. That's high school bully behavior. And then you laugh about it and celebrate?"

"That? Oh, come on, we do that kind of stuff in the locker room all the time. Last week I picked up our kicker and threw him in the pool, and then he got even with me later, set my shoes on fire. It's just guy stuff. We like to have fun."

She moved closer and poked her finger into his chest. "This isn't a locker room and he's not a football player, Jake. And it wasn't fun for Kyle. Everyone was laughing at him. I could tell he was hurt by the look on his face. You were nothing more than a damn frat boy picking on a guy half your size. Grow up and knock this shit off right now." She grabbed the beer from his hand and put it on a table. "And you've already had too much to drink."

Jake looked down at the floor. "Well, damn, I'm sorry, Lexi. I didn't mean anything by it. I guess sometimes I forget the rest of the world isn't like the guys in the locker room. I hope you don't think any less of me for it. If he got offended, I'll apologize next time I see him."

She took his chin and tilted it up so he was looking at her. "You need to apologize right now."

Jake looked around and pointed at the elevator as the door was closing. "I can't, Lexi. He just left."

Lexi grabbed her coat and ran through the lobby out of the building.

Just in time to see Kyle's car start to pull away.

"Kyle!"

She ran to the street, yelling his name and waving. But he obviously didn't see or hear her as the car pulled away. "Dammit!" She stood on the edge of the curb, stuck her arm out into the street and flagged down a taxi.

***

The cab pulled up to Kyle and Donna's home. His car in the driveway, the lights on in the house. She paid the driver, got out, quickly headed to the door and rang the bell. She saw a figure moving toward the door through the glass. Donna.

The door opened and Kyle's sister locked eyes with her. "You know, somehow I knew you'd show up. C'mon in."

"How's he doing?"

She shook her head and wore a sad look as she closed the door. "I'd say he's used to it, but he didn't expect that kind of stuff as an adult. Seeing you should cheer him up. C'mon, he's in the living room."

Donna led her down the hall. She turned a corner and saw Kyle slumped in a reclining chair, drinking a beer. "Kyle, someone's here to see you."

He looked up at Lexi but didn't smile. "Lexi. What are you doing here?"

"Uh, you left without your date." She shook her finger at him. "That is not acceptable, young man."

"I'm gonna turn in," said Donna. She moved over to her brother and kissed him on top of the head. "Love you, sweetie."

"Thanks."

Lexi moved toward him. "Hey, that's not the proper response

187

when your sister says she loves you. You seem to have forgotten your manners tonight."

Kyle looked up at Donna and took her hand. "Sorry. Love you, Donna."

Lexi nodded. "Much better." Donna smiled at her as she left the room. Kyle was not looking at her, staring straight ahead.

Dear God, I hope he didn't see Jake kiss me.

Lexi moved toward him, sat on his lap and wrapped her arms around him.

"Lexi, you don't have to—"

"So, let me get this straight. You escort a woman to a party... and not just any woman." She pointed to herself. "*Moi*... and then I turn around and you're gone. For all I know you left with another girl." She looked around the room. "You're not hiding one of those top-heavy tramps in here somewhere, are you? Don't make me check all the closets in this house."

He finally smiled a bit. "There's no other woman."

"Good. I didn't wear this dress to get you all worked up and have one of those silicone skanks at the party reap the rewards."

"You wore that for me?"

"You were my escort tonight. Though I realize my outfit doesn't compare to the ones the other women were almost wearing."

"You were the only one with any class in the entire place. That *was* quite a collection of plastic women."

"I know! You sure were right about bimbos going for football players. Did you see the one in the gold miniskirt with the star linebacker? I swear, if I pricked her boob with a pin she'd fly around the room like a deflated balloon."

He laughed. "Well, you know what they say about fake boobs. You can buy new headlights for a minivan, but that doesn't make it a Porsche."

She cracked up. "I'll have to remember that one. Anyway, one thing you should know about me, Kyle." She sat up a bit and stuck out her chest. "You'll never have to worry about me tipping over."

"If you expect a response to that loaded statement, forget it."

"So, after seeing that silicone buffet tonight, you think I need a little more on top? Think I'd look like a Porsche?"

He shook his head. "Don't change a thing. You're already a Ferrari."

"What a perfect answer. It appears your manners have returned. I was worried I was going to have to give you a spanking."

"If that's the case, I'll be rude again."

She smiled at him, then lay her head on his shoulder as she squeezed him tight. "Nah, I like you polite a lot better. Besides, I don't need an excuse to spank you. As you know, I'm a girl who takes what she wants." She felt his arms wrap around her and pull her close.

"I'm glad you came by, Lexi. Thanks. It really means a lot."

"Shhh. No more talking. Just holding. Don't let me go."

***

Lexi extended her hand as Kyle opened the car door at one in the morning. He took it as she stepped onto the sidewalk. "You know, men are so lucky they don't have to wear heels."

"I thought you women loved shoes."

"We do. But after several hours in these things, my feet hurt. And it was already a really long day before the party. You know what I need?"

"Pair of flats?"

"With this dress? No way."

"And with those legs, no way."

"Very nice, Mister. Back to what I need."

"Foot massage?"

"Later, but right now I need a lift. I did so enjoy your door-to-door delivery service on Thanksgiving."

"You're the boss." He smiled as he reached down and easily scooped her into his arms, then headed toward her building.

She wrapped her arms around his neck. "I love old-fashioned chivalry. From old-fashioned guys."

"You're a paradox, you know that?"

"Why?"

"Well, you like the chivalry thing, but you also like to be in charge all the time."

"I don't *always* want to be in charge."

He cocked his head to the side and gave her a disbelieving look.

"Fine, just most times. But I still like the fact you're old-fashioned and a perfect gentleman with me."

"You deserve to be treated like a queen."

"Nah, not quite. Maybe a princess. Got some work to do till I can be considered a queen."

"Well, that's good."

"Hey, you're not supposed to agree with me."

He shrugged. "It just gives me time to build a throne."

"You can start building."

"What's that supposed to mean?"

"I thought by this time you'd figured out your surprise."

"Honestly, I forgot all about it."

"It means… I'm now dating just one guy."

He stopped and his face lit up. "I sure as hell hope it's me."

"I want you, Kyle, and I take what I want. If I wasn't so damn tired right now… but, ya know, the weekend is coming. And for our first time I want to bring my A-game with you."

CHAPTER NINETEEN

The overpowering scent of roses greeted Lexi as she opened the door to her office. The massive bouquet sat on Chandler's desk, blocking her view of him. "Chandler? You in here?"

"Behind the flower shop." He peeked around the side of the vase. "These just arrived. I presume they are from the one suitor you have who can afford four dozen roses."

"You counted?"

"Absolutely."

She moved toward them, took the card that was attached and ripped it open.

Sorry I behaved badly. Hope you can forgive me. It won't happen again.
-Jake

"Yeah, right. Like I'll believe this." Lexi shook her head and flipped the card to Chandler, who caught it and read it.

"Oh dear. Must have been something awful to warrant such a bouquet."

"Yes, and by the way, you can refer to him as the suitor I *had*, past tense. You were right. Kyle is the better man. Actually he's twice the man Jake is." She told him the story of the party.

"That's reprehensible."

"It was awful for Kyle. Poor thing looked so hurt. So I'm done with Jake, though I had chosen Kyle even before the party. Looking back I should have seen the red flags way before that."

Chandler sat there, hands folded in his lap. "Glad to hear it. You have chosen wisely."

"Things sorted themselves out, just as you said they would. People eventually reveal their true selves. Kyle is the man for me. No contest."

"You do realize that Jake is still a client."

"Soon to be past tense again, Chandler. He's not worth it. The minute he signs with Kyle I'll tell him to get lost as my client. But I can't jeopardize Kyle's business relationship with him."

***

Donna stood over Kyle as he sat at his desk, then tilted his chin up so he was looking at her. "Hey. Lose the death stare. We need this commission."

"I know, but… just being in the same room with Jake after what he did last night…"

"Think of your brother. Act like it was no big deal, sign him up, get the commission off the contract. Pay for Anthony's surgery and then tell Jake to go to hell."

"You're right."

"Look at it this way… you already took his girl, now you're gonna take his money."

He heard the office door open. "That's probably him."

"I'll go get him. Be strong for Anthony. And don't forget you won Lexi's heart."

Jake took the seat opposite Kyle's desk, wearing a huge grin. "So, time to talk contract."

"Yeah."

"I was gonna chat with you last night after the party, but I guess you'd left."

"Didn't feel very well, so I went home."

"Yeah, right. Anyway, before I sign on the dotted line I wanted to make sure we're on the same page so there are no surprises in the future."

"Sure. What sort of things are you looking for?"

Jake went through a bunch of items, all pretty standard for a contract between an athlete and an agent. "Everything sounds pretty boilerplate, Jake. I don't have a problem with any of that."

"Good. Oh, one more thing that isn't boilerplate. I want Lexi."

"Sure, no problem. She and I work well together and she's terrific at PR."

"I wasn't talking about her public relations skills."

"Not sure I understand."

"I want her, Kyle. As in, I want you to stop dating her. Now. She's mine. So break up with her. Or I'll find another agent."

***

"*Excuse me?*" Kyle's voice was so loud through the air vent, it interrupted Lexi's conversation with Chandler. "*Jake, who the hell are you to tell me what to do with my personal life, and who to date? You can't make me stop seeing Lexi. Only Lexi can do that.*"

"What the bloody hell is going on upstairs?" asked Chandler.

"I don't know," said Lexi, pulling up a chair and moving closer to the vent. "But I think things have sorted themselves out in a big way."

***

"Look, Kyle, obviously you can't take the hint. I tried to do this without confronting you, but you apparently miss the obvious. I sure as hell dropped enough suggestions."

"What are you talking about?"

"All those pictures of me and Lexi in the tabloids and newspapers? That give you a clue she was dating a millionaire celebrity?"

"I already knew about you two."

***

Lexi's jaw dropped. "Kyle knew?" she whispered. "And Jake knew about Kyle?"

Chandler put his finger to his lips, then pointed to the vent.

"Kyle, I was hoping that would get you out of the way—"

"How did you even know I was dating Lexi? What, you had us followed?"

"Standard procedure for people like me. Too many golddiggers want me just for my money, so when I start seeing someone I have a private investigator check into things. Once he told me you two were dating, I took steps to get you out of the way. But since they didn't work, it has come to this."

"What steps?"

"Oh for God's sake, Kyle. The photos on Page Six *and the tabloids. That should have been enough to make any guy jealous enough to hit the road."*

"Whoa, hold on. You actually had yourself followed and those photos planted?"

"It worked before, but this time it turned out to be a big waste of money. Though Lexi really enjoyed being in the public eye."

"Knowing her as I do, I seriously doubt that. No decent woman wants her photo looking like she did on the front page of that tabloid."

194

Lexi's eyes bugged out as she clenched her fists. Chandler reached over and took her hand.

***

Jake leaned back in his chair. "Oh trust me, she *wants* the life that only I can provide. I've taken her on a helicopter to the Hamptons, a ride on my yacht. She tell you about our little trip to London?"

"She didn't have to. I saw the video of you guys touring after the game. I'm sure you arranged that too."

"Absolutely. And, geez, you didn't even get the picture last night at the party when I kissed her. I made sure you were looking right at us, so don't tell me you didn't see it."

"I also saw her push you away. And walk away."

"She didn't push me away in London. Oh, didn't little miss old-fashioned tell you she slept with me?"

"Bullshit, Jake. I don't believe you. Lexi wouldn't do that."

"You are soooo naive." He opened a manila envelope and pulled out some photos, then started flipping them at Kyle. "Look, here's one of us in my London hotel suite. Here's one of us in a hot tub with her on top of me practically naked. Here's one of her giving me a back rub. Here's one of us on my bed. I must say, the woman does like being on top. And in the one of me in the towel the morning after, you'll notice she's wearing the same outfit. Which should tell you she spent the night with me."

***

Lexi buried her head in her hands. "Dear God." When she pulled her hands away she saw Chandler studying her face. She bit her lower lip as her eyes welled up.

He slid his chair closer and wrapped one arm around her shoulders as the argument in the air vent got more heated.

***

Kyle's heart slammed against his chest as he looked at the grainy photos.

Jake leaned back and smiled. "But if you still wanna believe she didn't sleep with me, go ahead and ask her. If you know one thing about Lexi, it's that she can't lie."

Kyle spit his words through a clenched jaw. "Unlike you. And you really think she's the kind of girl who wants a guy who pulls stunts like this?"

"She'll never know. And if you tell her, I'll simply deny it. You'll just be another little guy who didn't measure up and will say anything to save face."

Kyle's blood began to boil. He stood up and pointed toward the door. "Get! Out!"

Jake started to gather up his papers. "You're cutting your own throat, Kyle. All you have to do is stop dating Lexi and you're my agent. Get a huge commission off my next hundred million dollar contract and I'll send you a bunch more business. If you don't... well, I'll find someone else and pass the word that you can't be trusted. And you'll be out of business in a heartbeat. Last chance... let her go."

"Lexi is not a thing that can be bought and sold like the rest of your possessions! Get the hell out of my office before I throw you out!"

"Yeah, like that could happen. And someone your size should be careful about making threats you can't back up." He stood up and moved next to Kyle, towering over him as he looked down. "By the way, if I were you I wouldn't think about telling Lexi any of this. In case I didn't make my point at the party, let me remind you that I could crush you without even breaking a sweat. So if I hear that you've told her one word of this, I'll snap you like a twig."

Kyle didn't back down. "Don't ever threaten a Sicilian. It's not good for your health."

Jake laughed. "Whatever. But fine. Your loss. And you're about to have another one. I'm going downstairs to claim my prize. And tonight at dinner I'm giving her a fifty-thousand-dollar diamond necklace, which will put the final nail in your coffin. She would have ended up with me anyway, Kyle, so you're making a point for nothing. Face it, you can't compete with what I have to offer. You can't give her the life she deserves."

"She sure as hell doesn't deserve to be owned. Get out. Now."

***

Lexi heard the door slam, jumped up, grabbed her purse and headed for the closet. "I gotta hide. Tell him I'm out all day."

Chandler nodded. "Got it."

She pointed at the roses. "And get rid of those." She closed the closet door, still able to see the office through the crack. Her jaw clenched tight, she tried to get her heart to downshift, to no avail.

Chandler grabbed the vase and headed for the door just as Jake entered the office. "Ah, Mister Frost," he said. "Lexi will not be in today."

"All day?"

"Yes. She's out of town."

"Uh, where are you going with the flowers I sent her?"

"Oh, you poor chap. I assume she never told you she was allergic to these. Some malady called *rose fever*. So unfortunate for a young lady such as Lexi. Her last suitor sent her a hundred of these. Anyway, I was going to give them to the nice young lady in the next office. Unless you want them back?"

Lexi's hand went quickly to her mouth to stifle a laugh.

"No," said Jake. "Do whatever you want with them. Just make sure you read her the card when she calls in." Jake pulled the card from the bouquet and handed it to Chandler.

He looked at it and read it aloud. "*Sorry I behaved badly. Hope you can forgive me. It won't happen again.*" Chandler looked up at Jake. "Did you treat the young lady badly, sir?"

"No, I just did something stupid. Like all men do."

"Understood. As you Yanks like to say, *been there, done that*. But I'll take care of it, sir. Was there any other message you wish to convey?"

He reached into his pocket. "You know what? I'll give her a call right now."

"I'm afraid she's in a conference and told me she would have her cell turned off. But she will call in later."

"Well, then, just tell her I look forward to our date and I'll have a big surprise for her."

"Ah, she does so love a surprise."

"Thanks."

Lexi heard the door close and emerged from the closet. "Damn, Chandler, it was all I could do not to laugh in there. You're good."

"Thank you. I assume you still want these flowers removed."

"Absolutely."

"And should he call later, what should I say regarding his message?"

"Tell him I'm really looking forward to our date tonight."

Chandler's face tightened. "You're still going out with him?"

"One more time, though it will probably make me physically ill. When I dish out revenge, I do it personally. And Jake deserves it big time. Besides, I heard him say something which means I *have* to go out with him." She started to walk into her office, then stopped. "Oh, no."

"What?"

"While things have sorted themselves out, I do have one big thing to clear up with Kyle."

"What's that?"

She shook her head and exhaled. "Dammit. Something Jake said about me was true. I, uh, slept with him."

Chandler's eyes widened. "Surely not!"

"I was fully clothed! Nothing happened!" She told him the entire story… the back rub, jet lag, Jake with his pants on. "So, you think he'll buy it?"

"I would surmise any man would have a hard time accepting that as the truth, especially in light of Jake's physical attributes and the fact he took you to London. But…"

"But…"

"You're the Spin Girl. You'll think of something."

"The truth is not something you have to spin."

"Then the truth will have to be told gently. Ironic, isn't it."

"What's that?"

"Yesterday you had two men courting you. Now you're the one who has to court the one you want."

***

Lexi bounded up the stairs and burst into Kyle's office. She found Donna sitting at her desk wearing a worried look as she wiped a tear from her cheek. "He's not here, Lexi."

"When will he be back? I really need to talk to him."

"I dunno. Something really upset him this morning. He ran out of here and said he needed to think."

"Can't say I blame him."

"Huh?"

She shook her head. "I heard the whole argument through the air vent."

"Oh."

Lexi pulled a chair up to Donna's desk and sat down. "Kyle really knew I was dating Jake?"

"Yeah. He reads *The Post* cover to cover. Then he saw the tabloid when we were in a store. He really thought he'd lost you when he saw that one. Then, to add insult to injury, Jake stopped by a few days ago, tells him the Jets are having him followed and dumps all the photos on his desk, asking him to track down the source. Looking back, he was just rubbing it in Kyle's face. I tell ya, Lexi, it was all Kyle could do to keep from strangling the jerk."

"Jake certainly showed his true colors. I can't believe I didn't see it. Well, until the party last night. What he did to Kyle was a huge red flag."

Donna shrugged. "I'm sure Jake was previously on his best behavior with you. But after Kyle told me about what happened at the party, I don't think I've ever seen my brother look more defeated. That is, until you showed up. You're like his oxygen, Lexi. This morning he acted like he could conquer the world." She folded her hands and leaned forward. "So, let me ask you this… what made you come by last night?"

"Couple of things. One, I knew he was hurting. God, the look on his face when Jake lifted him up and wouldn't put him down… I was hurting for him and couldn't imagine what he felt. It was beyond embarrassing; it was humiliating. Two, Jake pulling a stunt like that really cleared things up for me. I ripped him a new one before I left. But I was going to choose your brother anyway."

"You don't want him by default?"

"Of course not. Please believe me, Donna, this has been a very difficult thing for me, dating two guys. But your brother had already proved he was the better guy. What he did for me when I was sick… well, that spoke volumes. And Chandler told me what Jake did at the commercial shoot to embarrass Kyle."

"Well, your stock went way up when you showed up last night. I don't think he ever expected that."

"I had to. What Jake did was really cruel. Of course, who knew how far he'd gone with all this paparazzi stuff? Speaking of stock, your brother's went through the roof after what I just heard. Standing up for me like that. Damn, Donna, he's got a set of brass ones not backing down to Jake like that."

"He is a tough little thing. And Jake has no idea that Kyle could kick his ass. But right now my brother's got a look that tells me he needs to be left alone. Too much emotion in the past twenty-four hours."

"So don't call him, is that what you're saying?"

"I'll let you know when the time is right. But he won't be gone long. He's gotta get back here and drum up business with Jake out of the picture. We were really counting on that commission to pay for Anthony's surgery."

"Oh, no! How much do you need?"

"Thousands. About thirty."

"Donna, if I had it I'd give it to you."

"I believe you would."

"Meanwhile, Donna, I need your help on something. It's about something Jake said." She looked down at the floor. "About what happened in London." She looked back up at Donna and bit her lip.

Her eyes went wide. "You mean you—"

"No! I mean, I did fall asleep in his bed, but nothing happened." She explained the whole story with Donna listening intently.

Donna shook her head. "Honestly, Lexi, if I didn't know you, I'd think that was a total bullshit story. You fell asleep fully clothed with a guy built like Jake?"

"You think Kyle will believe me?"

"I don't know. All those photos… well, they sure don't help your case. You've got your work cut out for you, Spin Girl."

CHAPTER TWENTY

"Damn, you are absolutely smoking hot tonight."

Lexi forced a smile as she headed toward Jake, who was waiting in her lobby. His eyes ran the length of her body as he took in the sleaziest, most revealing thing she owned: a very tight, very short, low-cut electric-blue band-aid dress she'd bought on a whim (after too much wine) at a fashion show and never had the guts to wear in public. A pair of sky-high stripper heels with straps that snaked around her calves. Along with about three times the amount of her usual makeup and her hair teased out. She had to look as cheap as possible and talk as suggestively as possible for her plan to work. "Thank you." She traced the lapel of his suit with one finger. "And you're as handsome as ever." She ran her hands inside his suit across his abs, then rested them on his chest. "Ooooh, is this a Torano shirt?" She gave his pecs a rub, then slid her hands around his back into a strong hug as she rested her head on his chest. "Mmmm, nice fabric."

"Uh… yeah."

"Well, I guess we could re-enact the commercial later."

He pulled back and took her shoulders, then tilted her chin up. "Lexi, are we okay? I mean, regarding what happened at the party. You're not mad?"

"Do I act like I'm mad?"

"No, you sure don't. Honestly, I was worried you'd cancel. You were pretty steamed last night."

"You get me steamed in a different way, big boy. And if I was still mad, would I dress like this for you and give you a big hug?"

"Guess not. So you dressed for me?"

"It ain't for the doorman, honey. It's part of my apology. I was worried all day you'd be upset with me." She stuck out her lower lip in a pout. "Please don't be mad at Lexi. She doesn't know how to behave around such big, strong men."

"*You're* apologizing?"

"Uh-huh." She dipped her head and looked up at him through her eyelashes. "So, is Lexi forgiven?"

"I guess, though I'm still not sure what for."

"Well, I was awfully hard on you at the party." She slid her hands down into his back pockets, gave him a squeeze and saw his eyes widen a bit. "Thought I'd make it up to you by wearing something you might like."

"That's an understatement. This is quite a change from last night. I figured I'd be apologizing to you."

"Well, I have some explaining to do. Oh, and thank you for the flowers. Chandler read me the card and he said they were beautiful."

"I had no idea you were allergic to those things."

"As the old saying goes, it's the thought that counts. But next time just send tulips."

"I'll make a note of that." He gestured toward the door. "Well, let's hit the road."

Lexi finally broke the embrace. She took his elbow and he flinched. "Oooh, sorry, I forgot that's the sore one."

He moved to her other side and extended his arm.

And as she took it, she couldn't hold back a smile as a great idea flashed through her head.

Lexi closed her menu and handed it to the waiter, who gave her outfit a raised eyebrow but said nothing. They had the private room of the exclusive restaurant to themselves. She leaned back with her glass of wine. "This is fabulous, Jake. And I really like being in a place where no one can take our picture. Privacy is very important to me."

"Yeah, I picked that up last night, so I thought you'd appreciate this place. I'm so glad you were willing to forgive me and see me again."

She shrugged. "Well, you know, I kinda went off on you after a little too much booze. We all do stuff we regret when we drink and I can have a bad temper. This morning I gave it a lot of thought. I finally realized that one of the men I'm dating simply has too much to offer to just throw away. And I do know that boys will be boys on occasion. Especially boys who play a physical game for a living. I get that you need to flex those muscles away from the field as well."

He flashed a wide smile. "Very happy to hear you say that. So does this mean you're beginning to understand the mindset of an athlete?"

It was time to lay it on thick and let him think she was like the other girls at the party. *You obviously need a cheap bimbo who wants a caveman, so here ya go.* "Oh, absolutely. But I wasn't expecting the scene last night with all that testosterone in one room. Look, I walk in the place and the first thing I see is one of your teammates carrying some blonde off to a bedroom. I'm actually a party girl, Jake, but a different kind." She locked eyes with him and dropped her voice to a sultry tone. "I can fulfil any all-night fantasy you can come up with, but the party has to be a private one."

"Fine with me."

"So when I saw the girl being hauled away and a bunch of other couples making out on the couch it got me off on the wrong foot."

"Yeah, not the best first impression, I guess. And then you said I didn't behave very well."

"Eh, but when I calmed down and gave it some thought I had

to go back to the *boys will be boys* thing and cut you some slack. Besides, I knew you were drunk. But so was I because I started before the party. Then I remembered what you told me in London, how you enjoy crushing an opponent who's smaller than you. So, yeah, I get it… the bigger and stronger rule, you're an alpha male, built like Thor, who towers over the average guy and you wanted everyone to know you could easily take care of any man by physically dominating him. It was really eye-opening… the contrast between you and Kyle, your huge size advantage and incredible strength. Lifting him so effortlessly and holding him up in the air. I needed to see that in order to confirm what I'd been thinking."

"What's that?"

"That one of you is actually twice the man of the other. And I love a man who can dominate the competition." She licked her lips and watched his smile grow wide. *He really thinks I'm talking about him.*

Got him.

Okay, the hook is set, now reel him in very slowly…

"So, you prefer a strong man."

"I would say there's nothing quite like a guy who is head and shoulders over the other men out there. Honestly, I wish I'd seen you do that sooner."

"Do you still think I'm a high school bully?"

"You know what I think? That in a very raw, primitive way you wanted to show off for your girl. That little demonstration of brute strength was for my benefit, I assume."

He smiled and looked down for a moment. "Guilty as charged. Yeah, I wanted to impress you."

"I thought so. And, again, I'm real sorry I went off on you in front of your teammates. I hope I didn't embarrass you."

"No problem. Oh, and before I forget, I promise I'll apologize to the little guy."

She waved her hand like she was shooing a fly. "Pffft. I wouldn't worry about him. Look, if he can't deal with a Greek god who's twice his size and strong as Superman, he shouldn't be a sports agent." She took another sip of wine to watch his reaction, and saw a sly smile. "So if you wanted to impress me, what made you decide to do it that way? And why Kyle?"

"Well, the opportunity presented itself. He was one of the few little guys at the party, I happened to be standing next to him and you were close enough to see everything. Perfect timing. So I scooped him up."

"Ah, you wanted me to see your dominance in the real world as opposed to the football field."

"That was the plan."

"Well, I must say, I've never had a guy try to impress me in that manner. And I would imagine it wasn't *just* for me... I'm sure it boosted *your* ego. I could tell you really enjoyed it when you held him in front of me and then raised him up to the ceiling. But what was really amazing... it seemed so effortless. My God! Those massive biceps of yours made it look like he weighed nothing." She flashed a big smile at him to let him know she was impressed. "C'mon, fess up. I saw that devilish grin."

He really thinks I'm eating this up.

"To be honest, yeah, I enjoyed it. I mean, showing you how easily I could scoop him up... and then toying with him for you. Women are impressed when I do stuff like that. And men get the message."

"You've done that before?"

"Once I caught a little guy hitting on my girlfriend at a party I hosted. I picked him up and carried him under one arm for ten minutes. He learned his lesson. You gotta let people know a girl belongs to you. I kissed you in front of everyone so they'd know you were with me."

Ewwww, he was actually marking his territory.

"Then I gave Kyle an overhead press to show them how helpless another man would be who challenged me. So, Lexi, did I make my point? Did he look helpless?"

"Are you kidding? We're talkin' David and Goliath here. Sheer power. You were holding him up so casually, his feet were dangling two feet off the ground and if he could get down he'd have no chance against you. Of course he looked helpless. So I gotta ask… what's going through that mind of yours while you're holding a guy up like that?"

Of course, David defeated Goliath…

His eyebrows did a little jump and he flashed a sinister smile. "Pure dominance. When I pressed him up and held him there, his head nearly touching the ceiling, powerless to get away… what a rush. Knowing that I could easily crush him without even breaking a sweat is an incredible feeling of superiority. Then he gets rescued by a girl, which makes him feel even smaller and me even bigger. But it would have been better if you hadn't made me put him down."

"Really?"

"Because I would have carried Kyle around until he begged me to let him go, like I did with the guy who I caught hitting on my date, like I've done with other guys who got in my way. Now *that* is a feeling of pure, primitive masculinity. Dominating another man so easily… toying with him, which I *really* enjoy… he knows if he tries anything aggressive I could easily finish him off. His only hope is that I'll let him go without hurting him. I eventually let him go, but not until he begs. Too bad you didn't get to see Kyle give up. It's actually a bigger rush than crushing a guy."

Keep smiling and try not to throw up.

"You usually make the guy actually beg?"

"Hell, yeah. He has no choice because he knows I can snap him like a twig. Look, it's not enough to simply be stronger. You have to show total dominance, demoralize him and make him give up. That's why toying with the guy is important to break his

207

spirit. Showing he's no match for you really sucks the bravado out of any man. And pumps me up like you wouldn't believe. If I had just scooped up Kyle and put him down right away, it wouldn't have made my point. I was going to carry him around the room and introduce him to all the women, then toss him over my shoulder. And trust me, he would have eventually begged me to let him go. Regardless, he learned his lesson."

"And that lesson would be?"

"Guys like me take what we want. He'll be at a lot of team parties and little guys need to know their place in the food chain when it comes to women."

Oh. My. God. How did I not see this before?

You chose to ignore it when you saw it at the Tower of London. Through those rose-colored glasses you were so fond of wearing.

"Wow. I'm *so* glad I'm finally getting to know the *real you.*"

"Well, I've been holding back. I wasn't sure a classy girl like you would appreciate an alpha male and I needed to know. I figured the party was a good time to find out. So, Lexi, the big question is, did all of it impress you?"

Time to reel him in...

She locked eyes with him, hers beaming. "Even though I got mad at the time, well... the amazing way you showed off your physical superiority over Kyle... *toying with him* to impress *me*... hearing you say you could have easily crushed him and made him beg you to let him go... wow. And knowing you were teaching him a lesson... that really opens my eyes. By the way, I have a confession to make. When I went to bed I have to admit I was really turned on."

However, not by you.

Huge smile. "You seem to have accepted my way of thinking."

"You know, I always said I wasn't the kind of girl to be impressed by a guy who is all muscle. But it's survival of the fittest, right?" She licked her lips. "And from personal experience you're physically the fittest man I know."

"I thought you noticed in London."

"Noticed? Good God, Jake! It's like you're chiseled out of granite. I love a guy who is unbelievably strong. While I want to be respected as an equal, there's something about a man who wants to carry me away. Sometimes a girl wants a guy to toss her over his shoulder and simply take her. And other times I look at a man like a starving woman and want to devour him like a five-course meal. Although you're big enough for ten courses. That body of yours would be a playground for a girl my size. And I love playground rides."

Jake's eyes went wide. "Uh, which time is it right now? Carried-away Lexi or starving-woman-playground Lexi?"

She shrugged. "Maybe both. Who says I have to pick one or the other on any given night? Maybe I'm greedy. I do like variety. In your case it might be fun to conduct a thorough search of your body for an ounce of fat, which I doubt I'll find. But the search would be fun. And, of course, those nights after a game when you're too tired you'd probably enjoy having a girl get down on her knees and worship you."

"Wow. This is a side of you I've not seen, Lexi. And I'll be honest… I didn't expect to see you in an outfit like that."

She feigned an indignant look. "You don't like it?"

"Are you kidding? You look like one of my fantasies. I was just surprised."

"Well, a girl doesn't play all her cards at once. You held back on me and I did the same with you. And I figured it was time you knew what I was capable of, since I have been rather conservative when we've been together. Besides, I'm an alpha female."

"I didn't know there was such a thing."

"Ah, we fly under the radar."

"So what exactly is an alpha female?"

Time to continue torturing the guy. I mean, how dare he threaten to ruin Kyle's business? "A woman who takes what she wants sexually. You say you like the rush of toying with your opponent and making him beg? I enjoy toying with a man and making him beg as well. But, unlike you, I finish him off every time."

He visibly gulped.

And he's… almost in the boat.

"The alpha female dominates her man when the mood strikes her. There's nothing quite like draining a man of bodily fluids to the point he can barely walk the morning after. Of course, you need a man who can physically keep up with that."

"And you're one of these alphas?"

"Yep. Let's put it this way, I'll never be one of those girls who says, *not tonight, honey, I have a headache.* Just because I'm monogamous doesn't mean I'm a nun. I have a voracious sexual appetite. And with your body, a girl would never go away hungry."

"Good to know. Listen, your assistant told me you like surprises."

"Hey, what girl doesn't? So, you got a hovercraft outside? We going for a blimp ride?"

"Nothing that unusual." He reached into his jacket pocket, pulled out a rectangular velvet box and slid it halfway across the table. "Something more traditional."

She stared at the box and flashed a wide smile. "For me?"

"If I'm not being too forward in giving you a little Christmas present."

"Hey, tis the season."

He nodded at the box. "Well, it doesn't have a *do not open till Christmas* tag on it. Go ahead."

She took the box, gave him a quick look, then opened it, getting ready to fake a surprised look. She didn't have to fake anything. Her jaw dropped as she saw the necklace with several large diamonds and one massive emerald in the middle.

"Lexi, after I saw you at the Tower of London, I got the idea you liked shiny rocks."

"Again, they are not rocks! They're jewels! And this is spectacular! Oh my God, Jake, this is too much!"

"It's only—"

"But I ain't giving it back!" She handed it to him and locked eyes. "Put it on me. Right now."

"My pleasure." He got up, moved behind her, swept her hair out of the way, took the necklace out of the box and draped it around her neck, then kissed her on her exposed shoulder and put her hair back in place. He moved back to his chair and gave her an admiring look. "You look like a goddess."

"You make me feel like one. Appropriate, since you're built like a Greek god. And every goddess needs a god." She opened her purse, took out a compact and looked in the mirror. "I'm not gonna want to take this off. Jake, it's beyond beautiful."

"Should be. It's from Hansen's. I put the receipt in the box in case you didn't like it and wanted to exchange it for something else."

"Are you out of your mind? Why in the world would I want something else?" She looked at the receipt. "Whoa, Jake, this really is too much. But I'm still not giving it back because I know you can afford it."

"You're worth it. Like I said, what good is money if you can't enjoy it?"

"Damn, I could get used to this."

"Just let me know when you want to start."

She kept staring at the mirror. "You know, I think this is the perfect time to give you *my* Christmas present. Hope you like surprises."

"Sure. But you didn't have to buy me anything."

"I didn't." She cocked her head to the side and gave him a dreamy-eyed look. "Looking at you right now... this incredible gift... what we had together in London and how I really wanted to take you... and your amazing display of physical strength at the party to impress me... I realized right this minute... well, I've decided it's time I dated just one guy. Tonight proves there's only one man who can give me the life I deserve and that I have chosen the right man."

Jake beamed.

He swallowed the hook and is in the boat. Bring on the filleting knife.

She traced the necklace with her finger. "So, I was thinking… I'd love a man's opinion of whether I look good wearing *just* this necklace. You know… and nothing else." She stretched out her leg and ran her toe up his leg. "Though I could keep the shoes on, since I get the impression you like them."

His eyes lit up as she stole his breath. He started to get up and she knew he was coming over to kiss her. Suddenly she reached for her purse. "Hang on a minute, Jake. I thought I heard my phone vibrate and I've been waiting for something important. Please excuse me." She pulled out her cell, tapped it and her face dropped. "Oh no."

"What?"

"It's not good." She bit her lower lip. "Oh, no, I am so sorry, Jake. What horrible timing. I have an emergency. I have to go." She tossed her napkin on the table and got up.

"Something serious?"

"Yes. Someone I care about a great deal needs me."

"Can I help? You want me to go with you?"

"No. It's really something very private and I can't talk about it. Really, I'm so sorry to throw cold water on such a wonderful moment. Just call me a cab."

Jake walked her to the taxi and opened the door for her. "Call me if you need anything, anything at all."

"Sure."

"I'll wait up if you think it might not take long." He wore an eager look.

She shook her head. "Nah, it'll be quite a while. What I need to do will take an entire night. Listen, Jake, thanks for the great evening and the incredible gift. Sorry the night had to end this way."

"No problem. I'll see you soon."

"You'll be hearing from me."

He leaned down and kissed her. She grabbed his crotch and winked at him, making his eyes bug out. She got into the cab and told the driver her address.

The cabbie looked in the rear-view mirror and turned around. "Hey, was that Jake Frost you were with?"

"Yeah."

"Damn, those athletes get anything they want. May I ask how much a girl like you charges?"

"Excuse me? I'm not a hooker!"

"Stripper?"

"No! We, uh, just came from a costume party."

"Right. And I guess his costume was a guy in a suit."

She folded her arms and glared at him. "Is there a taxi ride somewhere in my immediate future?"

He smiled as his eyes ran the length of her body. "Well, helluva *costume*. Bet you'd look good as Wonder Woman too." He turned around and put the car in gear. "You could tie me up with your magic lariat."

"Just drive!"

The cabbie laughed and pulled out into traffic.

Lexi turned around and saw Jake get into his limo. She couldn't hold back a huge smile. "Enjoy the cold shower, you jerk." Then she started to laugh. "Damn, considering he was so overheated, there wasn't much there for me to grab. Who woulda guessed?"

CHAPTER TWENTY-ONE

The security guard in the suit unlocked the door and welcomed her. "Good morning."

Lexi returned the greeting and strode into the exclusive jewelry store in a classic knee-length gray business suit, her hair up, while oversized sunglasses hid her eyes. She spotted a sharply dressed fortyish brunette at the counter, walked toward her and smiled.

The woman returned the smile. "Good morning, may I help you?"

She pulled off her sunglasses. "Good morning. I have something I wish to return." She reached into her purse, pulled out the velvet box and placed it on the counter. "Receipt's in the box."

The woman opened the box and looked at the necklace while pulling out the receipt. "I never thought I'd see this piece returned. Is it not to your liking?"

"Oh, it's incredibly beautiful. My compliments to the jeweler who created it. It's the man that gave it to me who is not to my liking."

She studied the receipt and nodded. "Ah, I'm not surprised."

"Really?"

She dropped her voice. "Let's just say the gentleman in question is a regular customer and we've had several… *returns* over the years."

"Well, somehow I'm not surprised at that either."

The woman chuckled. "Would you like to exchange this for

something else? We have some beautiful new pieces in the same price range. Or I can give you a store credit to use at a later date."

"I'd like a refund if that's possible. I really don't want to wear anything that remotely reminds me of him."

"Certainly. Since this is a rather large amount I'll have to get our manager to cut a check. I'll just need some identification so we can make it out to you."

Lexi pulled a slip of paper from her purse and handed it to the woman. "It's not for me. Make it out to this charity."

She looked at the paper. "The Anthony Caruso Foundation. I'm not familiar with that one."

"Disabled veteran who needs surgery and has a ton of medical expenses. It's legit." Lexi pointed at the note. "Their tax ID information is on there."

"Ah, I see. How very generous of you."

"It will save a life. And this may seem like sacrilege in a place like this, but in the grand scheme of things, they're just a bunch of shiny rocks."

***

The receptionist led Lexi through the hallway of the Jets complex toward the last office, which housed her contact, Jeffrey Dell. She saw the slender, thirtysomething public relations man behind the desk get up to greet her. "Ms. Harlow, so nice to see you again." He shook her hand and pointed to the chair opposite his desk. "Please, have a seat."

"Please call me Lexi, and thanks for seeing me on short notice."

"Hey, after what you did for Noah Washington, I figured it was important. Hope none of our players is in trouble."

"Not in the way you think." She turned and saw the office door still open. "Uh, could we have some privacy?"

"Sure." He shut the door and sat behind his desk. He studied

215

her face with his dark eyes. "So, you said you had some important information."

"Right. And before I give it to you, you have to promise me that you did not get this from me."

He shrugged. "Okay. This sounds serious."

"I'm worried about retribution from the player in question."

"Apparently this *is* serious. My lips are sealed, Lexi. So what have you got?"

"It's about Jake Frost. And his upcoming contract negotiations."

"Yeah, that's gonna cost us and probably screw up our salary cap. What about him?"

"Well, before you guys give him a contract for a kazillion dollars, you should know he needs major elbow surgery."

"Really? To my knowledge I've never seen anything from our team doctor."

"That's because he's not seeing your team doctor about this. He knows if it got out that he needed surgery that could possibly end his career, you wouldn't offer him a contract."

The man ran his hands through his dark hair, but didn't say anything.

"You *have* noticed that this year he doesn't throw the long ball like he used to. Right?"

"That could be attributed to any number of things."

"But for a guy called the Mad Bomber, who is known for having the best arm in the league, doesn't that seem out of character?"

"I suppose that of late he hasn't thrown downfield much."

She pointed at his computer. "You can look up game stats on that thing, right?"

"Sure, why?"

"Please pull them up and I'll illustrate my point. Game by game." She waited for his screen to fill with statistics. "Remember the Dolphins game? When Jake hit his elbow on the linebacker's helmet?"

216

"Yeah. He said it just hit his funny bone."

She pointed at the computer. "Okay, how many passes did he attempt longer than fifty yards before that game?"

The guy scanned the stats. "A bunch."

"How many after that game?"

He looked again. His face tightened as he turned to her. "None. Now that you mention it, lately he's been saying no one has been getting open downfield."

"In fact, you'll find he attempted nothing longer than twenty-seven yards since the Dolphins game. Because he destroyed his elbow when he hit it on the helmet and can't throw long. That's why he's been throwing everything short lately. But if you wanna sign a quarterback who can only throw twenty-seven yards, hell, sign me, cause I can do it."

"This is unbelievable. But I have to ask... how did you come by this information?"

"I've been dating him for several months." She pulled the tabloid and a bunch of paparazzi photos from newspapers and placed them on the desk. "Let's just say I've gotten close to him. And men aren't exactly good at keeping secrets when they're thinking with the wrong head."

The guy studied the photos, then looked at Lexi. "So you're the mysterious redhead I've been seeing in the gossip pages."

"Trust me, I ain't that mysterious."

"Are you still dating?"

She shook her head. "Last night was our last date."

"Lexi, what you're saying makes sense from a statistical stand-point, but with all due respect, this sounds like the actions of a woman scorned."

She nodded. "I agree, and I'm not offended by your statement. But if a woman my size can make Jake Frost jump by simply resting my hand on his elbow, what does that tell you? Am I the proverbial woman scorned? Sure. He did something unconscion-able. Ask any of the players at his Christmas party what he did to his agent, who threw him out of his office the next day after Jake threatened him."

"Really? Wow, talk about tossing away an easy commission. Who was his agent?"

"Kyle Caruso. And you know he only takes squeaky-clean clients. What does that tell you?"

"It's… strange. Because I do know his reputation."

"The agent has scruples. Jake doesn't. But as for me, I also don't lie, and I don't like people who do. Look, all I'm saying is that you guys need your own doctor to give him a complete physical before you sign him to anything. And make sure he pays close attention to that elbow. Even if you don't believe me, you owe it to the team to check him out. And don't wait too long, since you know damn well that talented backup you have is ready to move on."

"We'll definitely do that. Thanks, Lexi. I owe you one. I'll steer some clients your way."

"Speaking of which, is Jonathan Egan around? He's already one of my clients."

"Yeah. Just saw him in the weight room. I'll point you in the right direction."

***

She started to walk toward the weight room with her head held high.

Part one of her plan, taking down Jake Frost, was underway.

Part two, getting Kyle Caruso back, wouldn't be this easy.

Her cell rang. She pulled it out of her purse, hoping it would be Kyle, but saw it was Donna. Maybe things were looking up. "Hi, Donna."

"Hi, Lexi. I wanted to give you a heads-up on something."

"Is Kyle ready to talk to me?"

"Not even close. Can't get those photos out of his head, I'm afraid. But… a toy store in our neighborhood is having a fund-raiser for Anthony on Saturday, selling photos with Santa. Kyle will be there playing Saint Nick. I think it would be safe for you to drop by. He's not going to make a scene with that going on."

"I'll be there. What time?"

"Come at three when things are wrapping up with the kids."

"Sure thing. It almost sounds like you're in my corner, Donna."

"Look, all I know is that you make my brother happier than I've ever seen him. And right now he's as miserable as I've ever seen him. There's one common denominator, and it's you. I don't know if you can fix things or if he'll ever believe you about what happened in London, but this might be a good place to start. After all, you are the Spin Girl."

She finished her call with Donna and headed into the weight room. A few players were working out and she spotted the Jets backup quarterback on a bench press machine. She headed toward him and he smiled as he saw her approach. "Hi, Lexi. Didn't expect to see you here."

"Hey." She dropped her voice. "Listen, you're about to be offered a starting job with a big contract."

"You know something I don't?"

"Let's just say you need an agent you can trust. And right away."

"Yeah, I've been shopping for one."

She handed him Kyle's card. "Well, your search is over. Trust me, Kyle is a lot like you. Give him a call Monday."

"Why not now?"

"Because you won't need him till Monday. And you didn't get any of this from me."

***

Donna greeted Lexi at the door of the toy store. "You're right on time. We're almost done."

Lexi walked into the crowded store, decorated for Christmas and wall to wall with frazzled parents and kids high on sugar who were bouncing off the walls. At the far end of the store she saw a short line of small children waiting to see Santa.

Kyle, in a red suit and white beard.

He was bouncing a little boy on his knee, then pointed to the camera set up on a tripod. A photographer took a photo as his brother, Anthony, seated in his wheelchair nearby, took a donation from a parent.

"He looks like he's enjoying this, Donna."

Donna nodded. "It's taken his mind off of things."

"Is he any better today?"

"Unfortunately no. The Sicilian grudge chromosome is a dominant one."

"He doesn't know I'm coming, right?"

"Of course not. Today all he cares about is his brother. But we're still way short of what we need as far as money is concerned."

"Don't worry, Donna. Things are about to change."

"You know something I don't?"

"Next!" A woman at the front of the children's line pointed to a kid in line, who headed for Santa.

Donna cocked her head in that direction. "That's the last kid. As soon as they take the picture, you're up."

"You think he'll talk to me?"

"Don't know. But good luck. I'm rooting for you."

"Thanks, that means a lot. I'm rooting for you and Chandler too."

Donna flashed a wide smile. "No rooting necessary there."

"So I've heard."

"I'm surprised you didn't hear me scream in ecstasy last night."

"Donna!"

Lexi caught a flash in her peripheral vision. She turned and

220

saw the last child get off Santa's lap. "I'm up." Donna patted her on the back as she walked toward Kyle. He was talking to his brother and didn't notice her until she was right in front of him.

He turned and his smile vanished. "Lexi, this is neither the time nor the place for this."

She pulled a check from her pocket, unfolded it and handed it to him. "I'd like to buy five minutes with Santa."

His eyes bugged out as he looked at it. "Where the hell—"

"I returned a certain necklace that a certain sleazeball gave me in an attempt to buy my affections."

Kyle handed it to his brother. "Anthony, look."

Anthony's jaw dropped. He couldn't contain his joy as he looked up at Lexi. "I didn't know you were rich."

"I'm not. Let's just say that fell in my lap and I knew of a good cause."

Anthony extended his arms. "Get down here and give me a hug." She moved forward, leaned down and hugged his shoulders as he gave her a strong squeeze. She leaned back and saw his eyes were moist. "God bless you, Lexi. You just gave me my life back. You're a real life superhero."

"A female superhero is a superheroine. But, yeah, I patrol the streets at night protecting women and children from ne'er-do-wells."

"I gotta tell Joanne." He put the check in his pocket and wheeled away.

Lexi turned back to Kyle. "So, what about that five minutes with Santa?"

He nodded. "After what you did, how can I say no?"

She smiled, moved toward him and sat on his lap. "Oooh, I've forgotten how comfortable this is." She patted him on the stomach. "Ah, good, it's a pillow. I was worried you'd gotten fat."

He slid his hand around to the small of her back. "You know, no one would argue that you deserved the money after what Jake put you through."

"Please do not mention he-who-must-not-be-named."

"Sorry. I can't thank you enough. But, Lexi, I'm just not sure I'm ready—"

She put her finger on his lips. "If I'm only getting five minutes, I'm doing the talking."

"Go ahead."

"Thank you. First, I cannot tell you how sorry I am about the whole situation. I know you have been terribly hurt and that I didn't handle things properly, but I had never been in this position before. And while you may think I'm a horrible liar, I wish there was some way I could prove to you that nothing happened in London. I understand the photos—" She saw him cringe and stopped. "I, uh… well, let me just say I miss you terribly and will do anything to get you back. And since you're playing Santa, the one thing I want for Christmas more than anything this year is your forgiveness and trust. But I certainly understand if that's not possible."

He locked eyes with her and nodded. "That all? You've got about four minutes left."

"For once in my life I'm at a loss for words. I've been rehearsing what I was going to say and now that I see you…" her words grew thick in her throat and her eyes welled up.

He brushed a single tear from her cheek. "Give me some time and space, Lexi."

"Usually it's the woman who says that."

"Just give me some time, okay?"

"Sure, Santa. I know I deserve coal in my stocking, but I'll leave that up to you." She kissed him on the cheek, squeezed his hand and got up.

"Lexi, thanks so much for what you did for Anthony."

"I'm glad I could help. See ya. Merry Christmas."

"You too."

She turned and headed for the door but was met by Anthony's wife Joanne, who ran toward her and gave her a strong hug. "Oh my God, Lexi, you are a lifesaver. I don't know what to say."

She looked at the woman who was in tears. "I think your look says it all."

"I saw you talking to Kyle. That go okay?'

She shrugged. "It's a start. I've got a lot of damage control to do."

"I'll work on him from this end. Poor guy… he's devastated about you and his business is about to go under with Jake torpedoing him."

She patted Joanne on the shoulder. "I wouldn't worry about his business. Don't worry, Joanne, I've got that part covered."

"You've got some new clients for him?"

"Trust me, in a few days, people will be beating down his door. One guy in particular who's about to be offered a big contract."

***

Donna approached as Kyle and Anthony added up the donations. "So, how'd we do?"

Anthony beamed. "Seven hundred from Santa pictures and fifty thousand and change from a redheaded guardian angel."

"Yeah, how about that girl? Kyle, I saw you talking to her."

Kyle looked up at her. "And gee, I wonder how she knew I was here?"

Donna shrugged. "Guess she was in the neighborhood shopping for toys."

"Uh-huh."

"Well?"

Anthony stacked up the money. "He's in love with her."

"Really?" said Donna with a smile.

"And she's in love with him."

Kyle rolled his eyes. "Do I have any input into this conversation?"

"No!" They answered in unison.

223

"I told her I needed some time and space and she seemed okay with that."

Anthony leaned back in his wheelchair. "You're not really gonna cut loose a great girl like that because of something she *may* have done, are you?"

"It's complicated, my brother."

"Bullshit. The other guy is out of the picture, what's past is past, and any girl who would give fifty grand of what should have been her own money to someone she met once... well, to me, she's a real gem. She looks at you like Joanne looks at me. And you look at her like I look at my wife. Kyle, she's a heart-and-soul girl. And if you let her go you're a damn idiot."

CHAPTER TWENTY-TWO

Kyle went through his contact list on Monday morning, determined to call every single person in search of new clients. If Jake followed through on his threat to kill his business, he'd need to look up some new people, and quick.

His train of thought was broken when Donna tapped on the door. "Uh, Kyle, a reporter is here from one of the sports networks wondering if you have a few minutes for an interview."

"What about?"

She dropped her voice. "Something about Jake Frost getting released by the Jets this morning."

"What?"

She shrugged. "Talk to the woman and see what's up. I'll check talk radio and the Internet."

"Sure, send her in." He straightened his tie and stood up as a young, attractive blonde sports reporter he recognized was ushered into his office. "Ah, Ms. Jenkins, nice to meet you. I enjoy your stories on the Sunday shows."

"Thank you. Nice to hear. And you can call me Brenda."

"Sure. You actually dig up some interesting stuff. So what can I do for you?"

"I assume you know your client Jake Frost has been released from the Jets?"

"Actually, I didn't and I dropped him as a client last week. What happened?"

"He'd been hiding the fact that he blew out his elbow and

needed major reconstructive surgery. Team doctor says he'll never play again." She studied his face. "And I can tell from your expression you didn't know."

He shook his head. "I had no clue. But, as I said, he's no longer my client."

"May I ask why?"

"Do you know my reputation?"

"Yeah, you represent decent human beings, for the most part. So if you dropped him you must have known—"

"This was about something else entirely. Let's just say Jake Frost was not the type of client I wanted to represent. We got into an argument last week and I asked him to leave."

"Was he your biggest client?"

"Had I negotiated his next contract he would have been."

"Wow. An agent who actually throws away a commission. Talk about an exclusive. Mind if we set up and get an interview on camera?"

"Sure, no problem."

***

Lexi heard the door to the outer office bang against the wall. "What the hell?" Chandler was out running errands so she went to investigate.

And ran right into Jake, who had fire in his eyes.

"You little bitch!"

Oh, shit.

She backed up into her office as her heart rate rocketed. "Jake, calm down. What's wrong?"

"As if you didn't know! The Jets released me this morning! Somehow they found out I need major surgery on my elbow!"

"Did the team doctor—"

"You're the only person I ever told! There's no other way they

226

could have known unless you told them! And I know you were in their office the other day. My career is over! And I thought after the other night you were mine. Now I know why you haven't taken my calls for the past few days."

He started to back her into the wall and she put up her hands. "Jake, calm down."

But he didn't.

He slapped her hard across the face. Pain shot through her jaw as she staggered back against her desk. He then grabbed her by her arms, hard, picked her up and glared at her in utter fury. "How much did you get to sell me out?"

***

The TV reporter sat opposite Kyle's desk as the photographer adjusted his camera and turned on the light. "Okay, and we're rolling."

"Mister Caruso, first please tell me how you came to represent Jake Frost earlier—"

You're hurting me! Please let me go!

The TV reporter stopped and looked at the air vent. "What the hell was that?"

Kyle put up his hand as he moved toward the vent. "Hang on a minute."

***

Jake was squeezing her harder now, still holding her in the air. She tried to kick him, but it had no effect.

He lifted her higher as he yelled at her. "You don't wanna date me any more, fine. You destroy my career, we've got a problem."

The pain in her arms was excruciating. "You're crushing my arms! Let me go!"

"Fine." He lowered her a bit, then threw her into the wall. Lexi slammed into it, shattering the drywall, then fell, her head banging hard against the concrete floor. She saw stars as pain shot through her head. She noticed her face was right up against the air vent. She mustered up as much strength as she could to yell. "Somebody, help! Help!"

**

"That's Lexi!" Kyle turned and headed for the door. "Call the police!

The TV reporter followed. "What's going on?"

"She's in trouble! One floor down in seven-oh-four! Call nine-one-one! Now!" He flew out of the office and ran to the stairwell, then down one flight, taking the steps two at a time. He sprinted into the reception area, past Chandler's empty desk and into her office.

Jake had Lexi by the throat, pinned against the wall, her eyes wide with fear.

His karate instincts kicked in.

He rushed toward Jake and unleashed a furious punch to his side right at his ribs. Jake groaned and released Lexi, who slumped to the floor. He turned and glared at Kyle. "Well, look who it is." He balled his hands into fists. "I'm gonna enjoy this."

"Bring it, Jake." Kyle assumed a defensive position as Jake charged him and swung wildly. Kyle blocked his punch and delivered three quick shots to his exposed ribs. Jake doubled over for a moment, grabbing his side. But he didn't go down. The guy was huge. It would take everything he had. As soon as Jake stood back up Kyle unleashed a spinning kick that landed square on his opponent's jaw. He went down in a heap. "Oh, what's the matter, Jake? You like beating up women because you're afraid to take on a guy? A man who hits a woman is a damn coward."

Jake was breathing hard. Blood dripped from his mouth onto his hand. He reached up and ran a finger inside his mouth. "You sonofabitch, you knocked out two of my teeth. I'll break you in half, you little shit."

"Hey, this is what a coward looks like from a *grown man's* point of view." Kyle made a "come on" motion with one hand. "Let's rock."

***

Lexi was barely conscious as the young blonde woman, who looked familiar, rushed to her side. "Police are on the way. Hang in there." She looked past the woman, who was holding her hand, and saw a man in the doorway with a television camera pointed into her office at the commotion at the other side of the room.

Where Kyle was wiping the floor with Jake.

The guy she wanted, the calm, gentle, kind, old-fashioned, chivalrous gentleman she knew looked like a man possessed as he pummeled the football player, who was a foot taller and probably outweighed him by a hundred pounds. One martial arts move after another staggered Jake, until Kyle spun around, fast as lightning, and kicked him in the face. Blood gushed from Jake's nose as his eyes rolled up in his head and he fell forward, face first, like a tree. He hit the floor with a thud, unconscious. Kyle ran to her side, getting down on the floor with her and taking her head in his hands. "Lexi, you okay? Lexi?"

She started to answer but then the world spun and went black.

***

229

Her eyes flickered open and her vision began to clear. She found herself looking up at bunch of white ceiling tiles.

Her entire body ached.

Someone was holding her hand.

She looked to the side and saw Kyle, asleep in a chair, his fingers entwined with hers. "Where am I?"

He woke up and turned to her. "Oh, thank God."

"Where am I?"

"In the hospital. You're gonna be okay." He stood up and sat on the edge of the bed.

She started to raise her hand to her aching head, but it felt heavy. "Shit, everything hurts."

"Lay still, Lexi. Let me go tell the doctor you're awake."

He started to get up but she didn't let go of his hand. "Wait. Are *you* okay?"

"I'm fine, but you've got a concussion, a broken arm, a black eye and a bunch of bruises. So try not to move. Let me get the doctor. And there's a police officer waiting to talk to you."

She still didn't let go. "Hey."

"What?"

"You saved my life. He would have killed me."

He looked down at the floor. "Yeah."

"You're my hero, Kyle."

The female police officer followed the doctor, who had given her something for the pain. The young woman sat on the edge of the bed while Kyle remained in the chair. She reached out and took Lexi's hand. "Hi, Lexi, I'm Officer Krista Haines." She was a tall brunette, with her hair up under a hat, with kind blue eyes and a soothing voice. "How you doing?"

"My earlobes don't hurt, but that's about it."

"You feel up to telling me what happened?"

"Sure. By the way, where's Jake?"

"Down the hall in another room."

Lexi's eyes widened in fear.

The officer squeezed her hand. "He's under restraints, Lexi, handcuffed to the bed and another officer is guarding his room. But he's in worse shape than you so he's not going anywhere. Four broken ribs, a broken nose, teeth knocked out. Among other things."

Lexi exhaled and relaxed. "He deserved it."

"You wanna tell me what happened?"

"Sure." She recounted the whole story as the officer took notes. Then she turned to look at Kyle. "And if he hadn't shown up, you'd be talking to me in the morgue."

"Well, the doctor says you're very lucky. Thankfully we have citizens like Kyle."

"I'm gonna buy him a cape for Christmas."

"Yeah, that would be good. So, Lexi, I know this might be a difficult decision, but I would encourage you to press charges."

"It ain't difficult at all. The sonofabitch needs to be in jail. Where do I sign?"

The officer smiled. "Great. You'll be helping a lot of women come forward who might not otherwise. This is a very high-profile case."

"Really?"

"Famous NFL quarterback involved in something like this? It's lead story on all the networks." She smiled as she cocked her head at Kyle. "And there's video footage of your white knight kicking the hell out of your assailant. We were hoping we might convince him to join the force."

Kyle laughed a bit. "Thanks, but hopefully I'll never have to use those skills again."

"Anyway," said the officer, closing her notebook, "I'll get the paperwork started and as soon as Mister Frost is well enough, we'll haul his sorry ass in front of a judge. Meanwhile, you take care." She stood up and handed a card to Kyle. "If she needs anything, call me immediately."

"Sure. Thanks, officer." He put the card in his pocket and shook her hand. The officer left the room and he turned back to Lexi, who was caught in a yawn. "You need to get some sleep."

"I just woke up. What time is it anyway?"

"Nine o'clock."

"Good God! How long have you been here?"

"I dunno. A little while."

"Little while my ass. The whole thing happened before lunch."

"Donna and Chandler were also here."

"But you've been here the whole time?"

He nodded. "You need to get some rest."

"Wait. Before you go… the officer said there's video of the fight. I do remember someone with a camera. How did that happen?"

"There was a TV crew in my office interviewing me about Jake when we heard you scream for help through the air vent. Thank goodness for that old decrepit building. Anyway, they followed me. You remember the blonde woman helping you? That was the reporter. Her cameraman came up and shot the whole thing."

"I wanna see it."

"Trust me, it's gone viral, and you can see it anytime. Right now go to sleep." He took her hand and squeezed it. "I'll see you tomorrow, okay?"

"Yeah." She locked eyes with him and hers welled up. "You're an amazing man, you know that?"

"Just a guy helping a damsel in distress."

"Yeah, right. I'll say it again, you're my hero. Regardless of what happens in the future, you will always be that to me. And when you go to sleep tonight I want you to hear my voice saying those three words."

***

232

Lexi sipped her orange juice as the morning sun spilled into her room. She'd slept long and hard, and though she was still extremely sore her head was at least clearing up. She was hoping Kyle would be here soon. A gentle tap on the door broke her train of thought. She looked up and saw a man in a dark suit standing in the doorway.

"Ms. Harlow?"

"Another doctor, huh?"

He shook his head as he walked into the room. "I'm not a doctor, I'm an attorney."

Her face tightened. "I shoulda noticed the hole in your shoes from chasing ambulances. I don't need a lawyer."

"No, I'm not trying to solicit you as a client. I'm Mister Frost's attorney."

She narrowed her eyes and glared at him. "Get the hell out of my room."

"Hear me out, Ms. Harlow. Just for a minute."

She reached for the nurse's call button and pressed it. "You and your client can go to hell."

He reached in his pocket, pulled out a slip of paper, unfolded it and put it on her bed. "Mister Frost has authorized me to offer this settlement in return for you dropping the assault charges."

She looked at the check.

One hundred thousand dollars.

"That's what he thinks I'm worth?"

"He knows you are not financially secure and it would help you get back on your feet. We would, of course, also cover all medical expenses."

"What's your name?"

"Fred Welton."

She pointed at her face. "Look at me, Mister Welton. You think this is worth a hundred grand? A million? You think a woman wants to get the hell beaten out of her by a guy the size of Jake and have her life flash before her while he chokes her

233

and she thinks she's gonna die? And that money will make it all go away?"

He looked at the floor.

"I thought so. And since I don't have two hands to tear up that check because he broke my arm as well, you can stick it up your client's ass. By the way, even if I dropped the assault charges it wouldn't help your client because the District Attorney is considering an attempted murder charge as well."

The lawyer's eyes widened.

"That's right, sleazeball." She pulled down her gown to reveal the dark bruises around her neck. "The doctor said a little more pressure on my throat and he would have killed me. I think that's a pretty good case for a prosecutor, don't you? Two- hundred-and-forty-pound professional athlete against a hundred-and-ten-pound woman, squeezing her arm so hard it breaks, picking her up and throwing her across the room, then choking her against the wall?"

The lawyer said nothing as he picked the check up off the bed. The nurse arrived. "Need something, Ms. Harlow?"

"Just this piece of shit lawyer removed from my room."

She grabbed his arm and shoved him toward the door. "Out! Don't make me call security." The nurse turned back to Lexi. "Sorry."

"No problem."

"Tough keeping the ambulance chasers outta here."

"He's Jake Frost's lawyer. Trying to buy me out of pressing the assault charges."

"You're not—"

"Hell, no. That man is gonna pay. And I don't mean with money."

The nurse flashed a smile. "I knew I liked you."

CHAPTER TWENTY-THREE

Lexi signed the discharge papers as she put her feet up on the supports of the wheelchair. She handed the clipboard back to the nurse and smiled at her. "Thank you so much for taking such good care of me."

"We're all proud of you for staying strong, Miss Harlow. You take care."

"You too."

The nurse left just as Kyle entered the room with the Manhattan District Attorney, Kate Bradwell. Lexi looked up at the tall blonde in her forties, dressed in a blue business suit. "Didn't know you were coming, Ms. Bradwell."

"There's a horde of media people outside waiting for you. I thought I could run interference… or we could sneak you out the back door. Mister Caruso told me you don't like the spotlight."

"That barn door has sailed. Besides, I want the world to see what he did to me."

The DA looked at Kyle. "You sure were right about her."

Lexi turned to him. "What did you tell her about me?"

"Just that you can take care of yourself." He moved behind the wheelchair. "And that you have an attitude."

"Why, thank you for the compliment."

"It was more of a warning."

Kyle rolled her out into the sunlight toward a waiting gauntlet of media people, who rushed forward to meet them. The DA put up her hand. "Okay, guys, give her some space. I've got some developments for you and then if she feels up to it, Lexi can take some questions."

Lexi looked up at her and nodded.

The DA turned back to the media. "Obviously this is a good day in that Lexi Harlow is going home today, but she still has a ways to go before she is physically recovered from this ordeal. However, the mental part of what she went through will never go away. But she has been incredibly brave in agreeing to press charges against her assailant, Jake Frost. After much discussion in my office and with the medical professionals here, we will be pursuing attempted murder charges against Mister Frost."

The media reacted strongly and peppered the woman with questions. After she answered a few, she turned to Lexi. "Okay, we don't need to keep this young lady waiting too long to go home. If you have any questions for her, now's the time."

"Lexi, was it a hard decision to press charges?"

She shook her head. "Not at all. The guy beat the hell out of me and needs to face the consequences." She pulled down the collar of her shirt. "And the world needs to know this is what domestic violence looks like. This is what happens when a two-hundred-and-forty-pound athlete throws a hundred-and-ten pound woman around like a rag doll. He broke my arm just by squeezing it. He choked me to the point I could barely breathe. When women are assaulted, they need to take action and not be silent."

"Have you had any contact with Mister Frost?"

"No, I don't ever want to see him again, but his attorney paid me a visit and tried to buy me off. Brought a check for a hundred grand if I would drop the charges."

"Did you consider it?"

"Well, since I can only use one hand right now and couldn't tear it up, I told him where he could stick it."

The media chuckled. "What was going through your mind during the attack?"

She turned serious. "That I was going to die." She reached up and took Kyle's hand. "Thank God Kyle showed up when he did or I probably wouldn't be here and you'd be covering my funeral."

"Mister Caruso, what were you thinking when you walked in on the attack?"

"I didn't have time to think. I saw Lexi being choked and had to stop him."

"Were you worried for your own safety?"

"Like I said, didn't have time to think. You see a woman in trouble and you have to help. Any man would do the same thing."

"Like hell," said Lexi, taking his hand as she looked up at him. "Bravest man I know."

The DA put up her hand. "Okay, guys, she needs to get home and recover. I'll keep you posted on any new developments, but please, give her some time and space."

Kyle started pushing the wheelchair toward his car. The media parted, clearing a path as they shot video and took pictures. He brought the chair to a stop in front of the car, stepped around and opened the car door, then kneeled down and flipped up the footrests so she could get up. "Okay, Lexi, take your time getting up."

"Do me a favor?"

"Sure."

"I'm a little unsteady. Can you pick me up and put me in the car?"

"No problem." Kyle reached under her legs and behind her back, then easily lifted her out of the chair, cradling her in his arms as the media surrounded them.

She wrapped her good arm around his neck and heard a ton of camera clicks. "Hang on a minute."

"What?"

She turned to the media and raised her voice. "One more thing… this is what a *real hero* looks like." She turned back to him and kissed him on the cheek. "My hero!"

"You tricked me." Kyle kept his eyes on the road as he pulled out into traffic. "I know you can stand up."

"You deserved the title. You're too modest about what you did. And I wanted the world to see how grateful I am. I'm the Spin Girl, so I spun some publicity for you and gave you a nickname. That you deserved. Kinda like one of those old-fashioned serials where the guy saves the girl on the railroad tracks from the speeding train."

"Any guy would have done the same."

"Stop saying that. You're a hero. Shut up and enjoy it. Hero, hero, hero."

"I guess you're feeling a little better."

"A little. Just getting out of the hospital helps. And being with you." She looked at the road sign as they headed away from the hospital. "Hey, my apartment's in the other direction."

"We're not going to your apartment."

"I'm in no shape to go to Coney Island."

"Very funny. You're staying with me and Donna for a few weeks until you get well."

"Kyle, you don't have to do that."

"Yeah, like you're in any shape to take care of yourself."

"I'll be okay."

"Dammit, you're a stubborn little thing. What, you gonna cook a steak and cut it with one hand? I'm taking care of you. End of discussion. So shut up and enjoy it."

She bit her lower lip and looked out the passenger window. "I feel guilty about you doing this."

"Why?"

"Because of everything that's happened of late. Because I know you're hurting inside. Because I'm worried that Santa won't give me my Christmas wish of forgiveness and he's stuck taking care of a woman he doesn't trust."

"Lexi, let's just get you well, okay? Right now that's our top priority. And please don't feel guilty about anything. I'm not *stuck* with you."

"You said you needed time and space and you're moving me in with you."

"It's a clever ruse to give a hot woman a sponge bath. I'm not stupid."

"I'm being serious, Kyle."

"And I'm being serious when I say I don't want to discuss… just let me get you well, okay?"

She slowly nodded. "Okay. But when I am well you have to let me make it up to you."

"You don't owe me anything, Lexi."

"Like hell. I owe you my life."

***

Kyle pulled up to his house, got out and opened the car door for Lexi. "You wanna try to walk?"

"Yeah." She extended her free hand and he pulled her out of the car. The cold wind smacked her in the face. "Wow, chilly."

"Let's get you inside." He wrapped one arm around her. "Lean on me. Take your time."

She started to walk very slowly and saw the front door of the house open, as Joanne stood in the doorway. "At that rate she'll be here for dinner. Carry her in, Kyle."

Lexi looked at him. "Go ahead. Glaciers move faster than me right now."

He easily scooped her up into his arms and quickly got her inside. Joanne pointed to the hallway. "Guest room is all set up for her." Kyle carried her down the hall and into a beautifully decorated bedroom, then set her down on the bed. Fresh flowers on the dresser filled the room with a wonderful fragrance.

Lexi grabbed a pillow and propped herself up. "This is really nice of you, guys."

"Not a problem," said Joanne. "I assume you're hungry after a few days of hospital food."

"Starving."

"I've got breakfast ready for you. Kyle, you get her settled."

"Hey, where's Donna?"

Kyle tucked her in. "She's doing a half day at the office, I'm doing the other half. We're tag-teaming things for a while." He sat on the edge of the bed and pointed to the nightstand. "TV remote. Books to read. Magazines. There's a bell and a whistle if you need anything."

"Oh, for God's sake! I'm not the Queen of England."

"Just in case you wake up and need help right away."

"Fine. So I ring the bell and you'll come running?"

"Yep."

"Ah, I've got you well trained. Every woman's dream." She reached over and took his hand. "Seriously, Kyle, I cannot thank you enough."

"No problem."

"Listen, I know you said you wanted some time and space—"

"Can we not talk about this now?"

"I've got one thing that's bothering me and I really need to get it off my chest. Please. And then I'll leave things alone."

He slowly nodded. "Sure. What's on your mind?"

"It occurs to me that I'm getting what I deserved."

"Seriously? You deserved to get beat up?"

"No, not that. I mean, it's sort of Karma that you don't trust me because the reason I went to London was because I didn't trust you."

"Huh?"

"Okay, so Jake asked me to go and I thought it was too big of a step, especially since I was dating you as well. Right after that I see the check for your nephew and I jump to the conclusion that I can't trust you because I thought you had a kid and an ex-wife and were hiding that from me. I figured I'd be saying

240

goodbye to you anyway, so I called up Jake and told him I'd go."

"So you were gonna break up with me?"

She nodded. "Remember how I confronted you with it at Thanksgiving?"

"Yeah."

"Bottom line, if I didn't trust you, it's fair that you don't trust me."

He exhaled and looked around the room. "I never said I didn't trust you."

"But you don't."

He turned back to her and ran his hand across her cheek. "Give me some time, Lexi. All that's happened in the last few days… it's a lot to process. I need to sort things out in my head, okay?"

"Sure." She felt her eyes well up and looked down.

He noticed and tilted her chin up. "Hey."

"What?" She wiped a tear from her eye.

"I'm glad you're alive and glad you're here. For now, let me take care of you, okay?"

"I'll settle for that any day of the week."

He kissed her on the forehead just as Joanne came in carrying a bed tray filled with food.

"Busted! Kyle, let the girl get well before you start making out with her."

"I wasn't—"

"Just yankin' your chain." She placed the tray on Lexi's lap. "And you, young lady, better clean your plate. This is an Italian household and we don't waste food."

"You won't have to worry about that with her," said Kyle.

Joanne looked at the plate. "Oh, sorry, I forgot your arm is in a cast. You can't cut the sausages."

Lexi shrugged. "I can eat with my hands."

"I'll do it," said Kyle.

Joanne winked at Lexi and left the room as Kyle picked up the knife and fork. He cut the sausages into bite-size pieces and put the utensils back on the plate. "There you go."

"Oh, this is too much fun. Feed me, big boy."

"Seriously?"

"While my other arm isn't broken, it still hurts like hell."

"Okay, then." She smiled at him and opened her mouth wide. He speared a piece of sausage and fed it to her. "You're enjoying this, aren't you?"

"A clever ruse to get you to spend more time with me. I'm not stupid either. And I probably will need a sponge bath at some point."

"Just ring the bell for that. I *will* come running."

"Seriously, I'm kidding about my arm, though it does hurt. I can feed myself. I just wanted to see if you'd do it."

"I can go into the attic and get Donna's old hula hoop if you'd like to make me jump through that too."

"Nah, you don't need any more training."

"I can tell you're getting well in a hurry, Lexi."

"Like I said, just being with you makes me feel better."

***

"Hey there, sleepyhead."

Lexi was just waking up from her nap when she saw Donna standing in the doorway of the guestroom. "Hi, Donna."

"How you feelin'?" She moved forward, sat on the edge of the bed and took Lexi's hand.

"Still tired and sore, but much better getting out of the hospital. And the personalized care here is stellar."

She leaned forward and whispered in her ear. "All part of the plan, sweetie."

"Huh?"

242

"You're not the only Spin Girl in this house. I'm going to—" she stopped as Kyle entered the room. "I'm going to be home the rest of the day with you. Kyle's going to the office now." She reached into her purse and pulled out a wad of message slips. "I had to hire a temp since the phone's ringing off the hook."

Kyle stared at her. "Donna, we can't afford—"

"We will shortly. I swear, every female athlete in the country must have called today wanting you as an agent. They obviously need a hero in their corner." She started handing him the slips, one by one. "Meanwhile, the mayor called, wants to give you the key to the city when Lexi is well enough to attend the ceremony. A sandwich chain called, wanting to name a hero sandwich after you."

He rolled his eyes. "You gotta be kidding."

"I find it appropriate," said Lexi. "Maybe something with ham."

"Very funny."

Donna handed him another slip. "Oh, the White House called. The President wants to give you some sort of medal."

"Seriously?"

"No, he wants you to be his agent. Of course, seriously. Oh, and Jonathan Egan is coming in this afternoon. He said the Jets want to lock him up right away with you-know-who out of the picture and he wants you to take care of the contract. You've got some serious leverage against the team."

"Wow, that's great, Donna."

"He's also Lexi's client and she told him to call."

"You called him from the hospital?" Kyle asked.

"No, I had already told him he'd be needing an agent since I knew the Jets would be cutting you-know-who loose."

Donna then started handing Lexi some slips. "Chandler gave me these, figured you could return a few calls if you're up to it. Half a dozen companies want some PR. A domestic- violence group wants you as a keynote speaker in January. Congress wants you to testify in regard to some law they're proposing on the subject. Some friend of yours from *The Post* called to check on you. I wasn't sure if it was a real friend or a reporter looking for another story."

She looked at the name. "No, he's a real friend." She shuffled through the slips. "I don't get a sandwich named after me?"

"Most delicatessens don't stock that much ham," said Kyle.

"Smartass."

"Anyway," said Donna, "I think it's safe to say we'll all be moving out of Motel Hell shortly and into a decent office. Oh, almost forgot. Some light reading material." She reached into her satchel and pulled out a stack of newspapers, then placed them on the bed. "You guys are front page."

Lexi beamed as the shot of Kyle carrying her at the hospital filled the front page with the caption provided by her own words. *My Hero!* "Wow."

Kyle shook his head. "It's too much."

"Hell," said Donna, "it's not enough."

***

Lexi heard Donna say goodbye to Kyle and the front door close. Then his sister walked into her room. "Okay, he's gone."

"You are seriously up to something, girl."

"No shit."

"So what did you mean when you said I wasn't the only Spin Girl in the house?"

"You're not the only one who can do damage control, sister. Remember how I wanted to fix you up originally? How I knew you were perfect for each other? Well, I'm gonna get you two back together."

"I dunno, Donna, he's still pretty hurt."

"Trust me, I know him better than anyone. First, you need to know that he was in love with you way before things went wrong."

244

"Really?"

"Yeah. Probably after the first date. I guess I should ask if you're in love with him too before I put things into motion."

"Yeah. I guess I was too stupid to realize it. And right now I'll be devastated if I can't get him back."

"Women can think with the wrong head too, Lexi, and considering what the other guy looks like and the places he took you, it's certainly understandable. Trust me, it was my biggest mistake with my ex. Anyway, we're dealing with two problems; the images of those photos in London he can't get out of his head, and the fragile male ego."

"I don't think the second can be fixed with any man."

"Yeah, but that front page pumped him up, even though he won't admit it. Nice going on your part."

"I knew the media would lap it up and thought it had *viral image* written all over it. Donna, I really want him back, but I don't know how I can make him ever trust me again."

"He will, just give it time. Anyway, I'm going to insist you stay here at least a month—"

"A month? It won't take me that long to recover."

"Yeah, but he doesn't know that. You want him back, right?"

"Of course. Just tell me what to do."

"Best way to do that is to show him what it will be like for both of you to live under the same roof. While he may never get over your past, I'm betting the future will be our trump card. By the time I get through with him, he won't be able to live without you."

CHAPTER TWENTY-FOUR

Four days later Lexi walked into the kitchen, where Donna was seated at the table sipping coffee. "Ah, you're up."

Lexi rubbed the sleep out of her eyes. "I overslept."

"Nonsense. You're not on any schedule. Your body needs rest. Why do you think you need to get up at a certain time?"

"I wanted to be up before Kyle went to work."

"Ah, well you missed him by an hour. Though he kept peeking in your bedroom to see if you were up. He wanted to say goodbye to you before he took off."

"Oh, really?"

"Yes, really. He's coming around slowly. And you seem to be getting around better."

"Yeah, I've got my balance back. And I need to get out of bed more." She headed for the coffee pot.

"You want me to fix you a cup?"

"Nah, I can do it. I need to learn how to do stuff with one hand anyway." She poured herself a cup and sat down with Donna. "You don't need to be here with me all the time. I'll be fine."

"You're not out of the woods yet. Besides, with each of us doing a half day at the office we both get things done. And it gives you and me a half day to plot while you get a half day alone with Kyle."

"So we're plotting?"

"Damn straight."

"Aren't we a little old to play games?"

"Damn straight. You want him back or not?"

"Damn straight."

Donna pointed to her black eye. "That still hurt?"

"Not really. But it looks awful."

"How about you let me cover it up a bit? And I've got a turtleneck to hide those bruises too."

"What's the point? I'm not going anywhere."

"You'll feel better about yourself and he won't be reminded of what happened."

***

Kyle walked into the house and was immediately greeted by the smell of something wonderful. "Wow, what is that?"

Donna put on her coat and headed for the door. "Lexi's making something."

"She's up? And cooking?"

Lexi turned and smiled at him from the kitchen. "I can't cook. But I can bake."

Donna kissed him on the cheek. "Okay, I'm off to the office. Anything I need to know?"

"I left everything on your desk."

"Okay. See you tonight at dinner." She headed out the door, leaving him alone in the house with Lexi.

He walked into the kitchen. "So, what's in the oven?"

"Cookies. Old family recipe that's in my head."

"You did this all by yourself? With one arm in a cast?"

"I need to learn to take care of myself. Anyway, have a seat, they'll be out shortly."

"You look like you're feeling better."

"I am."

"And you're starting to look like your old self."

"Oh, so I'm old?"

"Sorry, that came out wrong. You're starting to look normal."

The buzzer on the oven went off. Lexi opened the door, grabbed a potholder, took out a cookie sheet and set it on the stove. "Okay, let 'em cool and then you can have one."

"Those look great. What are they?"

"Just a chocolate concoction." She sat down next to him. "So how was your day?"

"Busy. But really good. Lotta new clients."

"Me too. Chandler emailed some stuff for me to work on."

"You feel up to working?"

"Writing press releases and proposals isn't exactly strenuous. But I can't type with one hand, so I'm doing everything longhand and then Chandler or the temp can type it up."

"I can do it for you."

"Nah, you're busy enough."

"You baked cookies for me, I can type for you."

***

Lexi turned as she heard the front door open and saw Donna returning from the office. Kyle's sister stuck her nose in the air. "Something smells good in here."

"Kyle's teaching me to make spaghetti sauce."

"And you're helping."

"Well, a little."

Kyle looked up from his frying pan of meatballs. "She's stirring the pot. I figured that's appropriate."

Lexi shot him a dirty look. "Smartass."

Donna entered the kitchen and dropped her purse on a chair. "Another busy day, dear brother. You've got three more clients to sign tomorrow morning. And Lexi, Chandler's coming by for dinner and he's bringing all your stuff. Apparently you're very much in demand as well."

248

"Well, thankfully your brother is a wonderful secretary. Typed up all my work today."

Donna moved toward him and wrapped one arm around his waist. "So, you've got him trained already."

"No, he's just the world's nicest man." She shot him a sweet smile.

"Least I could do," he said, as he carried the pan of meatballs toward the pot of sauce. "Okay, once the meatballs are halfway done you slide them into the sauce, then the heat from the sauce cooks them the rest of the way while picking up the flavor. It also makes the meatballs nice and soft."

"Ah, very clever, you Sicilians."

Lexi leaned back after a very filling dinner. "That was excellent."

Chandler nodded as he took Donna's hand. "My compliments to the chefs. Both of them."

"I didn't do much," said Lexi. "But I learned a lot."

Kyle patted her on the shoulder. "When you get rid of that cast you can roll the meatballs next time."

"Good to know there will be a next time."

"Why wouldn't there be?"

Kyle sipped his wine, his free hand in his lap. Lexi reached over and took it, slowly entwining her fingers with his.

He didn't resist.

**

Kyle woke up early before anyone else, went out to pick up the morning paper off the doorstep, and saw his photo on the front page with the one word headline:

SLINGSHOT

He rolled his eyes as he went back inside to the kitchen, poured a cup of coffee, opened the paper and started to read.

MEET THE DAVID WHO BEAT THE JETS GOLIATH

Nearly one week after former Jets quarterback Jake Frost put public relations woman Lexi Harlow in the hospital while his former agent Kyle Caruso did the same to him, the city has been wondering:

Who is this guy whose total destruction of Frost has gotten several million hits on YouTube?

According to the woman he saved, he's nothing short of a real-life superhero.

"He's an amazing man," said Lexi Harlow, now recovering at the home shared by Kyle Caruso and his sister Donna. "Not only does he save my life, but he took me in to help me get well. We think of superheroes as comic-book characters, but Kyle is a real-life superhero."

Caruso, a thirty-year-old agent with a reputation for only taking on squeaky-clean clients, had been serving as Frost's representative for a few endorsements since the quarterback's previous agent had gone to jail. Shortly before negotiations on a new contract with the Jets began, Caruso dropped Frost as a client, throwing the player out of his office and costing himself a huge commission. "I couldn't believe it," said college-wide receiver Jerry Haynes, who was waiting to see Caruso in the outer office while this happened. "I hear this huge argument, and then the agent tells Frost to get the hell out. I couldn't believe an agent would cut loose such a high-profile client, but that spoke volumes about the man."

As it turned out, the argument was about Ms. Harlow, who through a weird turn of events had been dating both men. When Caruso became Frost's agent, it left her with an uncomfortable situation. Finally the candle burning at both ends met in the middle. "Jake found out I had been dating Kyle and told Kyle to stop seeing me or he would drop Kyle as an agent and ruin his business. That's when Kyle threw him out."

Ms. Harlow dropped a dime on the Jets front office when Frost told her he had been keeping the need for major surgery from the team. "I couldn't let the guy con the Jets out of a hundred million dollars. That's just flat out stealing." Frost found out, which led to his attack on her. Caruso, who has an office one floor above Harlow's in the same building, heard her screams for help through the air vent.

The result was an amazing martial-arts beating he dished out to a pro athlete, who outweighed him by nearly a hundred pounds and is nearly a foot taller. "He was bullied a lot in school," said his sister Donna. "So he took up karate and became a third-degree black belt. He only had to use those skills once before, when my ex-husband hit me. But he doesn't go around broadcasting his skills. He's really a modest guy." Apparently true, since his office has turned down all requests for interviews from every media outlet.

Still, the David and Goliath video remains viral. "I confess, I watch it every day," said Ms. Harlow. "Kyle is my slingshot."

He heard footsteps and looked up to see Lexi shuffling toward him, looking dishevelled. "Morning, sunshine. You're up early."

"Ugh. I'm not in my body yet. Coffee ready?"

"Yeah, I'll fix you a cup."

She put up her free hand. "I'll get it."

He held up the newspaper. "Interesting article in *The Post*."

She looked at it and smiled. "How about that! You made the front page again. What a surprise."

"Yeah, right. So, when did you and my sister do the interviews?"

"When you weren't here. Because if you were here, you wouldn't have let us do them."

"And since when do you girls obey me?"

251

"Yeah, good point."

"I told you I didn't want any more publicity."

She started to pour a cup of coffee. "Shut up, hero, you deserve it and a ton more. Again, we don't obey."

"So I'm your slingshot?"

"David beat Goliath with a slingshot, I thought it was appropriate. I am the Spin Girl, after all." She sat next to him and put her hand on top of his. "You still don't get it, do you?"

He shook his head. "Not really."

"Look, while I'm an independent woman who can take care of herself, deep down every girl wants a guy who will stand up for her like you did. First, you defended my honor when you told Jake I was not a thing to be bought, and then you saved my life. You're in serious white-knight territory, young man. And please don't keep saying that any man would have done the same." She reached over and ran her fingers through his hair as she gave him a soulful look. Her touch sent a charge through his body. "You're that unique man who respects me as an equal while doing everything you can to protect me. You're the perfect combination of chivalry and respect. Very hard to find these days, and a lot of women are looking for just that." She leaned back and pointed at the paper. "And I love bragging about you."

CHAPTER TWENTY-FIVE

Two weeks later...

Lexi woke up with a powerful thirst. She looked at the clock and saw it was just past midnight. She started to head for the kitchen when she heard voices in the living room.

And a conversation she didn't need to interrupt between Donna and Kyle. About her.

She stopped in the hallway to listen.

"Kyle, you need to make a decision."

"I still need time."

"Bullshit. You're running out of time. Look, the doctor came by today and said she was recovering faster than he expected. And then I heard her on the phone talking to someone, saying she was going home soon."

"She can't go home! Who will take care of her?"

"She's taking care of herself pretty well around here."

"Yeah, but—"

"Sounds like someone doesn't want her to leave. Admit it, Kyle, you love coming home every day and finding her here. You love having her here every night to watch TV or play cards with or whatever. And if she's not up when you leave in the morning you're bummed because you didn't get a chance to say goodbye."

He nodded and looked down. "I do love her being here all the time. I would really miss her."

"So what's the problem?"

"You know what the problem is."

"Fine. Let me ask you a few questions. You love her, right?"

"I have for quite a while. Probably since the third date."

"You know damn well she loves you."

"I know."

"And she'd never cheat on you."

"I know that too."

"Therefore... through deductive reasoning... you trust her."

Long pause. "Donna, I know she'd never cheat but... the London thing is still in the back of my mind. I've tried but I cannot get it out of my head. I worry that it will haunt me, hang over the relationship. Ruin things eventually."

"What, you think she's lying to you about nothing happening between her and Jake?"

"Lexi's not a liar. But I think in this case she's protecting me. She probably knows I was jealous of Jake and if she admits she slept with him it would really hurt me."

"Okay, fair enough. But put yourself in her shoes... she goes off to London assuming you can't be trusted because she thinks you have a kid and an ex-wife that you haven't told her about. She's pretty sure she's gonna dump you and she's on this whirl-wind vacation with a rich, famous guy. Even if she did sleep with him, surely you understand her thinking and can cut her some slack?"

He didn't respond.

"Let's put it this way. Suppose the shoe is on the other foot and you think you're about to break it off with her. You're whisked off to some exotic island with your dream girl, Nicole Kidman, and she jumps in a hot tub with you wearing a string bikini and climbs all over you. Would you be able to resist?"

"Nicole Kidman? Probably not."

"Okay, so maybe this guy was Lexi's fantasy. You saw how I reacted when I met him. But Kyle, even though he had all that stuff going for him it was all superficial. He's nothing more than eye candy. She saw through that *before* the night of the party and she came to you after the party too. She told you that you were the one. Doesn't that tell you something?"

"But I won by default, because Jake was such an idiot."

She shook her head. "Not according to Chandler. Lexi told him she was gonna choose you after you took care of her when she got sick. My brother, who has to clip coupons and get creative, beat the rich, famous, incredibly good-looking millionaire. Who happened to be a total ass and did everything he could to make you jealous?"

"That part worked."

"And remember how Lexi told you she had a big surprise when you were walking into the party? She had already chosen you. Did you forget that?"

"You're right."

"Everything involving Jake is in the past, Kyle. Doesn't a future with Lexi outweigh that?"

"I suppose."

"You don't *suppose*, you *know*. And we both know that girl is the best thing to ever happen to you. Well, I'm not sure what else to say. All I can tell you is that you need to shit or get off the pot. Because once that girl leaves this house, she's gone. She's famous now. Men will be beating down her door. Speaking of which, that's been happening to you with women, right?"

"Yeah, they keep hitting on me and giving me their phone numbers."

"Pretty women?"

"Some are stunning. Beyond gorgeous."

"And how many have you called?"

"None."

"Because… wait for it…"

He slowly nodded. "Because I'm in love with Lexi."

She got up and kissed him on the head. "And with that, the defense rests."

"You're right, Donna. I'll tell her tomorrow."

"You'll tell her… what?"

"That I love her, want her to be my girl. That I trust her. As for the thing in London with Jake, I'll just have to live with it."

"It'll fade, sweetie. With time and her love, it'll fade. A girl like that will make it disappear very fast."

"I sure hope you're right."

"One thing you're gonna have to do, and this is important. Never, ever let her know it bothers you."

"That's the hard part."

Lexi tiptoed back to her room, beaming. Kyle was finally going to accept her.

But she knew she would have to work very hard to defeat an image that only existed in his mind.

***

An early meeting meant Kyle hadn't had a chance to talk with Lexi before leaving the house. She was still asleep.

He tried to focus on his work at the office, but his mind continued to wander. What would he say to her when he got home? Would he be able to pretend the London thing didn't matter, that he had put it behind him? Would he be able to be romantic with her without the memory of Jake interfering?

His thoughts were interrupted by a gentle tap on the office door. He looked up and saw a short guy carrying what he recognized as a photographer's bag. "Can I help you?"

"Sorry to barge in, but your secretary's constantly on the phone."

"Yeah, it's been that way for a while."

"Not surprised." The guy moved forward and extended his hand. "I'm Frankie, Lexi's neighbor. The paparazzo."

"Oh, she's mentioned you a few times." He shook hands.

"How's she doing?"

"Much better. Getting back to normal, even though she's still got the cast on her arm."

"Glad to hear it."

"So what can I do for you, Frankie?"

"More like what I can do for you." He reached in his pocket and pulled out a thumb drive, then handed it to Kyle. "A while back I told Lexi I thought Jake Frost was being followed, and told her I'd look into it—"

"Yeah. Turned out Jake was having himself followed."

"Right, I know the whole story, how he tried to use those photos to make you jealous."

"How do you—?"

"Lexi and I are good friends, known each other a long time. Anyway, after Jake shows up here, shoving those London photos in your face, Lexi told me the whole story. And she was really worried you'd believe everything Jake told you about what happened in London."

"Photos don't lie."

"Yeah, but people do." He pointed at the thumb drive. "And Jake was a big liar. Anyway, I managed to track down the paparazzo who Jake hired in London. Since Jake had already paid him and the guy's going to jail, he knew the rest of his work wasn't worth anything. And he'd seen what the guy did to Lexi. I told him what he had could help her, so he gave it to me."

"Not sure I understand how this helps. And I really don't want to look at more photos of the two of them."

Frankie shook his head. "That drive contains video, not photos. What Jake gave you were screen grabs. Basically he was across the street with two cameras. One rolling continuously on Jake's room and the other on Lexi, who had the room next door."

"They had separate rooms?"

"Yeah. Anyway, pop that thing in your computer—"

"I don't wanna watch."

"Trust me, you need to. It proves Lexi's story. She, uh, told me about the thing that's, ya know, holding things up on your relationship. I'm just trying to help her."

Kyle studied the guy's face and could tell he was being sincere. He sat at his desk and slid the thumb drive into his laptop. The screen filled with a grainy view of Jake's hotel suite.

Frankie pointed at the laptop. "Okay, scroll forward two hours and eleven minutes in."

"What am I looking for?"

"You'll see."

Kyle used the mouse to slide the control to the correct point. "Now hit play."

He took a deep breath and hit the button. The video rolled, showing Lexi lying on top of Jake. He had his shirt off while she was fully clothed. He grimaced as he watched.

Frankie patted him on the shoulder. "Sorry, dude, I know this is painful. Keep watching."

Kyle saw Lexi roll off and lie next to Jake. They talked for a minute, then she rested her head on his chest and closed her eyes.

"It gets really boring for the next eight hours," said Frankie.

Kyle began to quickly scroll through the video. Nothing changed for the next eight hours, until Jake got up, leaving Lexi asleep on the bed. He later returned wearing a towel, obviously out of the shower.

Lexi was still asleep.

"Okay," said Frankie. "Roll it right there. There's no audio but watch her reaction when she wakes up."

He saw Lexi wake up with a start, looking shocked. Then she got up and went to her room. "Wow."

"See, she didn't do anything. She simply was jet-lagged and fell asleep. And he was probably tired from the game and fell asleep. Bottom line, Kyle, she didn't have sex with the guy. Or even take her clothes off. She made out with him a bit, but that's no big deal. That screen grab of him wearing a towel and her in the same outfit… well, if you didn't know what really happened, I can see where you would jump to the conclusion that she was about to do the walk of shame wearing the same clothes as the day before. Nothing much happened in the hot tub either. If you wanna see that part—"

"I've seen enough." He bit his lower lip and turned to Frankie. "God, I feel terrible."

"I'm sorry. I know it was hard to watch—"

"No, it's not that. I feel terrible that I didn't believe her. I didn't trust her when I had no reason to distrust her." He pulled the thumb drive from the laptop and handed it toward Frankie.

"That's yours and my friend assures me it's the only copy. You should burn it," the paparazzo said, giving it straight back.

"Frankie, I don't know how to thank you. And I don't want to be rude, but I need to go home right now."

"I hear ya. Dude, don't ever let that girl go. She's one of a kind."

***

Donna noticed Lexi wore a big smile as she leaned against the kitchen counter sipping her coffee. "You look like you're in a good mood."

"You might say that."

"Not so sore anymore?"

"It's nothing physical, Donna. I, uh, well… forgive me for eavesdropping last night, but I heard you guys talking about me. The part about Kyle being in love with me and being willing to accept me."

Donna got up and hugged her. "Well, I've been about to bust

waiting for him to get home tonight to tell you. I'm really happy for you."

Lexi leaned back and looked at her. "I can't thank you enough, Donna."

"I told you it would work. Though honestly, if you weren't here it might have happened faster. I mean, he misses you during the day when he's at work. Imagine if you hadn't been here every day."

"Doesn't matter. And please know I will never hurt your brother."

"I know you won't, Lexi."

Suddenly the door opened and Kyle rushed in, walking fast as he headed for the kitchen.

Donna put down her coffee. "Kyle, what are you doing home? Everything okay?"

He didn't answer, but moved toward Lexi and gave her a strong hug. Lexi looked at Donna, who put her palms up and shrugged. She hugged him back with her one good arm. "What's wrong, Kyle?"

"Lexi, I am so, so sorry."

"Sorry about what?" He was still hugging her so she leaned back to try and see his face. "What's wrong, sweetie?"

"I know nothing happened in London. I saw the proof. And I hope you don't hate me for not trusting you. God, Lexi, can you ever forgive me?"

"Whoa, hold on. What proof?"

He wiped his moist eyes. "Your friend, Frankie, the paparazzo, dropped by. He found the guy Jake hired to take those pictures in London. Only they weren't pictures, they were screen grabs from video which was running twenty-four-seven and it showed you falling asleep in your clothes and waking up eight hours later and looking really upset that you'd fallen asleep in his room and you didn't have sex with him—"

She put her finger on his lips. "Slow down, Kyle. Everything's okay."

"And I hate myself for not trusting you and you never gave me any reason not to trust you and—"

"Donna, will you please tell your brother to shut the hell up."

"Zip it, Kyle. Let the lady talk."

He exhaled and nodded. "Sorry."

Lexi studied his face. "Someone had too much caffeine this morning."

"Lexi, I—"

"Only one way to get you to stop talking." She pulled him close and kissed him, long and hard, as she ran her free hand through his hair. She finally let him go and looked right into his soul. "I love you, got it? Do I have to spell it out for you?"

He stood there, mouth hanging open. "You're not mad?"

"Hell no. Look, I didn't trust you a while back for no good reason, so we're even. Besides, you're gonna have to forgive me for something I did last night."

"What did you do?"

"I eavesdropped. I got up to get something to drink and I heard you and Donna talking about me. I heard you say you loved me and that you wanted me as your girl." She ran her hand over his cheek. "Kyle, can you ever forgive me for finding out you loved me before you had the chance to tell me?"

He took her face in his hands and kissed her. "I love you, Lexi. Now it's official."

Donna moved forward and patted him on the shoulder. "Little brother, at this point I think it's time for me to go to the office so you guys can have the house to yourselves. Scream and yell all you want. Please don't break anything."

Lexi laughed. "Donna, I appreciate the thought but my first time with your brother isn't happening with me in recovery mode and my arm in a cast."

"Well, a woman can do a lot with one hand."

"Donna!" Kyle began to seriously blush. "Geez, you're my sister."

261

"Fine, then go decorate the tree in the nude. Which considering the look on your face will give Lexi one more place to hang an ornament."

***

Lexi's eyes widened as she looked at the dinner table filled with all sorts of Italian delicacies. It was a festive atmosphere with Donna and Chandler on one side of the table, Anthony and Joanne at each end, while she and Kyle sat close together on the other side. A bottle of wine started making its way around the table and she held up her glass. Chandler started to pour, but Kyle stopped him. "Whoa. Lexi, you can't have alcohol when you're on painkillers."

"I stopped taking them. For some odd reason I haven't needed one today." She gave him a soulful look.

"And the work on my cavity continues," said Anthony.

Lexi playfully swatted him on the arm. "Oh, leave me alone. We have a lot to celebrate tonight."

"Just yankin' your chain. If you're gonna be part of this family, get used to it."

"Trust me," said Joanne, "you won't."

Everyone laughed as Lexi took a sip of wine. "Oh, grape, I have missed you. And you taste so much better when all is right in the universe."

Donna started dishing out the food. "Good to see you so happy, Lexi."

"Hey, I got my man back and got even with the guy who tried to drive us apart."

Kyle patted her on the back. "Yeah, his career is toast."

"Well, that's just *part* of how I got even."

"I would think dropping a dime on the Jets was enough."

Lexi started spooning food on her plate. "Well, since all our stress has been put to bed, I would love to tell you the other part of the story. And how I got the idea to tell the Jets. I mean, if you don't mind me mentioning… him."

Kyle shrugged. "Okay by me. He's in jail, probably with his new girlfriend."

Lexi laughed as she grabbed a piece of bread. "Okay, here's the part I haven't shared. Of course you know after Jake's party I came here and told Kyle he was the guy for me, which I had decided before the party anyway. So the next day I go to work and realize I had a date with Jake for that night and I'm going to break it first thing and tell him we're done. Of course Jake had sent four dozen roses with an apology, as usual trying to buy his way into my heart. Anyway, before I get the chance to call him, Chandler and I hear the argument between him and Kyle through the air vent. All that stuff about Jake having us followed and planting the photos really pisses me off. And then he drops Kyle as a client because my sweetie here wouldn't break up with me." She patted him on the leg. "Even after Jake threatens him physically and says he'll ruin his business. At this point I never wanna see the guy again until he drops that one little thing at the end of the argument about giving me the fifty-thousand-dollar necklace. So I figure I have to go out with him on one more date. I knew Kyle was counting on the commission from Jake's contract to pay for Anthony's surgery and with that gone the only way to get the cash you guys needed was to accept the necklace from Jake but then sell it."

Anthony smiled as he shook his head. "I will never yank your chain again, young lady."

"Oh, go ahead, it's endearing. Anyway, back to our story. Remember, I left Jake's party seriously mad at him so the only way I'm gonna get that necklace is to make him think I've forgiven him and also that I've chosen him. So I put on the sleaziest dress I own, this tight, low-cut, incredibly short band-aid number. I picked up a pair of six-inch stripper heels with straps snaking all the way up my calves. And a ton of makeup. I looked like someone from cheap slut central casting."

Donna handed Kyle her napkin. "You okay, Kyle? I can open a window or turn on the air conditioning."

Lexi looked at him and saw his forehead was damp, with his mouth hanging open. "Something wrong?"

"I, uh, was just, you know, trying to picture you in something like that."

"Be happy to wear it for you when I'm well. But just at home. Lady in public, you-know-what in bed. Your eyes only, okay?"

"Uh-huh."

"Back to my story. So Jake goes gaga over this outfit and we start heading for dinner. I take his arm but I touch his sore elbow and he jumps, which reminds me he needs surgery and gives me the idea to tell the Jets. Then at dinner I tell him how I overreacted at the party, that he was just being an alpha male and I made him think I was so impressed with his actions. Luckily I hadn't eaten anything at this point or I would have thrown up listening him talk about how much he enjoys being a bully. Of course being the Spin Girl I was weaving my words in such a way that Jake thought I was talking about him when I was really talking about Kyle. I told him I had decided that it was time to date only one guy, that one was twice the man of the other."

"And he thought he was the one," said Donna.

"Right, because he thinks of everything on a physical level. Anyway, this is when I start laying it on thick, and I mean I have never talked in such suggestive terms before. After I've got him convinced that I am really attracted to his Neanderthal routine I start outlining the things I like to do to men in the bedroom, that I'm an alpha girl and sometimes like to be dominant and devour a man like a five-course meal."

"Turn up the air," said Kyle. Everyone laughed.

"Don't worry, sweetie, I was talking about what I'm going to do to you. But you'll have to wait to find out what those things are. So now Jake is all hot and bothered and gives me the neck-lace. And right after that I tell him I have decided it's time to date only one guy, and again, he assumes I'm talking about him. So now that I've got the necklace I pretend to get an emergency text and have to leave. So he calls me a cab and before I get in he kisses me and I grab his crotch for good measure. And let me tell you, when I said one of my boyfriends was twice the man of the other... well, it wouldn't take much to be two times the amount of what I felt."

The whole room filled with laughter.

***

With everything cleaned up, Donna started turning off the lights in the house, then shook her head. "Aw, hell, I forgot."

Kyle, his arm around Lexi, turned to her. "Forgot what?"

"To make up Lexi's room. I washed the sheets and was going to make the bed, but it slipped my mind with everything that happened today. I forgot to put the sheets in the dryer." She shot a quick wink at Lexi.

Lexi looked at Kyle. "That's okay. I'll find another place to sleep."

Kyle beamed. "You want—"

"Not yet. I said *sleep*. I'm not fully recovered and I don't want our first time to be with my arm in a cast. And no comments on that from you, Donna."

She shrugged and put up her palms. "What'd I say?"

Kyle started to lead her to his bedroom. "This is gonna be wonderful and torture at the same time."

Lexi kissed him. "Sorry, you'll have to wait and settle for waking up with me."

"That's not settling at all."

CHAPTER TWENTY-SIX

Donna raised her glass. "A toast, to Lexi's left arm! Free at last!"

Everyone clinked glasses, Lexi holding hers with her left hand, then staring at it. "You have no idea how much I've missed you. Now I can cut my own steak."

"So everything's healed fine?" asked Joanne.

Lexi nodded. "Good as new. And the doctor said I'm completely recovered from everything else. So I'm back to normal. And now I can sleep with my sweetie without banging his head with my cast."

Kyle nodded. "Yeah, I'm not gonna miss that. Some nights it's been like going fifteen rounds with her."

"I can type again, get dressed without help—"

"Now that, I'll miss," said Kyle.

Lexi shrugged. "I'll make it up to you. You can help me get *un*dressed instead."

Anthony shook his head. "Damn, these dinner conversations have gone straight into the gutter of late." He tossed his napkin on the table. "By the way, I also had good news from the doctor today." He shot a big smile at Joanne.

"Show 'em, sweetie," she said.

"Here goes." He grabbed the arms of his wheelchair and pushed himself up till he was standing.

Donna got up and ran to him. "Oh my God, you can walk!"

"Not very far and not very fast, but eventually I'll be pretty good."

Kyle got up and patted him on the back. "Man, that's wonderful news, Anthony. I can't imagine how great that must feel."

Anthony sat back down and pointed at Lexi. "And this would not have been possible without your girlfriend."

Kyle sat back down and shook his head. "I wish you wouldn't refer to her as my girlfriend."

Lexi's face tightened as she turned to face him. "Excuse me?"

Kyle reached into his pocket, pulled out an ornate diamond engagement ring and held it out toward her. "I think *fiancée* might be a better term. If, ya know, it's okay with you."

Her jaw dropped. "Oh my God…"

Kyle got out of his chair and down on one knee. "Marry me, Spin Girl. Make me the happiest guy in the world."

Her eyes beamed. "Absolutely! But…"

He paled. "But?"

"I want you to know I'm only doing this because I'm hopelessly in love with you." She thrust out her left hand. "Oh, is my hand about to be happy."

Everyone clapped as he slipped the ring on her finger and kissed her. "About damn time your left hand was free."

Lexi beamed as she stared at the ring, a perfect fit. "This is absolutely gorgeous. Is it an antique?"

"It was our grandmother's," said Donna. "She was married more than fifty years, so it's got good luck in it."

"It's wonderful that you want me to have it. Thank you."

"Welcome to the family."

She held out her hand for everyone to see.

Chandler leaned forward to look at the ring. "That's lovely."

Donna gave it a longing look, her head leaning to the side. "Yeah. I've always loved that ring."

Chandler reached in his pocket and pulled out a diamond solitaire, then held it in front of Donna. "Do you find it as appealing as this one?"

Kyle leaned against the wall in the hallway, waiting impatiently as Lexi put on what she called a "special outfit" for him in the bedroom. After sleeping with her for several weeks, he was beyond ready for their first time. "How's it going in there?"

"Aw, keep your shirt on!"

Donna walked by. "Don't rush perfection." She tapped on the bedroom door. "Lexi, it's Donna. Can I come in?"

"Sure."

Kyle threw up his hands. "Of course, but I have to wait in the hall."

Donna patted him on the cheek. "She's worth it." Donna entered the bedroom and shut the door behind her as he leaned closer to listen in. "Wow. I'd never have the guts to wear that. But you really pull it off. And you've got the legs for it." She came out of the bedroom, closed the door and took Kyle's hands. "Sweetie, you've got no shot. See you in a couple days. I'll have the paramedics standing by. And in case you don't survive, it's been a pleasure being your sister. G'night." She leaned up and kissed him on the cheek. "And congratulations."

He gave her a strong hug. "You too, Donna. Thanks for everything." She headed off to her bedroom and shut the door.

Lexi's voice came through the door. "Okay, young man, your fiancée awaits."

"Finally." He opened the door and what he saw knocked him for a loop. "Oh. My. God." He closed the door behind him without taking his eyes off her. She sat seductively on the edge of the bed, dressed in the outfit she'd worn on the night she'd gotten even with Jake.

"You like?"

"Donna was right. I've got no shot. Just take me."

"Since the discussion of the band-aid dress and six-inch stripper heels got you all hot and bothered, I figured it would get your motor running in real life." She beckoned him to come closer with her index finger. "C'mere. Lexi won't bite." He moved toward the bed, his eyes laser-locked on her. She stood up and took his hands, then placed them on her waist. "So, is this what you expected when you asked me to marry you?"

"Not exactly, but I'm certainly not complaining. Damn, Lexi, you're like a fantasy come to life."

"And Lexi will always be here to fulfill your fantasies."

"Speaking of which, I wonder if Home Depot is open at this hour."

"Huh?"

"We could use a pole for the bedroom."

"Very funny."

"So you sent Jake home after seeing you in this? I better never get on your bad side. Talk about torturing a man."

"You're catching on, young man." She took his chin and tilted it up, then gave him a long, soft kiss.

He looked up at her as their lips parted. "This reminds me of our first date."

"Excuse me? I didn't wear anything this sleazy."

"But you wore platforms that made you taller than me. By the way, I knew what you were up to."

"Oh, really?"

"You wanted to see if I was secure enough to go out with a woman who was taller in her heels. Anyway, if you remember, I didn't say anything that night."

"Fine, you got me. I was testing you and also wanted to let you know I like to be in charge. So, now that we're official, do I have to put all my heels away?"

"Hell no. You should know I've always looked up to you."

"Awww. You know what, sweetie? Even with these taking me up to five-eleven, I look at you and still see the biggest man I know."

"Damn, Kyle." Lexi lay back on the pillow, glowing, breathing heavy, totally spent. "You're amazing. My God, I have never experienced a night like this."

He smiled at her as he lay on his side. "Glad I measure up."

"Measure up? When I said you were twice the man Jake was... well, I think we need a bigger multiplier. What do you feed that thing?"

"Redheads."

"And your recovery time is, shall we say, impressive."

"If you're not too tired we could go for round four."

"I think the hat trick is fine for our first time. If you can wait for tomorrow night for me to recover."

"I guess. By the way, your *A game* gets an A-plus."

"Thank you, kind sir."

He handed her a glass of wine. "We've come a long way since you kicked my ass on the basketball court."

She laughed a bit. "That was a lot of fun. Y'know, that's why I went out with you."

"Because you wiped the floor with me?"

"No, because your male ego was still intact after losing to a girl and you still had the guts to ask me out. And I loved the clever way you did it. A lotta guys would want nothing to do with me after losing like that."

"A lot of guys are stupid."

"You get no argument from me. So, now that you've seen another side of me in the bedroom, do you have a preference?"

"Are you asking if I like stripper Lexi better than traditional Lexi?"

"Yeah. Do I put the band-aid dress in the closet forever, or do I need to go shopping for more stuff like that?"

"I liked the variety provided by both women, so stripper Lexi should take my credit card and feel free to accessorize her wardrobe."

"Ah, how nice of you."

"Does she have a stripper name?"

"I think with a name like Lexi Harlow I'm all set."

"Good point." He started to play with her hair. "Hey, wanted to run an idea by you. The house next door that you always say you love went up for sale yesterday."

She rolled on her side and raised her head. "Really?"

"Yep. And it's as beautiful inside. My best friend lived there when we were kids and I've been in that house hundreds of times. Anyway, there's also a huge mother-in-law apartment in the back, which we could convert into an office for both our businesses. Chandler would move in with Donna when they get married and we'd all have New York's shortest commute. Let's face it, we really don't need offices in Manhattan."

"I love that idea."

"Then we get to spend the whole day together, and have lunch."

"Ooooh, I like the idea of spending our lunch hour together."

"Yeah, there are a lot of good restaurants in the neighborhood."

She ran her hand over his chest. "I wasn't talking about food."

"You're an insatiable little thing."

"Absolutely. Anyway, let's buy the house. Tomorrow. The minute we wake up. Then we hang up a shingle. Harlow & Caruso."

"Oh, so your name goes first."

"And why wouldn't it?"

He smiled. "Not changing your last name?"

"Never gave it much thought. But I refuse to do that hyphenated bullshit. I mean, suppose we had a kid named Joe Caruso-Harlow and he married Jane Smith-Jones and they had a kid with four last names. Poor child would take forever doing a signature."

"Good point. Anyway, whatever you wanna do about the name thing is fine with me, Spin Girl."

"Only one thing I definitely want to be called. Your wife."

He leaned over and kissed her. "So, when do you wanna make it legal?"

"How about this summer, when it warms up?"

"I gotta wait that long?"

"What, you wanna go to Vegas and get married by an Elvis impersonator?"

"No, I'll be fine. I guess I won't believe I'm going to marry a girl like you until the ring is on my finger."

"A girl like me?"

"Total package. Smart, sweet, beautiful, kind, independent, old-fashioned… and pretty damn incredible in bed. I can't believe I won your hand."

"Still don't get it, do you? *You're* the total package. And *I'm* the big winner. I'm the girl who took New York's most eligible bachelor off the market."

"Spin Girl, I was off the market the moment I met you."

Also by Nic Tatano

Twitter Girl

Cover Girl

It Girl

Boss Girl

Wing Girl

Jillian Spectre & the Dreamweaver

The Adventures of Jillian Spectre